EMERALD GREEN

LINDSAY MARIE MILLER

Praise for *EMERALD GREEN*

DON'T MISS THESE OTHER BOOKS BY
LINDSAY MARIE MILLER

The Girl in the Woods

Me & Mr. Jones

Mr. Jones & Me

Jungle Eyes

Island Smile

Coastal Spirit

Single

An Arrangement

An Accident

Mercy

AND LOOK FOR HER NEW NOVEL

Available in November 2017

For my grandmother, Martha

You were right.

~ ~

Chapter 1

I stepped out into the cold dark night, searching for a familiar face in the parking lot. With a crumpled fold of white chiffon in my hand, I gently shut the car door, wondering why Eric was nowhere to be found. Locking my silver Volkswagen Beetle with the push of a button, I glided across the black pavement. The incessant clicking of my heels against the ground made me even more aware of my presence in a formal white gown.

The Winter Ball had never been my idea, but Eric had insisted, since his antiquated high school did not host dances. Maple Creek High, on the other hand, had no problem renting a Hilton hotel ballroom for the evening. With the rate of tuition increasing every year, the PTA felt no remorse in demanding what they wanted.

Inside the ballroom, a cluster of students migrated towards the center of the dance floor. Teenage boys jostled into each other, too distracted by the cleavage-baring dresses worn by their teasing girlfriends. Junior quarterback, Ricky Travis, danced at the front of the crowd with his very own Barbie doll, Nicki Caldwell.

Nicki wore an ocean blue dress with aquamarine jewels scattered along the neckline, though she looked more like a mermaid than a princess. Her white blonde curls were stacked atop her head, clasped together with a lavender seashell clip, while a string of pearls clung to either of her small, bony wrists. Even in December, Nicki was ready for the beach.

To achieve her picture-perfect appearance, Nicki frequented salons on a weekly basis, where she allowed beauticians to bleach her hair, burn her skin, and coat her nails with a new shade of candy-colored polish. Once the tanning process was complete, Nicki laid down ample amounts of cold, hard cash, so that a professional could wax the places on her body where she had rather not have hair. And yet, Ricky pressed his body against hers, wrapping his arms around her stomach, as if she had woken up like this.

I could not help but roll my eyes.

Ricky Travis had spent the past two years tugging at my hair in math class. Somehow, every semester, at least one teacher's seating chart always indicated that Ricky would be sitting in the seat directly behind mine. If I ever turned around, Ricky would let go of my hair, holding his hands in the air as if he were an innocent man. "I didn't do anything," he would smugly remark, his thin lips held apart.

The truth is, I had developed a crush on Ricky at the start of freshman year, when we all began taking classes at Maple Creek High. He was tall, dark, handsome, and athletic. But it only took two weeks for me to discover his wicked ways.

I sauntered around the edge of the dance floor and removed the cream-colored coat from my shoulders. No one stood at the punch table, so I poured myself a drink. The cherry flavored liquid felt pungent on my tongue, as I shriveled my face in disgust. When I looked up, a young girl approached, who could have been no older than fifteen.

"Ricky poisoned it," the girl said. Her black bob

slightly bounced as she spoke.

"What?" I set the plastic cup down on the table, carefully looking her over.

"I mean with alcohol." She shrugged her shoulders, then turned towards the dance floor to look at Ricky. "He's my brother."

"Oh." I raised my eyebrows, then placed a hand at my waist. "My condolences."

The girl laughed at my snide remark, drawing attention to her doll-like figure. "I'm Jeanine." She stuck her small hand forward, shaking mine. "And you're Addie Smith."

"Yes." I nodded. "How do you know my name?"

"Ricky." She pointed over her shoulder, while her older brother gyrated against Nicki's tight-skirted bottom. "He talks about you all the time."

"Really?" I caught Ricky's eye across the dance floor. He froze in place, then passed Nicki off to another football player, as the next techno-pop song began.

"I better go." Jeanine grew stoic and frightened. Her red lips looked as though they were quivering. "Don't tell him what I told you."

"All right." I watched her scamper away, not understanding our brief, yet telling conversation. When Ricky approached, I turned my back to him, studying the punch bowl before me.

"Hello Addie," Ricky murmured. I could feel his breath at the back of my neck.

I turned to face him. "What do you want?" I pressed my palm into his chest, pushing him away. Ricky leaned against the punch table, reclining on his elbows.

"Just to tell you how beautiful you look tonight."

Ricky pulled at my hair. I slapped his hand away, sighing in frustration. Nicki walked up to me, the hatred evident in her eyes.

I looked at Ricky, then grabbed the folds of my white gown. "You're ridiculous." I stormed off, in search of the bathroom, leaving Nicki to contemplate the behavior of her boyfriend.

On my way down a long corridor, I heard the sound of someone crying. Jeanine sat in the hallway, with her back against the wall. Her bright red party dress fell in ruffled folds, just above the knee.

"Jeanine, what's wrong?" I knelt down beside her, not minding that I might stain my white dress.

"Can you drive me home? Please! I don't want to go home with Ricky." Heavy tears streamed down her face, pulling streaks of black mascara with them.

"All right," I succumbed, resting my hand on her shoulder. "You're a freshman aren't you?"

"Yes." She nodded.

"And we had a class together?" I squinted my eyes in a questioning manner.

"Study hall," she whimpered, unable to look me in the eye.

I took a deep breath, blowing hot air through my teeth. "Wait here, I'll find the back door to this place." I rose, slipping back into my winter coat.

"Addie, thank you," she whispered, choking on her own tears. "And I'm sorry I ruined your night."

"It's all right, honey. My date didn't show anyway." I patted her on the shoulder before walking off.

I turned at the end of the hallway, noticing a red EXIT sign above a door. I pushed the door open and climbed three flights of stairs, before reaching an old wooden door at the top. Turning the tarnished metal knob, I crossed the threshold and found a dark, empty room.

"Hello," I called out, stepping forward. But as I let go of the heavy door, it swung back into the door frame, slamming in place. I twisted the doorknob, frowning at its immobility. The door was locked.

"Hello." I banged my fist against the door, yelling for help. "Jeanine!" But she wasn't going to hear me. I had left her in the hallway three floors below.

After fifteen minutes of hollering, I set my purse down and removed the thick warm coat that hung over my gown. The room smelled of dust and sweat. I wondered why the hotel had yet to remodel it, as renovations had been completed on the rest of the building just before the Winter Ball date had been set.

All was dark in the room, except for a small, square window that revealed a sliver of moonlight, which shone down on the floor below. I stepped into the pale white light and watched the half-moon hang in the black sky. A translucent layer of dense fog surrounded the moon, drawing further attention to its true silvery radiance.

"Addie," a strange voice said. I felt a cool hand touch the bare skin of my shoulder. My heart thumped loudly inside of my chest as I swallowed, too terrified to turn around. Lifting my eyes to the window, I spotted his reflection in the glass. His black, neatly cropped hair looked like Ricky's, though not exactly. Unable to resist my fear any longer, I turned around. The man who stood before me was not Ricky.

"Hello." He smiled, standing much closer than I would have liked. A pair of straight white teeth glimmered in the moonlight as I recoiled, pressing my body into the window. Privy to my fear, he held his hands up in innocence and backed away from me.

Breathing heavily, I closed my eyes, and then opened them again, only to find him staring at the stretch of wall beside me. He kept still, letting his arms hang down at his sides, as I took a step towards him. Once I followed his gaze, I realized that he was not staring at the wall, but at the painting that hung there.

It was a portrait of a young woman, no more than eighteen. She sat still in the moonlight, gently holding her palms together, over her lap. Long thick locks of golden blonde hair framed her face and fell to the middle of her back. The hair was silky, wavy, and looked as though it had been fashioned from an angel's wings.

The woman's frame appeared thin, fragile even, yet her complexion was less fair than one would have imagined, presumably from hours spent beneath the summer sun.

Though of all her soft, gentle features, the most remarkable was the magic, liquid luster of her emerald green eyes. She was beautiful.

"You remind me so much of her," he whispered in the darkness.

A white satin gown was draped over her shoulders, flowing around the rest of her slim body. I looked down at my own dress, unable to deny the similarities. *The hair. The eyes. The skin.* It was all the same. If not for the emerald stone around her neck, I would have thought I was looking in a mirror.

"Who is she?" I extended my hand, moving close enough to touch the portrait. But before my finger could trace the stone, all of it disappeared.

* * *

I woke in the darkness, lying on a bed of white sheets. Recognizing my bedroom, I turned to the lamp on my nightstand and switched it on. The clock by my bed indicated that it was three o'clock in the morning. I pulled the sheet back, sank my feet into the carpet, and lost my balance. Stumbling to the wooden chair near the window, I found my white formal gown and winter coat that lay draped over the seat. For the life of me, I could not remember putting them there.

I thought about the strange dream. The boy seemed familiar to me, somehow. He had jet black hair and a tall, muscular build, like Ricky. Yet, there was something different about the two of them. Both had brown eyes, but they were not quite the same. Ricky's eyes had always been a strange mixture of red and brown, like the color of a maple leaf. But the boy, the stranger, his eyes were golden brown, almost the shade of honey, with flecks of yellow sprinkled throughout.

I spent the next several nights sketching the boy's eyes. I started with a thin gray pencil to outline the shape of them. Then, I filled the pupils with black before coloring the irises with a blend of orange, yellow, and brown. By the time I was finished, the eyes reminded me of autumn, when all the leaves begin to change in color and hue.

I looked out at the tree that stood before my bedroom window. All of the leaves were gone.

Chapter 2

After New Year's, Maple Creek High was back in session. It had been over a week since I had seen Jeanine Travis at the Winter Ball, yet she found me just after the first bell rang. I was carelessly shoving books into my locker, not minding who was standing close enough to notice.

"Hey Addie," Jeanine said. She was wearing a candy apple red headband over her black bob. It rested just behind the line where her bangs began.

"Hi," I replied, smiling at her. I tried to remember if I had driven her home that night, but the last thing I could recall was finding her in the hallway, crying. "Did everything work out all right at the dance?"

"Yeah," she piped up, her voice escalating in pitch. Then, her eyes flicked to the side and she turned her head down. "I'm sorry about my brother," she whispered, discreetly glancing over her shoulder to see if anyone else was listening.

"It's okay." I shut my locker, beaming in her direction. Jeanine nodded, her voice turning quiet all of a sudden. "Well, don't be late for class." I turned on my heel and waved, as I walked down the hall towards homeroom.

I sat down in the front row, waiting for Mrs. Thompson to hand out our class schedules. I retrieved a sketchbook from my backpack and began drawing on the first page.

"Addie Smith," Mrs. Thompson called. I took the schedule from her, looking down to see what the semester held.

Name: Addie Smith

Year: Junior

Homeroom

1st period: Chemistry

2nd period: British Literature

3rd period: Trigonometry

4th period: Gym

Lunch

5th period: Western Civilization

6th period: Latin

7th period: Psychology

I was happy to see that I no longer had gym class first period. I curled my lip at chemistry and nearly barked at trigonometry. The curriculum had been tolerable for fall semester, but this spring semester schedule made me cringe.

Maple Creek High was ranked in the top five for college preparatory schools in Georgia. Atlanta always nabbed the top four spots with their top of the line educational facilities. In all honesty, we were lucky that Savannah had even made it on the list, much less received a fifth place standing.

At the sound of the bell, I packed my things and headed upstairs to the chemistry lab. I knew that Mr. Martinez was an easy grader and gave out bonus points for showing up. Nonetheless, I felt a nest of butterflies flutter around in my stomach when I entered the lab. The entrance was at the back of the classroom, with all of the tables and chairs facing the opposite direction, towards the whiteboard.

Each table held two chairs that sat beside each other. Looking around the room for an empty seat, I found a vacant table at the front of the classroom and decided to sit there. Nicki caught the corner of my eye, as I walked to the table. She glared in my direction, then whispered to her fellow cheerleaders. Their laughter echoed across the room.

Mr. Martinez swung the door back and entered the classroom. "Welcome back, students," he began, setting his books on the podium, once he reached the front of the room. He turned his back to us, holding a green marker to the board as he began to write out his name. "If you have not had one of my classes before, my name is Mr. Martinez." I looked down at the thick textbook on the table in front of me, losing focus when he continued with the introduction.

"Is this room 302?" A voice interrupted Mr. Martinez in the middle of his speech. I lifted my head at the sound of it. I knew that voice.

"Tom! Yes, I'm sorry I left you waiting downstairs," Mr. Martinez said. "Class, we have a new student joining us this semester, Tom Sutton." Mr. Martinez gestured in the boy's direction. "I trust that you all will do your best to make Tom feel welcome. Why don't you take a seat up here in the front, by Addie?"

I froze, too afraid to look into his eyes and acknowledge the truth.

Tom sat down beside me, in the chair to my left. I turned my head, though only slightly. He smiled at me, and then nodded his head in politeness. I looked away, refocusing on Mr. Martinez's lesson for the day. When the sign-in sheet made its way to our table, I let him write his signature first. Tom pushed the piece of paper towards me. I grabbed it without meeting his eyes, making sure that our hands did not touch.

When class ended, I packed my bag, then waited in silence. Tom stared at me and refused to move, even though I wanted nothing more than for him to leave quietly. Unable to stand the tension any longer, I rose from the table and took one last glimpse of him before I left. His eyes were the color of honey.

* * *

British literature class felt much less restricting. Mrs. White softly trotted across the front of the room, passing out the reading list for the semester. We would be reading *The Strange Case of Dr. Jekyll and Mr. Hyde*, *The Picture of Dorian Gray*, *Dracula*, and *The Woman in White*. I smiled down at the book titles. I had already read them all.

Afterwards, I stopped by the bathroom to splash cool water on my face. Someone had turned the heat up in the building, and I had grown hot in my thick gray sweater. I grabbed a few paper towels from the dispenser to dry my hands, and then looked in the mirror as I tied my hair back into a ponytail.

"Addie could never be homecoming queen." I immediately knew that the voice belonged to Nicki. I rushed towards the nearest bathroom stall and closed the door.

"Why not?" It was the voice of a cheerleader, though I couldn't be sure which one. They all sounded the same to me.

"The same reason why Ricky would never go out with her," Nicki chimed. "She's not pretty."

I felt my brow furrow in response. A cold feeling came over me, despite the sweat that had collected at the ridge of my palms. I listened for them to leave, and then bolted once they had. I didn't look in the mirror.

Chapter 3

Thankfully, Nicki was not in my next class, but Ricky was. I walked to the front of the classroom, standing in line behind the other students. Mr. Mason was a complete stickler about the seating chart. On the first day of class, he posted the chart at the front of the classroom, with the seats facing the opposite direction on the paper. So, everyone usually ended up seating themselves in the mirror image of the actual seating chart, because the angle he used to lay it out was just too confusing.

I followed a group of students to the back of the classroom, keeping my head down, as I looked at the seat number that was assigned to my name. I had written it down in my notebook, but all I noticed was the sketch of Tom's eyes that I had drawn earlier. I stopped in the fourth row, behind a very recognizable head of black hair.

"Ricky," I spoke with a sharp edge to my voice. "What are you doing in my seat?"

He turned around, but the "he" was not Ricky. The boy in my seat was Tom.

"Oh," I chirped, too startled to keep quiet. "I'm sorry. I thought you were–"

"Your seat is behind mine," he interrupted. Tom quickly glanced into my eyes, offering a hint of the yellow-gold in his.

I sank down into the chair, accepting the fact that I

would have to stare at the back of his head for the next fifty minutes. Mr. Mason entered the room, clapping his hands together as he did so. He was not a very tall man, and his thin, wiry body most closely resembled a toothpick.

"Pop quiz!" Mr. Mason exclaimed, running to his desk. He picked up a thick stack of papers, while I sighed in misery. "Mr. Travis," he declared, "nice of you to join us."

I turned back in my seat, cringing when Ricky sat down in the desk behind me. He pressed his lips out, kissing the air in front of him. I handed him a quiz over my shoulder, once the remaining pages for our row reached me.

"Hey Mr. Mason!" Ricky leaned over my shoulder. "Can I borrow a pencil?"

"Sure," the teacher replied. Mr. Mason opened his desk drawer to retrieve a pencil. Without any foreseen warning, he threw the pencil at Ricky, and it hit him in the head.

"Ow!" Ricky scratched his head. "What was that for?"

"Maybe next time you should come to class more prepared, Mr. Travis." Mr. Mason paced the floor, walking up and down every row. "I will not tolerate coming to class unprepared!" He stopped in front of Ricky's desk, hovering over him. "Even from the star quarterback," he added. Then, Mr. Mason lowered his voice, and only those around him heard what he had to say next. "Football season's over Ricky. Get a clue."

I chuckled to myself, making a mental note to remember the day Ricky Travis got showed up in trigonometry class. "What are you laughin' at?" Ricky tapped my shoulder with his pencil. I turned my head, offering a sassy smirk. "Mr. Mason, Addie's cheating off my quiz!" Ricky yelled in the tone of a tattle-telling preschooler.

"There's nothing written on your page yet, Mr. Travis," Mr. Mason said from the front of the room, though his back was turned to us. I laughed a little louder this time, holding a hand over my mouth to muffle the noise.

Just as I bent my head down to start the quiz, Ricky grabbed the ponytail at the back of my head and forcefully jerked it out of place. My neck slammed into the desk behind me as I cried out in pain. All of my hair fell down in thick, wavy locks, while Ricky continued tugging it at the ends.

Enraged, Tom rose from his desk and leapt on top of Ricky. By the time I was able to sit up in my own desk and look at what was happening, the two boys were on the floor, brawling. I held a hand to the back of my neck, overcome by a sudden migraine.

Ricky pinned Tom to the ground, battering his fist against Tom's face. Mr. Mason rushed to the back of the room, leaping over desks like an Olympic hurdler. But before Mr. Mason could reach them, Tom jabbed Ricky with a strong arm, and that was when Ricky's nose started bleeding.

Mr. Mason grabbed both of the boys by their shirt collars and marched them out the door, down the hall, and into the principal's office. When he returned, Mr. Mason collected the quizzes whether we had finished them or not. I hadn't answered a single question.

* * *

Before gym class started, I changed clothes in the locker room and tied my hair back into a ponytail.

Afterwards, I followed a group of junior girls onto the track. I heard them complaining about the cold, but I liked the winter weather. It was nice to see my breath in the open air before me.

Coach Coleman appeared with a group of junior boys, both Ricky and Tom among them. Ricky had a light brown bandage covering his nose, while Tom wore a strip of white tape over his cheekbone. Suddenly, it felt as if everyone's eyes were on me.

"All right, kids," Coleman began. "Run five. Walk five." Coleman lifted a silver whistle to his lips, signaling the start of our laps. Ricky sat down on a row of bleachers, touching his nose in agony. "That's all right, son," Coleman said. "You can sit out the first week."

Coleman was the varsity football coach. Go figure.

My classmates rushed by in a blur of skin and clothing, as I caught a glimpse of Tom dressed in a black t-shirt and black sweatpants, with a white pin-stripe on either side of them. He walked past me, quietly staring into my eyes, before turning his head and running after the others. Bewildered, I shook my head and shrugged, because the boy from my dream was the same one who was distracting me now in gym class.

Coach Coleman noticed the distraction and came running after me, blowing his whistle all the while. I chased after Tom, hurriedly escaping the wrath of Coleman. When I caught up with Tom, he looked over his shoulder at me.

"Hi," I softly greeted. "I just wanted to thank you for what you did, earlier today." I motioned over my shoulder at the bleachers, where Ricky sat holding his nose.

"So now you'll talk to me." Tom kept a steady pace, breathing deeply. "That's right." Tom snapped his fingers and looked up at the sky. "You're one of those who has to be rescued first."

I exhaled, looking to the football field that rested in the middle of the track. "How did things go in the principal's office?"

Tom turned his head towards me. "Fine," he said. "How does your neck feel?"

"Fine," I echoed. We both started laughing at that. After another half mile of keeping pace with him, I worked up the nerve to tell Tom that I had seen him before today.

"So, this is going to sound so crazy, but..." I hesitated, not wanting him to think that I needed to seek mental help. Tom looked back and forth, between me and the track, until I spoke again. "I had a dream about you. I was at this dance that our school has every year, in December, and-"

"I know," he interjected before I could go on.

"You know?" I stopped on the track, tugging at his shirt sleeve to make him stop with me. "How could you possibly know?"

Tom stood before me, leaning his face towards mine. I could feel his breath on my lips. "Because you weren't dreaming." Tom took off running again, as the rest of the gym class came barreling towards me. I stepped back at the sight of the stampede and fell into the end zone on the football field.

Before I could regain my bearings, Coach Coleman ran after me, whistle in hand. Frantic, I jumped to my feet and sprinted onto the track with a hand over each ear.

Chapter 4

After gym class, I changed back into my school clothes and headed to the cafeteria. I saw Tom up ahead, on the breezeway, walking with his hands stuffed into his pockets. He was alone.

Picking up the pace, I hurried after him, enjoying the sight of my breath misting in the air. I watched him enter the building and flinched when the door slammed shut behind him.

Just before I reached the entryway, Ricky appeared out of thin air. "Hey Addie," he beckoned, sliding his arm behind my neck. "Where ya goin'?"

"Stop touching me," I demanded, pulling myself out of his grasp. I entered the cafeteria and searched for Tom in the crowd. Grabbing a sand-colored lunch tray, I followed the handrails until I had reached the back of the line. I quickly spotted Tom and smiled. There were only two middle-school boys standing between us.

Once I reached the long, buffet-styled food station, I grabbed a turkey sandwich, carrot sticks, a fruit cup, and a bowl of banana pudding, and then placed them each on the tray in that order. Moving along in the line, I waited to grab a bottle of water, until the two boys between Tom and me scampered off, in search of the soda fountain.

Tom spoke over the protective layer of glass that covered the food, asking the lunch lady for a fork.

"They're over there," I butted in, pointing to the table by the soda fountain. It was covered with silverware and condiments. The lunch lady nodded, pointing in the same direction.

"Thank you," Tom said, looking at the lunch lady. He turned to me and nodded before walking off.

"Hey girl." Ricky stood behind me with a tray of hamburgers, potato chips, and Snickers bars. How he was able to maintain his clear complexion with that kind of diet was a mystery that I had never been able to solve.

I grabbed a small milk carton from the food line and peeled the opening back before setting the carton down on my lunch tray. Ricky placed his hands around my waist and squeezed my stomach with his muscular arms. "Ricky, let go," I whimpered, barely able to breathe. I could feel his hot breath against my neck. The stubble of his beard felt tingly and strange against my skin. "Leave me alone," I complained, while students stopped and stared.

Ricky picked up the bowl of banana pudding from my tray and poured it all over my hair. I froze, pulling my fingers through the creamy yellow substance. The pudding dripped down my face, falling into my eyes and mouth. In anger, I picked up the milk carton and poured it down his shirt. Ricky's eyes widened as the stinging cold liquid ran down his chest.

I smirked in his direction, then puckered my lips into a fake kiss, mimicking his earlier behavior in Mr. Mason's class. Instantly provoked, Ricky grabbed the back of my ponytail and pulled, sending me to my knees. I slapped his arms and screamed to be let go, until I felt two arms wrap around my stomach and pull me away from him. But Ricky pursued me anyway, while I flailed around, eventually kicking him in the jaw. When I did, Ricky staggered backwards and sank down to the floor in front of me.

Tom still had his arms around me when Principal Caldwell approached us with a clipboard in hand. "You three," he coldly commanded, pointing to each of us. "Follow me."

Tom helped me to my feet and glared at Ricky before we all followed the principal back to his office. Ricky walked beside Caldwell, talking with him the whole time as if they were old pals. Principal Caldwell was Nicki's father; it was so unfair. But I forced myself to be quiet, and even bit my tongue, to keep from yelling the obscenities that I was thinking in my head.

When we reached Caldwell's office, he sat down in a brown leather office chair that rolled in front of his desk, a nice piece of furniture with a cherry oak finish. "Which one of you would like to tell me what happened this time?" Caldwell looked me in the eye. "Addie?"

We stood before him in a row of three. Somehow, I had been sandwiched in between Tom and Ricky. The former stood to my right, the latter to my left.

I cleared my throat, reminding myself that Caldwell would favor Ricky above all else because of Nicki. "Well, we were in the lunch line and Ricky attacked me."

"What?" Ricky intercepted. "That's not true. She attacked me," Ricky pleaded, motioning to the bloody nose that Tom had given him in math class and the swollen jaw that I had given him ten minutes ago. I lunged for Ricky's throat, disgusted with him for lying, because I knew that he would get away with it. Caldwell would see to that.

Tom pulled me away from Ricky and into his grasp. With his arms locked around my clavicle, Tom held me back to prevent me from pouncing on Ricky again.

"Let her go," Caldwell demanded. Tom released me, and then stepped in front of Ricky, taking my place between them. Caldwell gripped a pen in his hand and pointed it at me. "Detention," he said, sending a soft heat through my body. Then, he raised the pen towards Tom and did the same. "Detention," he repeated.

"What about him?" Tom and I said in unison. Ricky held his nose, complaining that it had started bleeding again.

"Ricky," Caldwell addressed him, though without the condescending pen. "I want a five page paper on the importance of Southern hospitality, due on Friday."

"What?" I argued, leaning over Caldwell's desk. "We get detention and all he has to do is write a paper!" I motioned from us to Ricky as the sentence lengthened.

"Ms. Smith, let's see," Caldwell sputtered, opening a file on his desk. "You're eligible for that art program, at the institute in Atlanta this summer. Is that correct?"

"Yes sir," I answered, resenting the scruples that require one to respect authority.

"Wouldn't want to spoil your chances now, would you?" Caldwell raised a gray eyebrow, while his sinister gray eyes failed to blink.

"No sir," I spoke through my teeth, holding my hands behind my back to keep from strangling him.

"Well then." He smiled, revealing two crooked front teeth. "I suggest that you apologize to Mr. Travis, and then be on your merry way."

I turned to Ricky, sighing in discontent. Tom grabbed my wrist and then spoke into my ear. "Just do it," he whispered, nudging me on.

"I'm sorry, Ricky," I offered, then quickly averted my eyes.

"That's all right," Ricky remarked. "We all make mistakes. Isn't that right, Tom?"

Tom kept his hand around my wrist, sensing that my blood had yet to stop boiling.

"All right," Caldwell said. "Off you go." He pointed towards the door, prompting us to leave. "Oh, and take a shower." Caldwell waved a hand in front of his nose. "Ya'll smell like food."

Ricky left first, and then we sauntered out afterwards. Caldwell slammed the door behind us, just as I crossed the threshold. Tom walked with me down the hallway, shoving his hands into his pockets.

"I can't believe that guy," Tom snapped, kicking one of his black boots into the side of the wall. "Does Ricky always get out of trouble so easily?"

"Yes," I complained, running a hand through my hair. It felt sticky and gross.

"Man, my first day at a new school and I've already got detention," he said, studying the floor beneath him.

"How mad are your parents going to be when you get home?" I searched his face and smiled when he found mine.

"They shouldn't be too mad," he began. "They died when I was a little boy. I never knew my parents." Tom grew quiet, looking through the glass windows at the end of the hallway.

"Tom, I'm so sorry," I sympathized, holding my palm to my chest. "I didn't know." Tom nodded, as if the matter were of no importance. "What about your parents? Will they be mad?"

"Oh yeah," I chuckled, "Mom's gonna flip."

Chapter 5

"Addison Elizabeth Smith!"

A cold shiver came over me at the sound of Mom's voice. "Yes Mother." I entered the foyer with a backpack slung over my shoulder. We never spoke this formally to each other, unless I had gotten into trouble. Mom was great about paying attention to me when things were going badly. She never said anything when they weren't.

"Please tell me why I received a call from the principal's office today," she snapped, still dressed in scrubs.

"Hey Mom." I waved. "It's good to see you too."

"Cut that out right now." She pointed her finger at me, reminiscent of Caldwell. "You served detention today?"

"Yeah, so?" I opened the pantry, searching for something crunchy to eat.

"You've never served detention in your entire life, Addie. This just doesn't sound like you at all," she murmured, placing her hands on her hips.

"It's Ricky, Mom," I insisted, turning from the pantry to face her.

"Who?" A fine line formed between her eyebrows. Two pairs of crow's feet crinkled at the outer edges of her eyelids.

"Ricky Travis," I hesitated, "the quarterback."

"Oh yeah." She moved towards the telephone as it

began to ring. "He's cute." She grinned like a Cheshire cat. "Hello?" Mom and I don't really look anything alike. She has deep brown eyes, dark brunette hair, and olive skin, convincing me that I must have inherited my lighter features from someone else in the family. "Yes, I'll be right in," she declared and hung the phone back up on the wall.

"Back to the hospital?" I lifted myself onto the counter, letting my legs dangle beneath me.

"Yes." She looked down at the cell phone in her hand as she left the kitchen. "A cesarean and then two sets of twins," she announced. "I'm staying in town tonight. I only stopped by to stock the fridge with more food." We lived in the country, on a plot of sixty beautiful acres. Funny thing is, I was the only one who noticed.

"What about Dad?" I walked behind her, following her footsteps like a house dog.

"He's got that deposition in Atlanta tomorrow, and then court for the rest of the week." She did not look up from her phone when she reached the front door.

"Goodbye, Mom," I called after her. She crossed the threshold, already talking to someone else on the phone again. The door slammed shut behind her. "Love you," I whispered to myself. It wasn't like she was going to hear me.

Every night had been like this since I turned thirteen, when I was old enough to stay at home by myself. I looked in the fridge. Mom had stopped by an Italian restaurant, a Chinese restaurant, and a Mexican restaurant and ordered enough food for a week. Everything looked delicious, but I wasn't hungry.

I watched TV in the living room for a little while, flipping to a new channel each time a commercial came on. Any homework that had been assigned was due later in the week, since today was the first day back at school. So, I headed upstairs to my bedroom and picked up the phone.

I had been trying to get in touch with Eric all week, since he never showed up at the dance. We had been friends since childhood, but when his sister Emily went missing two years ago, the entire family moved to Atlanta. I understood the need for a change, because Emily had been my best friend.

"Eric," I sighed in relief, glad to hear the sound of his voice.

"Hi Addie," he replied, cheerful enough.

"What happened to you at the dance? You never showed up. I've been trying to get a hold of you all week." I sat in the chair by my window, rubbing a thumb over my fingernails.

"Sorry Addie, I got held up." Eric grew quiet, pensive even. Neither of us said anything on the phone for a long time, until he broke the silence. "Mom and Dad don't want me coming back to Savannah anymore," Eric murmured.

"What?" I could not believe it. Eric was the only piece of Emily that I had left.

"They don't think it's safe." I could hear him breathing in the background.

"Okay," I accepted. "I understand."

"Be careful, Addie," Eric said before hanging up the phone.

"I will."

* * *

Back at school, Mr. Mason rearranged the seating chart. Ricky and I were now separated by three rows of desks. It was nice to let my hair down.

Jeanine joined me for lunch on Friday, complaining about life as a freshman. I gave her advice, recalling my experience with the same teachers and courses. Jeanine was a sweet girl, with her cute childlike features. Except for the black hair, I did not see how she and Ricky were related.

"Have you seen my lipstick?" Jeanine opened her purse and began sifting through every pocket.

"No," I replied. Jeanine wore a cherry red shade of color on her lips. It was as much a part of her look as the black bob.

"It's okay." She waved her hand in the air, tossing the matter aside. "I have another one at home."

At the end of the day, Jeanine approached me on the way to our lockers. "What are you doing this weekend?" Her dark blue eyes glistened beneath the fluorescent lighting.

"I don't have any plans. What did you have in mind?" I held a notebook and two textbooks in my arms, as we neared my locker.

"I was thinking we could go see a movie," Jeanine offered, a desperate look in her eyes.

"Yeah," I agreed. "That sounds fun."

We paused in the hallway and noticed a group of teenage boys hovering around my locker. I recognized them as members of the varsity football team and close friends of Ricky. "Excuse me," I demanded, forcing my way through the crowd.

The group of boys parted like the Red Sea, splitting into two clusters, as I saw what lay between them. On the front of my gray metal locker, the word **VIRGIN** was written in red lipstick. I recognized the shade as the one Jeanine wore on her lips: cherry red.

I turned around and gave Jeanine a questioning look. "I didn't do it," she said, shaking her head from side to side. The ends of her black bob swayed to and fro.

Nicki stepped out from the girls' bathroom with her hands crossed over her chest. Her platinum blonde ringlets jostled with each forceful step of her high-heeled boots. I could make out the image of a small object in her hand that was the size of a chess piece. Nicki approached Jeanine and dropped the object before her feet. It was a tube of cherry red lipstick.

Tom appeared out of the corner of my eye. He took a slow step forward, looking at my locker and then turning his face to look at me. Jeanine knelt down, retrieving the tube of the lipstick from the floor.

"Thanks," Nicki sneered. She smiled down at Jeanine before turning to walk away.

I scowled in Jeanine's direction and stormed off, not bothering to stop by my locker. "Addie," Tom crooned. He grabbed my arm when I passed him, but I pulled away and bolted for the door.

"I didn't do it Addie!" Jeanine yelled after me, but I wasn't in the mood to listen. "Addie! I didn't do it!"

I spent the afternoon holed up in my bedroom, distracting myself with chemistry homework. I neither liked it nor understood it, but it took my mind off what had happened that day.

Before sunset, I trudged down our long dirt driveway. The mailbox stood at the end of it, on the other side of our locked gate. I hopped over the shortest part of the gate and checked the mail. I was the only one who ever did.

I found a handful of bills, two fliers advertising the

opening of a new pizza place in town, and one envelope addressed to me. I hopped back over the gate and folded the rest of the mail into a wad that was small enough to fit inside my jacket pocket.

A cool chill filled the air as I veered off the driveway, entering the wilderness. I walked with the envelope in my hand, striving to get as deep into the forest as possible. Once I felt secure enough, within the safety of the woods, I sat down at the base of a massive oak tree and opened the envelope. There was a folded piece of printer paper inside.

Confusion swept over me, because there was no return address on the back of the envelope. I scanned the stretch of wilderness surrounding me to make sure that no one else could see what I held in my hands.

I unfolded the sheet of paper and held a hand over my mouth. A pair of emerald green eyes stared back at me. I was looking at the portrait from my dream. Three words were scrawled in black ink at the bottom of the page: *Find the necklace.*

I folded the portrait into a small square and slid it into my pocket with the rest of the mail. Rising to my feet, I brushed away any dirt that had collected on the back of my clothing and headed for the house. I stopped along the way, watching the sun sink into the trees. Before the sunset was complete, a melodic harmony filtered through the woods. My ears perked up at the sound, so I followed it.

I soon found myself trailing beside the wooden fence that separated our land from the neighboring property. A row of trees lined the fence on the other side, so I wasn't able to see what lay beyond the border until I reached an open gap that spread into a stretch of pasture land. A man stood in the grass, no more than a hundred yards from me. He stared at the horizon, whistling to himself in glee.

"Tom?" I shouted in disbelief.

He turned around and lifted his hand in the air. "Hey," Tom called, walking towards the fence.

"What are you doing?" I leaned over the wooden railing, surprised by his presence.

"Just watchin' the sunset," he answered. Tom shoved his hands into his pockets and smiled in my direction.

"No," I clarified, "I mean, what are you doing here?"

Tom removed one hand from his pocket and slung it over the fence. "I live here," he said, as if it had always been true.

"Oh," I retorted. "Since when?" I had never known of anyone owning the lot next to us; it had always been vacant.

"My grandfather has a house here and I live with him." Tom's eyes glowed like the flames of a fire. The yellow edges of his irises appeared gold in the fading sunlight.

"Oh." I nodded. I remembered the envelope in my pocket, and it suddenly felt bigger. "While I have you here, I need to show you something." I reached into my jacket pocket and unfolded the picture. Tom held his hand over the fence and took the page when I offered it to him. "Now," I murmured, lowering my voice. "I think it's about time we talked about that dream."

Chapter 6

Tom and I approached his grandfather's three-story colonial style mansion. Ivory pillars stood in a perfect row at the front of the porch, which wrapped all the way around the house. The front door was painted in coal black, to match the trim and shutters that framed each window.

"Are you coming?" Tom beckoned from the doorway.

"Oh," I started, climbing the few steps up to the entrance. Tom shut the door behind me and walked down the hallway that extended from the foyer. I glanced into the entryway of the dining room and sitting area as we passed through the house. Fine furniture and décor had been artistically laid out in each room, while numerous landscapes lined the walls on either side of us. I had never seen so many paintings in someone's house in all my life.

Tom turned right at the end of the hall. I looked back over my shoulder to observe the kitchen as we passed it. Tom weaved his way through the dining room before entering the staircase that rested on the other side of the doorway. I followed Tom, taking two steps at a time to match his pace.

At the top of the staircase, I noticed a bedroom that sat snuggly in the right hand corner. But Tom turned in the other direction and stopped before an old wooden door. Tom jerked at the metal handle, sighing in relief when the door squeaked open.

We entered the dark room. It had no more light than what filtered through the small square window. A wooden board creaked beneath my feet when I took a step forward. "Can I see the picture?" Tom stuck his hand out. I unfolded the paper and handed it to him.

The original hung on the wall that lay just past the window. Tom held up the page beside the portrait. The two images were nearly identical in every way, except for the handwritten message at the bottom of the photocopy I had received in the mail.

"Who is she?" I stepped in front of the painting and rubbed my finger over the canvas, to feel the texture of the paint. A thin silver chain hung around the woman's neck, holding the stone over her breast. White diamonds circled the shape of the emerald, as it lay over her white satin gown.

"Antoinette Beaumont," Tom answered. He pointed at the base of the painting, where a tiny string of letters spelled her name.

"So, whoever sent this wants me to find her necklace?" I nodded to the portrait. Tom handed the printed picture back to me and shoved his hands into his pockets.

"That's what it sounds like," Tom sighed, glancing over the painting one last time.

"Well, why did they send it to me? And how am I supposed to figure out who this person even is?" I folded the picture and put it back in my pocket. The door creaked open, startling me as I moved closer to Tom.

"I know who sent you that picture." A stranger stood in the doorway.

"Grandpa," Tom called, walking towards him. "I

thought you were lying down." Tom placed his hand on the old man's chest. His face looked worn and ragged, with saggy, wrinkled skin bordering his eyes and mouth. But there was a look of intrigue in his beady blue eyes that could not be missed.

"Let me see her," the old man hissed. Tom stepped out of the way and motioned for me to come closer.

I swallowed, and then took three careful steps toward him. The old man placed his hand on my cheek and studied my eyes. I froze, widening my eyes at Tom when his grandfather began to examine a lock of my hair.

"All right, Grandpa." Tom grabbed his grandfather by the shoulders and turned him towards the window. The old man sat down on the windowsill and patted his head with a white handkerchief.

"Mr. Sutton?" I asked, growing bold enough to step into the moonlight.

"Please, call me Daniel," he insisted.

"Okay, Daniel," I paused, holding my hands together in a nervous manner. Tom nodded in my direction, urging me to continue. "Who sent me this picture?" I handed him the piece of paper, which was now covered with wrinkles and creases.

Daniel removed a pair of reading glasses from his breast pocket and slipped them on. After quickly scanning the picture, he returned it to me and said, "Tony DeMilo."

"Tony DeMilo," I repeated, letting the words roll off my own tongue to see if they sounded any more familiar. I shook my head, knowing that they didn't. "Who's Tony DeMilo?"

"He was Antoinette's husband," Tom said. "She

was murdered fifty years ago, right here in Savannah. They found her body floating in the river."

"Who killed her?" My heart was pounding. It sounded like it had settled at the base of my throat.

"Well, no one really knows for sure." Tom embellished the length of his words. I didn't like the tone of his voice; it was uncertain.

"I know." Daniel looked out the window, as if the glass were allowing him to see into the past.

"DeMilo," I guessed, turning my head from Tom to his grandfather. "Am I right?"

"Yes," Daniel whispered, disliking the truth.

"How did you know them?" I could not fight the urge to learn more. I had to know what happened in Savannah all those years ago.

"Antoinette was friends with my wife." Daniel looked down at his wrinkled hands, as they began to shake. "I think I better go lie down," he said reluctantly. "I've excited myself too much this evening."

Tom helped Daniel to his feet and said, "You need to take it easy, Grandpa." Daniel shook his head, not wanting to hear it. "Wait here," Tom said to me, "and I'll walk you home." I nodded, watching as Tom led his grandfather through the doorway.

I circled the room until Tom returned. There was a door at the back of the room, concealed beneath a layer of darkness. I had never noticed it before.

"Let's go," Tom called. I turned my face away from that far secluded space in the room and followed Tom's voice into the hall. He didn't say anything about Daniel, so I didn't either.

Tom grabbed a thick winter coat from a wooden rack in the foyer and slipped his arms through the sleeves. I stuck my hands into the gray jacket over my sweater, preparing for the cold. As we entered the wilderness, our boots crunching over dried leaves and branches, I looked to Tom and asked, "Do you know why DeMilo killed his wife?"

"No," he replied, looking straight ahead.

"Liar," I murmured. Tom stopped, jerking his face in my direction.

"Antoinette is the lady in the painting," Tom snapped, his words rushing past my face in foggy, white breaths. "She was married to DeMilo, and he murdered her. That's all I know." Tom turned his back to me and continued through the woods. I remained where I stood.

"I don't believe you," I softly spoke.

Tom stopped dead in his tracks. "Look, it's not my story to tell, all right?" He turned back to me, his face dim and gray in the moonlight. "Come back another time." I accepted, nodding my head in the darkness.

We continued through the trees without speaking. I found the silence to be louder than the shrieking owl in the distance. Once we reached the edge of my house, I looked up at Tom. "You sure know your way around these parts," I mentioned. Tom ignored what I said and stopped before the front door steps. When he turned to walk away, I asked, "Can we talk?"

Tom hesitated, rocking back on his heels. I detected the faintest glimmer of gold in his eyes as he searched my face, considering. "I really should be getting back to Grandpa," he explained.

"It will only take a minute," I urged, motioning for him to come to the door when I opened it. Tom tilted his head back, taking in the exterior of the house.

When he finally answered, it was through a pair of

chattering teeth. "Oh, all right," he consented.

I shut the door behind us, placed the mail from my pocket on the kitchen table, and then walked into the living room. "My room's this way," I said, pointing towards the staircase in the distance.

"Where are your parents?" I sensed the uneasiness in Tom's voice. We climbed up the stairs, while I explained their absence.

"Working," I chirped. "Mom's a doctor. Dad's a lawyer." I rattled my parent's occupations off like a drive-thru attendant at a fast food restaurant: *Two cokes, two fries. Will that complete your order?*

I opened my bedroom door, flipped the light switch on, and sat down on the edge of my bed to remove the warm winter boots I had been wearing. "They have an apartment in town," I continued, tugging at the laces. "They bought it a few years ago, so they wouldn't have to drive out here late at night, if either of them had to stay late at work." Tom stalled in the doorway, unsure if he was allowed to enter. "They stay there most nights, so I don't wait up."

Tom stepped into the room, content that no disgruntled parent would come barging in at any moment. "That seems unfair," Tom mused, studying the drawings on my desk and the cork board above it. I left my boots on the floor in front of my bed and rose to shut the door.

"What does?" I unzipped my jacket and hung it up in the closet. Then, I grabbed my boots from the floor and threw them in the closet before shutting it.

Tom shed his thick winter coat and sat down in the chair by the window. "They ignore you," he declared, as if there were no question. I grew quiet, sitting down in the swivel chair before my desk. "I didn't mean it like that," Tom said, backpedaling. "What did you want to talk about?" Tom leaned forward in the chair, resting his elbows against his knees.

"What happened on the night of the dance?" I crossed one leg over the other, determined to have an answer. When he wouldn't respond, I pressed him further. "I know you were there."

"I wasn't," he argued, folding his arms over his chest. When I groaned in frustration, Tom spoke again. "You really don't remember, do you?" he asked, searching my face.

"All I can remember is being at the dance, and then I was in the room we just left at your grandfather's house. And you were there with the painting. Then I woke up here," I declared, looking at my bed against the wall. "That's all I can remember," I admitted, holding a palm to my forehead. When I tried to recollect anymore about that night, my temples began to throb.

Tom stared at me, his eyes like two glowing beams of light.

"Well," I grumbled, "are you going to tell me what happened or not?"

"Not tonight," he muttered. Tom sat still beneath the moonlight. I glared at him and let my shoulders sag in disappointment. But then a bolt of energy surged through my veins. I had an idea.

"Can I draw you?" I almost laughed at the idea myself. In that moment, nothing seemed more out of place.

"Um." Tom pulled his eyebrows together, thinking to himself. "Sure."

I opened my sketch pad to a fresh sheet of paper. There was a wooden box of colored pencils stored in the top drawer of my desk. I selected shades of black, yellow, gold, and brown from the box and set those pencils by the sketch pad on my desk.

"Just sit still," I told him. "And try not to breathe." Tom widened his eyes in alarm. I laughed, and then explained that I was only joking.

Chapter 7

A loud clatter woke me the next morning. I recognized that the sound was coming from the kitchen and leapt from the bed. My parents were home.

I opened my bedroom door and took the stairs down two at a time, not bothering to change out of the clothes I had slept in. I entered the kitchen, noticing the blender on the counter. It was filled with carrots, tomato juice, blueberries, and ice.

"Hey Dad," I spoke, recognizing his figure on the ground, kneeling behind an open cabinet door. Dad hit his head on the wood and peered around the door.

"You scared me," he barked, pressing a palm to the top of his head. "Have you seen the lid to this thing?" Dad shut the cabinet door and stood up, blood rushing to his face. I opened one of the overhead cabinets next to the fridge and grabbed the lid to the blender. "Thanks," Dad said. He took the lid from my hand and placed it over the blender.

I lifted myself onto the kitchen counter and watched the tornado of red, blue, and orange swirl inside the container. When the mixture became one frothy liquid concoction, Dad pressed a button that silenced the machine. "How is school?" Dad poured the drink into a thermos, then took a sip once it was full.

"Fine," I droned. Dad set the thermos down and

cupped a hand over his mouth. The blended drink spewed from his lips, spraying across the floor. "Dad, what are you doing?" I slid down from the counter and retrieved a dish towel to wipe up the mess.

"That stuff's disgusting," he griped, rinsing his mouth out in the sink. "Your mother's insane," he said with his head bent under the faucet. I rolled my eyes, waiting for him to get out of the way, so I could clean the tile.

As if reading my mind, Dad stepped around the explosion of smoothie that remained on the floor, leaving it to me. There was a briefcase on the table, along with a jacket that completed his suit-and-tie ensemble. Dad was lucky to walk away with his work clothes unstained.

"How are you with money?" Dad slipped his arms through the jacket and straightened his tie. I stood with the dish towel in my hands, unsure of what he meant. "Oh, that reminds me," he began, reaching into his back pocket. "I just upgraded the credit card, and I don't think I gave you one yet." An ash-blonde hair fell across his forehead, but he smoothed it back into place. "Just cut up the old one," he instructed, handing me a new piece of plastic from his wallet.

"Thanks," I muttered, carelessly tossing the credit card on the counter. Dad walked towards the front door, briefcase in hand, so I spoke up before he was gone. "Where's Mom?" I followed him into the foyer and leaned against the doorway.

"The hospital," he answered. "And then she leaves for that medical convention in the morning." He checked his appearance in the mirror hanging next to the coat rack. "Well," he chirped, "call us if you need anything." The door shut behind him in one swift, final movement.

I cleaned the kitchen floor and then did a load of laundry. There was an expired carton of milk in the fridge, so I poured it down the drain and wrinkled my nose at the smell. I wasn't living with parents. I was living with a couple of self-absorbed workaholics, who had forgotten that they had a kid of their own.

* * *

Sheets of sketching paper lay scattered across the desk in my bedroom. I pulled the center sheet towards me. It was the drawing of Tom that I had done the night before. It was mostly black-and-white, with empty spaces left for me to color in the rest of his skin, clothing, and eyes. I turned around in my swivel chair and looked at the window where Tom had been.

In the drawing, Tom sat with his arms relaxed and feet spread apart. He was wearing a charcoal sweater, with sleeves that stopped at the elbow, as well as a pair of black jeans and boots. The sweater dipped down into a v-shaped opening at the top of his chest. It revealed the olive tone of his skin, still glowing with traces of the summer sun, despite the change in season.

I picked up a flesh-colored pencil and sketched within the outline of his lips. I had made sure to copy them exactly as they were in real life. Tom was not smiling.

Looking at his eyes, I traced a rim around the deep black dots of each pupil. Then, I filled in the irises with a rich golden color and bubbled over them in yellow. I lowered my head over the paper and blew away any traces of pigment that the colored pencils had left behind.

I collected the other sheets of paper on my desk and stacked them into a pile. A small white envelope fell through the pages. It felt lighter than it had the day before, so I opened the flap of the envelope and looked inside. It was empty.

* * *

"Tom!" I stood on his front porch and beat my fist against the door. "Open up," I demanded, "it's Addie." A cream-colored shade flicked against one of the windows. "Come on!" I yelled. "I'm freezing out here!" The door opened.

"What?" Tom leaned against the door with a hand on his hip.

"Did you steal the picture DeMilo sent me?" I accused, raising my voice.

"Shh," he whispered, holding a finger to his lips. Tom grabbed my arm and jerked me across the threshold. "Be quiet," he said. Tom closed the door behind us and led me into the den. Beyond the arrangement of fine furniture, a well-lit fireplace sat snuggly against the far wall.

"Well," I continued, "did you steal it or not?" Tom parted his lips to reply, but then hesitated. "Just tell me," I demanded. "Did you take it?" Tom nodded. I turned away from him and headed towards the hallway. I was prepared to search every room in the house until I found it.

"Addie, wait," Tom called, "you don't understand." He caught the sleeve of my jacket and pulled me back. "I only did it to protect you." I searched his eyes, unsure if I could find truth in them.

"Protect me from what?" I snapped, drawing my arm out of his grasp. I marched into the hallway when he didn't respond.

"Look, it's complicated, all right?" Tom stood at the end of the hall. "It would be really hard for me to explain it to you," he sighed. I looked back at him and then attempted to ward off the sudden pain in my chest.

"Oh," I piped up, "so what you're saying is that I'm too stupid to understand." The words left me trembling. I could not stand still any longer.

"No," Tom dissented, "that's not what I'm saying at all." I weaved my way through the house and did not stop until I had found the staircase. "You won't find it up there." My hand froze where I had placed it on the railing. Tom leaned against the wall with his hands in his pockets.

"Then where is it?" I demanded, stepping down from the handful of stairs that I had managed to climb. Tom studied the ground as if a map of Southeast Asia had been sketched onto the floor, and he was looking for a port.

"I threw it in the fire," Tom murmured, no louder than a whisper. He didn't look me in the eye until the words were out of his mouth. I retraced my steps to the den and knelt down in front of the fireplace. Pieces of ash danced beneath the flames.

"You never should have opened that envelope." Tom placed his hand on the mantle and glanced down at the fire.

"And why not?" I rose from my crouched position on the carpet. I could feel Tom's eyes watching me, but I could not bear to look at him.

Tom shook his head and shoved both hands into his pockets. It was the exact way that Tom behaved every time he felt cornered. I trudged to the door in disappointment. "Addie, wait a minute. Where are you going?" I walked out into the night and wrapped my arms around my chest to hold in the heat from my clothing. It was a long walk through the wilderness, but I was happy to be free of him.

When I reached my house, Jeanine had already called five times. I clicked through the voicemail messages she had left me, before deleting them altogether. I didn't want to talk about it.

I climbed up the stairs and walked into my bedroom, shutting the door behind me. Then, I removed my coat and draped it over the back of my desk chair. The drawing of Tom lay beside a box of colored pencils on my desk. I picked up my sketchpad and placed it over the drawing, covering Tom's face.

A thumping sound startled me as I turned to find Tom perched in the tree outside my window. I took a deep breath to calm myself before I opened the window. "What are you doing?" I leaned against the window frame, appalled by his very presence.

"I wasn't done talking to you," Tom gasped, positioning himself over the highest branch of the tree. I could see his breath in white smoky puffs.

"You could have just called me," I suggested, "or knocked on the front door." I raised a thumb over my shoulder to indicate the entrance of the house.

"No," Tom replied. "Your mom's here." He sat down on the tree limb and let his legs dangle beneath him.

"What?" I raised my eyebrows in concern. "No she's not," I insisted. "Mom's never home."

"Addie," Mom called. There was a knock on my bedroom door. "Addie," she repeated. "Who are you talking to in there?"

Tom smirked, as if to say, *See, I told you so.*

I scrambled, closing the window in a panic. Mom opened the door just as I turned around to face her. "Mom," I began, masking the surprise in my voice. "What are you doing home?"

"My flight got delayed and your dad left his laptop," she exhaled. Mom looked around my room and then walked towards me. I was still standing by the window.

"Oh," I said, "are you staying here tonight?" I knew that she wasn't listening to me, because her eyes studied the window pane like she had never seen glass before.

"No, I'm headed back to the airport in a bit." The words came out in a rush, so she could ask, "Who's that?" I swallowed, afraid that Tom had not concealed himself.

"Where?" I stepped back and made room for her as she approached the window. Mom gazed at the pane for a long moment, searching the tree.

"I thought I saw someone," she finally said, straightening her blouse into position over a pair of dress pants. "I guess not," she muttered unconvincingly.

"Dad's laptop is on the table in the living room." I followed her to the door, trying my best to get her out of my room. "I saw it after he left this morning," I added, wondering how cold Tom was on the branch outside my window.

"That's a good daughter," Mom mused. She patted me on the shoulder and then left me standing at the top of the staircase. I watched her from above as she slipped into her winter coat and collected the laptop. "Hey Addie!" she called. "Have you seen my red scarf?"

"It's on the coat rack, by the door," I answered. Mom walked in that direction and wrapped the scarf around her neck. And then, just like Dad, she was gone.

Chapter 8

I think she saw me," Tom stammered, his chattering teeth knocking together like two pieces of chiseled wood. I closed the window after Tom climbed through. He wasn't even wearing a jacket.

"It's freezing out there," I complained. Tom shivered by the window, so I pushed him towards my desk chair. "Sit here," I commanded. "I'll be right back." Tom obeyed, placing his hands under his arms to warm himself.

I went downstairs and found an old sweatshirt that Dad had worn in college. He would never notice if it were missing. I climbed back up the stairs, starting to feel like I had become everyone's mother.

"Here," I said, throwing the sweatshirt at Tom. "Now tell me what you came here to say and get out." I slammed the bedroom door behind me, then walked over to my bed. I threw myself on top of the covers and buried my face in a pillow.

"What's this?" I heard Tom flipping pages. "These are really good, Addie."

I leapt from the bed and snatched my drawings out of his hand. Tom huffed in response and spun the chair around to face me. I riffled through the pages, realizing that Tom had just seen the countless sketches I had drawn of his eyes. I had reworked the image several times, because I had yet to fix, on paper, the way his eyes looked in real life, the way they looked right now.

"You weren't supposed to see these," I explained, tossing them in the drawer of my nightstand. Tom looked to the ground, tugging at the sleeve of Dad's sweatshirt. I placed my hand to my forehead for a moment and stared into oblivion.

"Who's this?" Tom pointed to a photograph of Emily and me as children that was pinned to the cork board above my desk. We were at the beach, building sandcastles in our matching red-and-white polka dot swimsuits.

Tom removed the picture from the board and held it in his hands. "Do you have to touch everything?" I barked, leaning over his shoulder. I confiscated the photo and placed it in the same drawer as the sketches. "Tom," I began, sitting down on the edge of my bed. Before I could finish, the phone started ringing again. "Uh," I moaned, and then let my body collapse into the mattress.

"It's Jeanine," Tom relayed, after checking the caller ID.

"I know," I snapped back. "She's been calling all day." I beat my fist into the pillow beneath my head.

"She didn't write that on your locker," Tom said, turning somber and reserved. I sat up in the bed, balancing on my elbows.

"How do you know?" I searched Tom's face. He looked down, his gold eyes covered by a thick row of lashes.

"I heard Ricky talking about it in the boys' locker room yesterday, after gym class." Tom placed his hands on his thighs, then stood up in one slow, reluctant movement. "Nicki spent the night with him." Tom stood by the window and gazed through the pane into the darkness. I wondered if he would rather be perched on that tree outside than stuck in here, talking to me. "And she took Jeanine's lipstick to make you think that Jeanine was the one who wrote on your locker," Tom explained. "Nicki doesn't want you to be friends with Jeanine. I'm not sure why."

I stared at him from across the room, trying to make sense of it all. "Why didn't you tell me all of this?"

"I've been trying to!" Tom stood before me, aggravation present on his face. Dad's sweatshirt moved to the rise and fall of Tom's chest.

"If you could just tell me why you took that picture," I exhaled. Tom's eyes met mine. "What are you protecting me from?" We shared a long, desperate look until Tom sat down in the chair by my window. He sighed in defeat.

"Tomorrow," Tom began. "I'll call you and you can come by tomorrow." Tom rose, trudging towards the door in a state of regret.

"Why don't you stay?" Tom lingered in the doorway, unsure if I had been the one to say those words. "I'm not going to the movies with Jeanine now and," I hesitated, "well..." I didn't finish the sentence, because Tom had begun to nod.

We spent the rest of the night making hot chocolate and telling childhood stories. An old movie came on TV, so we watched it downstairs in the living room. An invisible barrier sat between us on the couch, with Tom clinging to the cushion farthest from me. I rested my head on a pillow, slinging my arm over the edge of the couch. The black-and-white image on the screen grew blurry before my tired eyes, and then there was nothing but darkness.

* * *

I woke to the sound of a telephone ringing. A soft, warm blanket lay over my outstretched body on the couch in the living room. I grabbed the cordless telephone from its stand on the small wooden table behind me.

"Hello," I murmured. My voice felt dry and scratchy.

"Hey, it's Tom." I relaxed into the couch at the sound of his voice and pulled the blanket up to my chin.

"What happened last night?" I held a hand over my mouth to stifle a yawn.

"You fell asleep when we were watching *Marty*."

"Oh," I exhaled. "How did it end?" I closed my eyes and rolled onto my side.

"Good, it was a really good movie." Tom coughed, but I could hear the smile in his voice. He hesitated, waiting for me to speak again.

"Well, at least one of us got to watch it," I mused. "What time did you leave last night?" I looked at the blanket over my body, knowing that I had not been the one to put it there.

"Midnight," Tom yawned. I heard a metallic clatter over the phone line. The sound echoed before finally fading out.

"Is everything all right?" I sat up on the couch, searching for the nearest clock.

"Yeah, just starting to make lunch," Tom remarked. "Why don't you join us?" I held the phone away from my ear at the sound of banging pots and pans. I giggled to myself, wondering if he knew what I had heard.

"What time is it?" I pulled the blanket away and

climbed off the couch.

"Almost eleven," he answered, clearing his throat.

"Let me wake up first, and I'll be over there in a minute."

I headed upstairs to take a shower and looked in the mirror. My hair was a disheveled mess of tangles and my breath tasted of stale chocolate. I undressed and stepped beneath the warm, foggy shower mist. The moisture felt like an oasis of soothing comfort around me. I washed my face and body with a gritty apricot scrub that left my skin feeling smooth and supple.

I opened the closet with a towel wrapped around my hair, deciding on a dark chocolate-colored sweater and a pair of blue jeans. The walk to Tom's house would be a chilly one, so I grabbed a pair of tan winter boots as well. The inside of the boots was lined with fluffy, faux fur. They would keep my feet warm in the wilderness.

On my way downstairs, I noticed that Tom had left Dad's sweatshirt on the recliner in the living room. I returned the sweatshirt back to its hanger in the closet, briefly catching a hint of the spicy musk that Tom's cologne had left behind.

I grabbed a scarf and coat from the rack in the foyer, carefully buttoning up before I faced the winter chill. A flush of red colored my cheeks when I crossed the threshold and stepped out into the daylight. I locked the front door and placed the key in the front pocket of my jeans. Then, I walked across the lawn, nearing the wilderness with swinging steps.

Skinny branches crunched beneath the weight of my boots as I strolled through the forest. I could see my breath forming into puffs of white air in the space before me. When I reached the fence separating our land from the Sutton's, I lifted my right boot onto the middle railing and swung the rest of my body over.

I paced the stretch of pasture land before me, until I had reached another stretch of wilderness. The mansion lay just through the trees, perfectly situated on its own tract of cleared land. I climbed the front steps and rang the doorbell with my elbow, not wanting to remove a hand from my warm jacket pockets.

"Hey," Tom greeted me in the doorway, standing back so I could enter. I stepped over the threshold, exhaling in relief at the feeling of warmth that circulated through the house. "Lunch will be ready in just a minute." Tom shut the door, and then helped me out of my coat. I unraveled the scarf around my neck, noticing the lit fireplace in the den. Tom grabbed the scarf, accidentally brushing his fingers against my neck in the process.

"Thank you," I murmured. The back of my neck tingled from Tom's touch. I followed him into the kitchen, where a pot of chili sat simmering on the stove. The table had been set, with sterling silver cutlery laid out beside each soup bowl.

"Addie," a familiar voice called. I turned on my heel to find Daniel lurking in the entryway to the kitchen, halfway between one room and the next. I walked towards Daniel, noticing that he was not that tall of a man, no more than average height. Regardless, his beady blue eyes exuded a sense of calming power that quickly filled the room. When Daniel pulled me into his embrace, I could not help but notice that he was freezing.

"All right, Grandpa," Tom interrupted, pulling us apart. "It's time to eat."

We sat down at the table, with a bowl of steaming chili before each of us. Daniel sat at the head of the table, while Tom and I sat to his left and right, respectively, so that we were facing each other. A plate of corn bread was passed around the table. I took a piece and dipped it into my bowl, biting at the chunk of chili.

"Tom tells me that you're an artist." Daniel lifted the silver spoon to his quivering lips. I felt Tom's eyes on me as I thought of the best way to respond.

"Yes," I answered. "I've been known to draw a thing or two." I gazed across the table at Tom. He knew what I meant.

"I'd be interested in seeing a drawing of yours some time." Daniel kept his eyes on the bowl in front of him. Tom clutched the spoon in his hand, skimming the edges of the bowl with it. Neither would look me in the eye until I answered, as if the fear of rejection had permeated the air around us.

"Sure," I agreed, nodding my head. "I don't see why not." I thought about mentioning the countless paintings that decorated the mansion walls, but when the moment turned silent, I bit my tongue.

Tom cleared the table after we had finished eating and left the dishes and silverware in the sink. When he returned to his seat, I spoke again. "So," I hesitated, choosing my words carefully. "How long have ya'll lived here?" The question was meant for Daniel, but when Tom answered, I looked at him instead.

"We've always lived here." Tom lifted a glass of water to his lips, keeping his eyes on me all the while. When Tom set the glass down on the tablecloth, I felt a warm, strange sensation come over me. His honey-colored eyes pierced right through me, sending a steady heat through my body. The look in Tom's eyes was frightening, but I did not feel afraid.

"Really?" I suppressed a nervous giggle at the back of my throat. "Then how come I've never seen you at school?" I held my hands together in my lap, digging my nails into my palm.

"I was homeschooled," Tom muttered. He pressed his lips together in a cautious manner, eyeing me carefully across the table. I swallowed, unable to escape his steady gaze.

"Why don't we head upstairs, Addie?" Daniel rose from his seat and led me to the staircase. Tom remained at the table, his fingers firmly gripping the glass in his hand.

Daniel slowly climbed each step, as I noticed the fragile state of his body. His posture was severely rigid, as if all of his flexibility had been sapped away. When we reached the top of the staircase, Daniel was out of breath.

"Are you all right?" I placed my hand at the small of his back, hoping to make the walk more bearable for him. We passed through the door on the left and entered the old, dark room, where that mysterious portrait hung on the wall.

"Yes, I'm," he mumbled, moving towards the windowsill to sit down. "I'm fine." Daniel took a handkerchief out to wipe his forehead, while I paced the creaky wood floor in front of the painting. "So I hear Tom burned the picture DeMilo sent you?" Daniel gazed at me from where he sat.

"Yeah," I huffed, sitting down on the floor in front of him. "Tom said that he was protecting me." I pulled my knees into my chest, rubbing my palms over the soft felt texture of my boots. "He thinks that," I paused, wondering if Tom could hear me, "I never should have opened the envelope."

"And what do you think?" Daniel placed his hands on his thighs, balancing himself along the windowsill.

"I don't know what to think." I rocked back and forth, pressing my face into the jean material around my legs. "If DeMilo murdered his wife, what would he do to me? And what does he want with me anyway?" I let out a long, bellowing sigh.

"Addie," Daniel whispered, leaning forward. "What I'm about to tell you," he stopped, wincing for a brief moment. Before I could ask if he were all right, Daniel spoke again. "It's not going to be easy for you to hear." Daniel pushed his palms into the windowsill, and then pressed his back into the glass, still searching for balance.

I nodded, unable to find the right words to convince Daniel that I was ready to hear whatever he had to say, no matter how bad it was. "Get up," he commanded, "and go stand in front of that wall." I did as he said, wondering if I had been placed in time-out for asking too many questions at lunch. "Now, look at the painting, Addie," he requested, "and tell me what you see."

I exhaled, setting my gaze on the artwork in question. "I see a woman," I said, narrowing my focus to study the delicate features of her face. "No, a girl," I corrected. "She looks about eighteen."

"Good," Daniel encouraged. "Now, go on."

I looked into the woman's eyes and examined the deep green hue of them. They resembled two emerald stones, glistening in the daylight. "Her eyes are," I hesitated, making a point to choose my words carefully, "different." I felt my eyes drifting. "And her hair," I stopped myself, swallowing before I continued. "It's like soft gold, angelic almost." I found my hand waving over the painting, in search of her halo. "And the necklace," I softly said, taking a step closer, "it's..." I stared at the emerald stone that hung from her neck, transfixed by the green liquid luster. But when I looked above the necklace, searching for the woman's eyes, the portrait turned to glass, and I was staring at myself.

Chapter 9

I woke up on the dusty hardwood floor. My hands and feet lay sprawled out before me, while a stream of cool water dripped down my face and along my throat. Tom stood over me with an empty glass in his hand.

"What happened?" I took several shallow breaths, looking around to see that Daniel still sat on the windowsill, as he had earlier.

"You passed out," Daniel said, opening his mouth to say more until I interrupted.

"I saw myself in the painting," I murmured, disbelieving my own words, even as I said them aloud. "I mean, in the mirror." I placed a palm to my forehead; it was still wet.

"What mirror?" Tom interjected. The tone of his voice was more accusatory than I would have liked. I gazed up at the portrait from where I lay on the ground.

"There was a mirror right there!" I pointed my finger towards the painting, frustrated that no one else had seen the flash of glass when I had. Tom and Daniel exchanged glances, neither sure of my sanity.

"What did you see?" Daniel's brow furrowed, then the expression on his face froze.

"My reflection," I answered. The woman in the painting sat in a motionless pose, mocking every statement I made. I buried my face in my hands, smoothing my hair back so that it fell over my shoulders.

"You were looking at Antoinette," Daniel insisted, nearly convincing me, for the sole purpose of securing my sanity. Tom placed a hand on my shoulder. "Make her a cup of tea." Tom moved away from me and left the room. "Shut the door, Tom." I sat up on my palms, looking at Tom across the room. He kept a careful eye on me before stepping out of view and closing the door behind him.

"I don't understand," I began, my lips trembling, "what happened."

"I've tried to think of the best way to tell you this." Daniel rose from the windowsill, keeping a hand on the wall to expand his rigid posture. "But I suppose there is no best way, so here it goes." Daniel lingered by the window, then turned to look me squarely in the eye. "Antoinette was your grandmother."

My eyes widened in surprise. "No, she can't be," I argued, stepping away from the painting. "I've met all of my grandparents, two grandmothers included, and she can't be," I hesitated, quickly eyeing the painting from where I stood. "She couldn't be." I forced a synthetic laugh, attempting to push the possibility as far from my mind as I could.

"Do you think it's a coincidence that you look just like her?" Daniel stood in front of the painting, rubbing his hand along the features of her face. "That you have her eyes, her hair, her smile?" Daniel placed his hands along his waist. The motion accentuated the frailty of his frame. A grin surfaced at the corner of his lips, for he felt he had won.

"I don't know." I looked from the painting to Daniel and then back again. "I don't know," I repeated, my head throbbing in effect. "I have to go." I rushed towards the door, reaching for the doorknob.

"Addie." Daniel took two narrow steps forward. "If you don't believe me, then take a look at your birth certificate. I wouldn't lie to you," he said, "not about this."

I opened the door, drawing in a quick breath at the sight of Tom in the doorway. "Sorry," I exhaled, holding a hand to my chest. "You scared me." I ran down the stairs, hurrying to the foyer where I slipped into my jacket and scarf before retreating to the forest.

The trees rushed by in a blur of gray and black as I raced through the forest, hoping to lose my breath in the bitter chill of winter. I ran until my lungs burned and my throat grew wet and dry all at the same time. Giving out, I sank onto the forest floor, resting my back against the base of a live oak tree.

"Addie!" Tom approached, resting his palms on his knees to catch his breath.

"You knew this whole time and you never said a word." I kept my voice calm, despite the biting tone. "How could you keep something like that from me?"

"Addie, it's complicated," Tom started, taking a seat at the base of the tree opposite me. Tom blew air through his parted lips and watched the puffs of white drift through the air until they dissipated. His golden eyes watched every move I made. I grew tired of his unwavering gaze and rose from the ground.

Tears sprung up around the edges of my eyes, as I trudged through the wilderness on a pair of shaky legs. I was still stunned by the realization that I didn't actually know who I belonged to. I had never looked at my birth certificate before, because I had never had a reason to. Why would I question where I had come from when I had never been led to believe anything different?

"Addie," Tom called after me. I could hear the sound of his boots crunching through fallen branches and leaves. I ignored him, pressing my fingertips against the water around my eyes. "Can't we just talk?" I stopped, turning around to face Tom.

"Talk?" I felt a painful lump form at the base of my throat. "What do you want me to say?" My voice broke, releasing a flood of fresh tears with it. I held my hand over my mouth to conceal a string of choking sobs. I did not want him to see me like this.

I turned to walk away, but Tom grabbed my arm and pulled me towards him. He pressed his lips to mine, sending a slow, steady fever throughout my body. Tom placed his hands at the small of my back, supporting my weight as I grew dizzy, losing my balance. When I sighed, Tom offered another gentle, lingering kiss before pausing to allow time for me to breathe.

A light, fluffy feeling overwhelmed me. Everything felt hot and cold all at once. He tasted of chili pepper and mint. I realized that nothing would ever feel the same.

Chapter 10

Jeanine was waiting for me on the breezeway on Monday morning. I approached her, pausing to say hello when she tugged at the sleeve of my shirt. "Addie," she began, a hint of loneliness in her innocent blue eyes.

"I know." I slung my arm over her shoulder, leading us through the double doors. In the hallway, students crowded around each lined wall of lockers, talking as much as they could before the bell rang. "Lunch today?" Jeanine smiled in agreement, relieved that our budding friendship had been mended.

We parted ways as I walked to my locker, exchanging books to prepare for my morning classes. Tom appeared out of thin air, casually leaning on my locker door.

"Hey," he murmured. "Did you want to go to the bank after school?" Tom lingered before me, searching my face for some sense of decisiveness. I zipped my backpack and then shut my locker, careful to click the combination lock back in place.

"Give me a few hours to think about it." I threw my backpack over my shoulders, ready for homeroom. School had become a convenient distraction since last weekend, now that I had real problems to worry about.

My parents kept a safe deposit box at the bank, and a copy of my birth certificate was inside of it. I knew that it was deceitful to unravel the past without telling them, but they had done their fair share of lying to me. If they cared so much, then why had we not sat down for a family dinner together in four years?

"Okay," Tom said. "Just let me know when you decide." He smiled and let go of my locker door, turning in the direction of his own homeroom. I watched him walk away until he was out of sight.

A swarm of students gathered around a locker at the end of the hall. Jeanine approached me as I walked over, curiosity just as apparent on her face as it was on mine. The crowd scattered at the sound of the bell, leaving behind the locker and the person who stood in front of it.

Nicki buried her face in her hands, tears streaming down her cheeks. She wept uncontrollably, not even noticing that Jeanine and I were standing there until I cleared my throat. "Are you happy now?" Nicki slurred her words, mumbling something about revenge that I could not make out.

"Nicki, what are you talking about?" I noticed how red her eyes looked, so bloodshot that one could fairly wager that she had not slept in a week.

"Don't act like you don't know what this is." Nicki stepped aside, revealing the locker that she had been blocking with her body. It was like last week all over again.

On the front of Nicki's gray metal locker, just as generic as the rest, the word **SLUT** was written in red lipstick... **cherry** red lipstick.

Principal Caldwell clunked down the hallway, rushing to the aid of his daughter. "Look what they did, Daddy!" Nicki pointed a light blue fingernail at each of us, accusing Jeanine first and me second.

"We didn't do anything," I argued, feeling the blood rush to my cheeks.

"Yeah, Principal Caldwell," Jeanine added. "We just got here."

Caldwell turned to each of us, studying the innocent expressions we bore. But then Nicki tugged at his sleeve, complaining of the inhumane bullying we had thrust upon her. If I had been a witch, I would have snapped my fingers to cast a spell that would make her disappear forever.

"Go to class," Caldwell commanded, wrapping his arm around Nicki to console her. "We'll discuss this later." Nicki buried her face in her father's chest. I looked at Jeanine, then continued down the hall to homeroom. Within two minutes, a voice came over the intercom, and I was being called down to the principal's office.

Jeanine waited outside the door to Caldwell's office, too frightened to enter the room by herself. "I am so sick of this," I complained to her, before placing my hand on the doorknob. She followed me inside, where Caldwell instructed each of us to take a seat.

"Welcome back, Ms. Smith," Caldwell barked. "Are we making a weekly ritual of these visits?" He shuffled through a slew of papers on his desk, then placed a handful of them in a folder. I rolled my eyes at him, slouching back in the chair.

"Nicki informs me that the two of you have been vandalizing school property. Is that true?" Caldwell held a pen in his hand, ready to write down my confession.

"What? No!" I protested, startling Jeanine with the noise my voice made. She sat quietly in the chair beside me, her eyes darting around the room. It was obvious that I would have to speak for both of us.

"Then how do you explain this?" Caldwell removed a printed picture from the folder on his desk and handed it to me. "Is this your locker?" The image had been taken last Friday, when red lipstick was written all over my locker.

"Yes, but-"

"And Ms. Travis," Caldwell interrupted before I could finish my statement. "The lipstick you're wearing is the same color as the filth that has been written on my daughter's locker. Is that correct?" Caldwell tapped his fingers against the surface of his desk, anticipating her confession. Jeanine pressed her mouth into a fine line, ashamed of the red on her lips.

"Principal Caldwell," I began, looking him directly in the eye when his head turned to me. "Why would I vandalize my own locker? That doesn't even make any sense." I waited for him to respond. Instead, Caldwell opened the top drawer of his desk and began filling out two rectangular slips of paper with his pen.

"Since you two girls have contributed to the expense of cleaning our fine facility here, you will spend detention with the janitorial staff." Caldwell offered a slip of paper to each of us, smugly regarding our presence.

"What?" I yelled, rising to my feet. "But that's not fair! We didn't even do any of this and Nicki is the one who wrote on my locker," I insisted, waving my hands in the air like a mad man. "Why aren't you punishing her for it?"

"My daughter would do no such thing," Caldwell declared. "Now, both of you return to class." I snatched the detention slip out of his hand and headed for the door. "And Ms. Smith?" He glared into my eyes, preparing to release another threatening command. "You can forget the art institute." Caldwell chucked the application in the trash can beside his desk.

A school administrator's signature was required on the application. If Caldwell refused to sign the form, I wouldn't be allowed to go, even if I was accepted.

I stormed into the hallway and ripped the detention slip into shreds. Pieces of white paper floated down to the floor like falling snow. Jeanine knelt down to collect all of the pieces, then placed them in her pocket when she thought I wasn't looking.

"What did he mean about the art institute?" Jeanine kept pace beside me, holding her hands behind her back in a childlike manner. Sometimes, it felt like she was my little sister.

"It's just this art program that I wanted to go to in Atlanta." I felt myself calming down. It was nice to talk about things that I actually liked. "Every summer, they host a workshop for two weeks and all of these really amazing artists show up and teach classes." I shoved my hands into my pockets, letting the disappointment sink in.

"Do you paint?" Jeanine held the door open for me when we reached the end of the hallway.

"Not really, I'm mainly a sketch artist." The words sounded strange on my tongue, because I had never defined myself by my art before. "But I would love to learn how to paint."

"I'm sure you will someday, Addie."

Chapter 11

I can't believe he gave you detention for that," Tom griped. He stabbed his fork into the heart of a round carrot slice. "You too, Jeanine," Tom added. Jeanine nodded in appreciation, then lifted a spoonful of tomato soup to her lips. They were bare and pink.

I looked down at the chicken pot pie on my lunch tray and curled my lip at the milky, tepid gravy. Tom sat beside me, chomping on shards of gravy-laden crust like it was candy. After a long, hesitant moment, I placed a chunk of chicken in my mouth and swallowed it down with a swig of water.

Jeanine cringed, narrowing her eyes on the bowl of soup in front of her. "What's wrong?" I asked, reaching my hand across the table to comfort her.

Ricky approached our table, walking with a cocky bounce to his step. He sat down beside Jeanine and slung his arm over her shoulder. "You've decided to join the dark side, I see." Ricky stared into my eyes and mouthed the words, *I love you.*

"Leave me alone," Jeanine whined, peeling his arm from her shoulder. "You're so annoying." Ricky sulked to himself and then folded his arms over his chest in disgust.

"So what, are ya'll dating now?" Ricky pointed a finger between Tom and me, indicating that he did not approve.

"It's none of your business, Ricky," I snapped,

holding Tom's wrist to keep him from leaping over the table at Ricky. A wayward football player called to Ricky from across the cafeteria, so he got up from the table and left.

"I hate that guy," Tom snarled.

"Tom!" I nudged his shoulder, not wanting to make Jeanine feel any more uncomfortable than she already did.

"It's all right," Jeanine admitted, shrugging the matter off. "Just because he's my brother doesn't mean I have to like him."

Jeanine held the same disinterested tone of voice after school, when we were stuck in detention, cleaning toilet seats and scraping the gum off desks. Eventually, we were condemned to the breezeway, where we collected trash and plastic bottles. I breathed in the fresh winter air and looked out at the nearly vacant parking lot. Only a handful of cars remained, mainly belonging to faculty and staff, except for those of students who participated in winter sports or detention.

Ricky appeared at the edge of the parking lot, rifling for car keys in his pocket. "Ricky, wait!" Nicki chased after him, tugging him halfway out of his letterman jacket.

"Hey Jeanine," I called over my shoulder. "Come look at this." She came to stand beside me, placing her bag full of recyclable materials on the ground.

"Shut up, Nicki!" Ricky banged his hand against the hood of his BMW. "I'm sick of dealing with you! We're over!" He climbed into the driver's side, but Nicki held the car door open, preventing him from closing it.

"I can't believe you!" Nicki leaned into the car and grabbed Ricky by the collar of his shirt. "After everything we've been through," she wailed, "and everything I've done for you." Nicki slapped him in the face, then flew back into the cement ground. It took me a moment to realize that her lip was bleeding. Ricky had hit her.

"I don't want you," Ricky demanded, holding the car keys in the ball his fist had made. "You're no good for me anymore." He sat back in the driver's seat and slammed the car door behind him. Then, Ricky rolled the window down, letting his elbow hang over the edge. "It's true," he hesitated, taking a moment to start the car. "You are a slut."

Ricky backed out of the parking lot and stepped on the accelerator, his tires burning rubber as he left school grounds. Nicki staggered to her feet and held a hand to her lips, noticing the blood on her fingers. She saw Jeanine and me watching in the distance, then turned her back to us and walked towards her SUV.

The incident was still on my mind when I was driving home. I reviewed every detail, unable to understand why Ricky had broken up with her. But then I remembered Ricky's last words, and all of the puzzle pieces fell into place. Ricky had been the one to write on her locker, because Nicki had written on mine.

* * *

When I got home, the garage was up and both of my parent's cars were parked inside. I entered the house through that entrance and walked into the kitchen, scraping my boots off on the *Welcome* mat. Mom and Dad sat across from each other at the kitchen table, as if they had been waiting for me for a long time.

"What's going on?" I walked past the refrigerator, then stopped in front of the table, not comfortable enough to sit down with them. Two pairs of eyes that looked nothing like my own stared at me, resenting every step I made.

"I received another call from Principal Caldwell today," Mom relayed, as if she were a telecaster reporting the news. "He said that you have been vandalizing school property. Is that true?" Mom held her chin high, accentuating the thinness of her nose. Dad just stared at me, like I was some illusion that was about to vanish.

"No," I huffed, growing defensive. "Of course it's not." I let my backpack fall to the ground and sat down at the kitchen table. "Caldwell just hates me. That's why he's not letting me go to the art institute." I tugged at a strand of my golden hair, wondering if this was how Antoinette's had looked in the flesh.

"The art institute?" A thin line formed between Mom's eyebrows. She looked at Dad, but he simply shook his head. I moaned in aggravation, recalling the countless times I had mentioned it to them when neither had been paying attention.

"Yeah, they have this summer art program," I began, hoping that one of them would remember. "For high school students," I muttered, scraping my fingernail against the table in frustration. "It's in Atlanta."

"Oh," Mom inhaled, opening her mouth wide. "Well, why would you want to go to that anyway?" I sank into the back of my chair, unable to believe what she had just said.

"Excuse me?" A wave of throbbing anger came

over me. I placed both hands on the seat of my chair, for her protection alone.

"Well," Mom sighed, and then tapped a finger against her temple. "Your drawings are nice, Addie," she said.

"Very nice," Dad interjected.

"But," she hesitated. I knew that whatever came next would change things between us forever. "Your father and I don't think that art is something that you need to pursue as a long-term goal." I blinked, taken aback by her statement.

"What?" I felt my face scrunch into a contorted manner. "I don't understand."

"What your mother's trying to say, Addie," Dad murmured, pausing to clear his throat. Mom grew impatient and finished the explanation for him.

"Is that we don't think Caldwell's interference with the art program is such a bad idea," Mom asserted, holding my gaze as her dark brown eyes pierced holes through my face. When I failed to respond, Mom rambled on about real life and responsibility. "Why can't you choose something more practical, like your father and I?"

I crossed my arms over my chest and stared at the ground.

"The quality of your life is dependent upon financial stability." Mom tilted her chin upward, as if she had just recited an awe-inspiring Bible verse. The way she gloated over her own self-importance made me sick.

"Stop talking to me like that! I'm not one of your patients." I rose from the table and stormed off, until Mom interrupted, as she has been known to do.

"Addie." She let the word rest on her tongue,

unsure if she liked the way it sounded. "Give me your car keys." I widened my eyes at her outlandish request.

"You must be joking," I snipped back at her. My backpack remained on the kitchen floor, so I scurried over to retrieve it, not trusting Mom and her domineering ways.

"Give me your car keys," she repeated. Mom held her hand out, with her palm facing the ceiling. When I tried to move past her, she snatched the backpack off my shoulders and stuffed her fingers inside the front pocket.

"How am I supposed to get to school?"

"You can take the bus," Mom answered, stepping back to show me the silver key ring that dangled from her hand. She jingled the keys in the air, reveling in her glory.

"Congratulations," I muttered.

Mom walked away with her heels clicking against the tile floor.

I headed upstairs to my bedroom, holding back tears until the door was shut. For the first time, I hoped that Daniel had been right. I had to belong to another family. I needed to.

Mom and Dad left ten minutes later. I breathed a sigh of relief when the garage door shut, sending a stale silence throughout the house. Most of my tears had dried, and I was tired of listening to myself think. I picked up the phone and called Tom.

"What's wrong?" he asked. I exhaled at the sound of his voice.

"Mom found out I had detention today, so she took my car keys." I sat down in my chair by the window and looked through the glass. "Can I ride with you tomorrow?"

"Sure." Tom did not hesitate. "What time should I pick you up?"

"Seven thirty," I answered. My eyes began to water at the sight of a small, white-bellied squirrel climbing the tree outside my window. The little creature studied my frozen posture through the glass and then lifted an acorn to its mouth.

"Are you all right?" Tom waited for an answer, then spoke again when I failed to provide one. "Do you want me to come over?"

"Sure," I replied, allowing the slightest bit of a grin at the corner of my mouth. "I could use some help with that trigonometry homework."

"No problem," Tom chuckled. "I'll be right over."

"Wait." I listened. "Tom?"

"Yes?"

"I want to go to the bank tomorrow."

Chapter 12

Atall, middle-aged man nodded for me to join him behind the counter. He had silver hair and a black mustache, with the pallor of his skin setting a deep contrast to both. Tom sat down in the waiting area and rifled through a booklet about interest rates and security options. I watched Tom from where I stood, and then followed the bank manager to a vault in the back.

The key to the safe deposit box sat in the front pocket of my jeans. I had taken it from one of the drawers in my mother's jewelry box. I remembered her showing me the shiny key, with its strange, jagged edges, many years ago.

It was my sixth birthday, and I was wearing the pink party dress that Mom had picked out for me. She covered my face in powder and blush, then dabbed my lips with gloss until they were the color of bubble gum. Before placing a silver tiara on my head, Mom opened the jewelry box to find sparkly adornments for my wrists and fingers. At the time, I had never seen the act for what it was. To my mother, I was no more than a doll.

"Do you have your key?" The bank manager slipped a key into one of the slots on the face of the box. I slipped my hand into my jeans and retrieved the key.

"Yeah," I said. My voice echoed among the rows

of safety deposit boxes. I pressed my key into the other slot and held my breath, as I pulled the box from its cubbyhole.

The bank manager led me to a private room, and then turned on his heel. "I'll leave you to it," he said, carefully shutting the door behind him. I set the box down on the table in front of me and opened it.

All of the documents sat at the bottom, beneath the weight of a gold pocket watch, two class rings, and a military pin. I held the pin in my hand, rubbing a finger over the silver edges. Mom's father had served in the navy for twenty years, so no surprise there.

The first two documents were birth certificates belonging to Mom and Dad. Then, there was a deed to the house and the sixty acres that it sat on. I placed the documents on the table, as well as the handful of trinkets, and then looked back down at the only document that remained.

Certificate of Birth

Name: Addison Elizabeth Smith

Mother's Name: Josette Addison Beaumont

Father's Name:_____

Chapter 13

Explain this to me." I slapped my birth certificate down on the dinner table in front of Daniel. Questions jostled over each other in my mind, nearly sending me into a fit of hysteria. Who is Josette? Did she have an affair with my father? Is that why my last name was still Smith? And how come the space left for my father's name was blank?

When Daniel wouldn't answer me, I spouted off the first question, impatiently seeking the truth. "Who is Josette?" I crossed my arms over my chest and tapped my foot in frustration. Tom stood by my side, knowing that I was too sullen to be touched.

Daniel studied the birth certificate, then sighed to himself. "Josette was your biological mother." I felt a stab of pain in my chest.

"Was?" I choked on the word.

"She died not too long after she gave you up for adoption," Daniel muttered. There was a steaming cup of tea in front of him. He took a sip, keeping his hands firmly wrapped around the cup to soak up its warmth. "Jeffrey Smith and Eleanor Jacobs," he hesitated, "they are your adoptive parents."

I sank down into one of the chairs at the dinner table. The last time I was sitting here, Mom and Dad had just been Mom and Dad. Now they weren't. I felt cheated, foolish, blind, and violated.

Burying my face in my hands, I wept over the

table, not caring who saw me cry. Everything made sense now. Why Jeffrey only cared about his law firm and Eleanor only cared about her medical practice. Why neither had ever understood me, nor tried to. I saw myself as a child and remembered all of the times that they had rejected my affection when I offered it. I couldn't remember the last time either of them had even given me a hug.

I lifted my head, leaning on my elbow for support. Tom sat down in the chair beside me and placed his hand on my shoulder. "Well, then what about my biological father?" I turned to Daniel, stumbling over the words as they left my mouth. "Why is his name missing?" Daniel mulled over the question, then opened his mouth to speak when he was ready.

"Because he abandoned Josette when she got pregnant." Daniel shrugged his shoulders. "They were only sixteen." I rubbed my thumb over my index finger to calm myself. Tom touched the back of my neck and flinched. I was ice cold.

"Well, what is his name?" I rose from the chair and towered over Daniel. "I'm going to go find him." I shivered in place, rubbing my hands over my arms to warm myself.

"Addie," Daniel complained. "This is not the time to go running after your past."

"Then why are you telling me all of this?" I paced the floor, then ran my hands through my hair until it hurt at the roots. "So if Josette was my mother." I counted each name off my fingers, trying to make sense of it all. "And Antoinette was my grandmother," I stretched the phrase out, waiting until Daniel nodded at the statement. "And DeMilo is my grandfather." I placed significance on the fact that DeMilo was the only existing relative left. "Then why don't either of them have his last name?"

Daniel held a hand to his chin, stroking the shadow of a beard. "Antoinette's portrait was done before she married," he explained, resting his head on the back of the chair to study the ceiling. "Beaumont was her maiden name."

"And Josette?" I rubbed my arms at the elbow, balancing on one foot and then the other. Daniel leaned over the table and smiled at me. It was more of a sardonic grin than a polite expression.

"Would you keep your father's name," he paused to take a sip of tea, then continued, "after he murdered your mother?" I felt dizzy and hollow, like all the life had been drained from my body.

"I think I need to lie down." I walked through the house until I had reached the den and collapsed onto the couch. Tom lit the fireplace and then sat down on the carpet in front of me.

"Are you all right?" Tom folded his arms over his knees. The look in his golden eyes reminded me of the way I had felt as a child, when looking through the window of a candy store.

"How would you feel?" I sunk my head into a pillow and threw an arm over my eyes. The couch cushions felt soft and inviting. I decided that it would be all right if I did nothing more with my life than lie there.

"Addie, your parents still love you," Tom insisted.

"Do they?" I draped my other arm over my stomach and turned to look him squarely in the eye. "How do you know?" I gazed up at the ceiling, letting out a deep breath. "How can anyone know?" My voice grew to a whisper as my mind traveled back in time, through forgotten memories and overlooked behaviors.

"DeMilo will come at some point," Daniel muttered. He entered the den with stiff posture, and then sat down in the middle of the love seat.

"What does that have to do with anything?" I complained in frustration, beating my fist against the back of the couch.

"He wants Antoinette's necklace," Daniel stated, as if there were no question about it. I huffed, allowing my teen angst to rear its ugly head.

"So?" I slurred the end of the word, though sounded more cynical than intoxicated.

"Don't you see, Addie?" Daniel leaned forward and clasped his hands together, as if that would make his argument more plausible. "DeMilo thinks you have it." Daniel pointed his finger at me, which caused me to grow all the more defensive.

"Why would I have it?" I placed a palm over my chest. The prospect of Tony DeMilo in Savannah sent chills up my spine, even if he was my grandfather.

"You're the only Beaumont left," Daniel explained. "Who else would have it?"

Firewood crackled in the distance, reminding me of the time Tom burned the picture. "Why didn't DeMilo come and find me?" I tugged at the sleeve around my wrist. "He could have raised me." I motioned from Tom to Daniel. The former ran his palm through the carpet, avoiding all eye contact, while the latter stared into my eyes, as if he were fishing for pieces of my soul. "I mean, I've never seen him in my entire life, and now he reaches out?" I shook my head from side to side, not minding when stray pieces of hair fell out of place.

"I need to go." I rose from the couch and walked out of the den. The birth certificate was still lying on the dinner table where I had left it. I picked up the document and then disappeared through the front door without saying goodbye to either of them.

Every person that I had ever loved was no more than a legal relation. It was all a lie.

As I bounded through the dark, chilling forest, an image came to mind. I was eight years old, shopping for groceries with Mom at the local supermarket. An old friend from high school approached her, asking questions to fill the gap in time since they had last seen each other.

"Who is this?"

Mom placed a hand on my shoulder, but it wasn't protective, just ornamental. "A daughter," she replied. A truthful answer, no doubt. But I never realized then what I realized now.

She hadn't said *my*.

Chapter 14

On Thursday, I stood at my locker, exchanging books between classes. A group of girls walked down the hallway, talking loudly enough for me to overhear their conversation.

"Did you hear that Ricky and Nicki broke up?" one of them said. "I heard that she cheated on him with another football player."

"Which one?" I kept my back to the girls, so I couldn't see what any of them looked like. But from the way they sounded, juicy gossip was the blood that they survived on.

"Not sure yet, but I'll find out."

"Are you sure?" a third girl piped up. "I thought he cheated on her?"

The question led to a debate, which carried the girls down the hall and through the double doors. I shut my locker and looked over my shoulder, listening to the sound of their chatter until it faded away.

"Addie," Ricky startled me with his voice. I stepped back at the sight of him. "I need to talk to you about something."

"Okay," I hesitated, not wanting to trust the desperation in his eyes.

"Not right now," he said. Ricky looked over my shoulder, as if someone were watching us. "Can you meet me here after school?" Without giving me the chance to respond, Ricky nodded his head. "Great, I'll see you then."

* * *

Tom stared at me from across the classroom in Western Civilization. Mr. Robinson was giving a lecture on the Ottoman Empire and Mehmed II. I looked out the window, too plagued with confusion to pay attention. Wind rippled through the trees outside. I wished that I could be there, hanging from the branches.

"Ms. Smith?" Robinson singled me out, recognizing that I had yet to flip to the next page of my textbook. "Would you please tell the class the time period in which Mehmed II reigned and the name of his successor?" I felt blood rush to my cheeks. Tom kept his head down, not wanting to watch Robinson humiliate me in front of the entire class. "Please, stand up." Robinson opened the palm of his hand and motioned for me to rise.

I stood up, holding my hands behind my back like we were in pre-school. "Mehmed II reigned from 1451, until his death in 1481 when his son, Bayezid II came into power. Bayezid II ruled from 1481 to 1512, during which time his two sons, Ahmed and Selim, raged war against each other. It was called the Ottoman Civil War. It lasted from 1509 to 1513." I held my head high in accomplishment. Tom held a hand over his mouth, trying to hide a tight-lipped smile.

"Who won?" Robinson placed both hands on his hips. His wire-rimmed glasses fell to the tip of his nose, as his bald head glistened with sweat beneath the florescent lighting.

"The youngest," I answered, clearing my throat

before adding, "Selim."

"Very good, Ms. Smith," he growled back at me through a pair of gritted teeth. "You may sit down now." I sank into my chair, relieved that I had survived the wrath of Robinson. He turned on his heel and began writing our homework assignment on the white board. When he stepped away, the bell rang, and I looked up to see what was written in black dry-erase marker.

Who was Bayezid's favorite, Ahmed or Selim?
10 pages, due Monday

A handful of students scowled at the assignment on the board. I walked past Mr. Robinson on the way out of the classroom and noticed the resentful glower on his face. Tom tugged at my hand, dragging me into the hallway.

"Nice job, Addie!" a classmate yelled from behind. I felt a stout lump rising in my throat when others did the same.

"Don't listen to them, Addie," Tom sympathized, placing a hand on my cheek once we reached my locker. But after ten students had walked by, all shouting similar complaints, I threw my Western Civilization book on the ground and screamed.

* * *

I watched the hallway until it had cleared, then crept towards my locker. Tom would come looking for me, now that school was out and he was driving me home every day. I grew anxious when Ricky kept me waiting and wondered why I had been foolish enough to meet him in the first place. Just as I began to walk away, I heard the sound of someone running down the hallway and stopped in my tracks. Ricky had finally arrived.

"Come on," he said, grabbing my wrist. Ricky pulled me into a dark, empty classroom and locked the door behind us.

"What are you doing?" I jerked myself out of his grasp and stepped away. Ricky reached into the back pocket of his pants and pulled out a small white square. As he began to unfold it, I noticed that it was a piece of paper that had been folded four times, so that it would fit in his pocket.

"Did you send this to me?" Ricky held the piece of paper in the air. Once again, I found myself looking at Antoinette's portrait.

"Where did you get that?" I snatched the picture from his hand and looked at it more closely. *Find the necklace* was scrawled in black ink at the bottom of the page.

"In the mail," Ricky muttered, as if I should have already known. He shoved a white envelope in my hand. Ricky's name and address were written on the front, but there was no return address. "I thought you sent it to me." Ricky's eyes darted from the portrait to me, searching for lies, searching for truth.

"Why would I send it to you?" I found the accusation absurd. Ricky knew how I despised him. Why would I send him anything in the mail?

"Isn't that you?" Ricky pointed to the picture in my hand.

"No," I said, shoving the piece of paper into his chest.

"Really?" He held the picture in front of his face. "Because it sure looks like you." Ricky suspended the picture in the air, so that he could compare

Antoinette's features with mine. His eyes bounced back and forth, between the picture and my face.

"Ricky, stop it!" I snatched the picture out of his hand, causing him to turn away from me. "It's not me, I swear," I gasped, pulling in breaths of stale classroom air.

"Well then who is it?" Ricky walked closer, towering over me. "And who sent it to me?" Ricky held his chin taut, pressing me for answers.

I turned away from him and began to pace the floor. "I don't know," I said, failing to make eye contact with Ricky. "Who all have you shown this picture to?"

"Well," Ricky murmured, looking to the ceiling as he scratched the top of his head. "My sister, my mother, a few guys on the football team, and you," he listed, as if he had just visited the grocery store and was telling me what he had bought.

"What?" I kept my voice low, too stunned to move. Ricky placed a hand on either hip, revealing the shape of his pointy elbows. "Ricky!" I screeched, sinking into one of the desks.

"What did I do?" Ricky hovered over my desk. "Look," he began, crossing his arms over his chest. "I thought it was a picture of you, and I've seen you drawing on your notebook in class before. I thought maybe you did it." I held my mouth ajar, not knowing where to begin.

"You thought that I drew a portrait," I hesitated, "of myself?" Ricky nodded. "And mailed it to you?" I raised my eyebrows, wishing he could see how ludicrous the idea was. "Why would I do that, Ricky?" I paused, tapping my fingers across the surface of the desk. "I don't even like you!" I stood up and marched towards the door, hoping that Tom had not left without me.

"I'm sorry about what happened on the night of the dance," Ricky apologized. "I was drunk, and..." he faded out, refusing to finish whatever he had intended to say. I remembered him at the punch table and Jeanine crying in the hallway afterwards.

"Ricky," I commanded, not caring for his vacant apologies. "Please, don't tell anyone else about this." He nodded and placed both hands in his pockets. "I'll find out what I can," I promised.

"Thanks Addie," he called after me, but I was already out the door.

Tom was waiting for me in his black Mustang at the edge of the parking lot. I knocked on a window when I reached the car and caught the glare in his honey-colored eyes. I opened the passenger's side door and climbed inside, placing my backpack on the floorboard.

"Where have you been?" Tom moaned in frustration. He sat in the driver's seat, with a hand held to his forehead. "I've been waiting here for over half an hour," he demanded, leaning over me to pull the door closed. Tom started the car and before I knew it, we were on the road, heading home.

"I was talking to Ricky," I said, waiting to study his reaction. "He gave me this." I showed Tom the picture and the envelope that it came in. When Tom's eyes widened in surprise, I went on. "He thinks that I sent it to him." Tom pressed his lips into a fine line. "Tom, what did you do with the picture DeMilo sent me, the one that looks just like this?"

"I burned it," Tom answered, guiding the steering wheel with one hand. "I told you that." I bit my lip and looked out the window, staring at the moving strips of pavement to distract myself.

"Well then how did Ricky get it?" I stared at Tom, disliking the way he clenched his jaw. Was Tom lying to me?

"I don't know." Tom kept his eyes on the road. "Maybe DeMilo sent the picture to more than one person," Tom hesitated, mulling over his thoughts. "Maybe he didn't send it to just you." I nodded to myself; it seemed rational.

"Did you get one?" I turned sideways in my seat, not minding when the seatbelt tightened around my waist.

"No," he replied, shaking his head. Tom pulled into my driveway and stopped just before the gated entrance. I hadn't realized that we had been driving for twenty minutes. We lived on the outskirts of town, but for some reason, the commute had not felt as long as it usually did. "Addie, please don't talk to Ricky anymore." Tom placed his hand over mine. I moved away from him and got out of the car.

I didn't like being told what to do.

Chapter 15

The next morning, I hopped over the gate and waited for Tom to pick me up. I could not stop thinking about what had happened the day before, and after fifteen minutes of waiting, I began to wonder if he had left without me.

Growing impatient, I climbed back over the gate and trudged down the dirt driveway. If I was late for school, Caldwell would have my neck in a noose. I cut through the trees, briskly striding across the forest floor, as my backpack jostled over my shoulders. Just before I reached the fence, a dark figure caught the corner of my eye. I froze in place, turning around to look over my shoulder, but no one was there.

I saw my breath billow out before me in quick, nervous clouds of air. I ran to the fence and climbed over the wooden railings. Once I had my feet firmly set on Sutton territory, I ran harder, until I was at Tom's front door.

The door was ajar, hinting at the hollow feeling in my stomach that something was wrong. I walked into the house with caution and let my backpack fall to the floor. Pieces of furniture and broken glass lay scattered throughout the hallway. I shut the door behind me, and then stepped over the fallen coat rack before my feet.

"Tom," I called. The walls on either side of the hall were bare, while the oil paintings that had decorated them lay scattered across the floor, damaged with puncture holes. "Tom," I repeated, making my way through the house.

"Addie," a weak voice replied, nearly devoid of breath. I reached the staircase and found Tom at the bottom, with Daniel's lifeless body atop his. "Help," Tom begged, as he struggled to remove himself from the weight of his grandfather. "We have to take him to the hospital." Tom stood up, holding a hand to his back.

"What happened?" I helped Tom carry Daniel to the car, as we lay him down across the back seat. If not for Daniel's moving chest, I would have thought that he was dead.

"Someone broke into the house." Tom started the car and drove through a stretch of pasture land, before we reached a canopy road that served as their driveway.

"What?" I loudly gasped, unable to breathe. Turning my head around, I checked on Daniel in the back seat. "Daniel," I cried, squeezing his hand. To my relief, he opened his eyes and looked around the interior of the car. I took a breath and did not let go of his hand until we reached the hospital.

* * *

Tom paced back and forth in the waiting area. I sat in one of the chairs and rubbed the inside of my hands together in a nervous manner. There was a table beside me with a pot of artificial flowers and a slew of celebrity magazines on it. I looked away from the table and wiped my palms against the fabric of my jeans.

I watched Tom's nervous, repetitive steps, as he walked in front of me like a caged animal. Tom and

Daniel had hidden upstairs when the intruder broke in, not long before I had gotten there. Once the intruder was gone, Daniel's body had grown so weak and stiff, that he collapsed on his way down the staircase. I wondered if this had been the first time Daniel had fainted.

Tom sat down in the chair beside me, nervously biting his lower lip. I rubbed my hand over his back, trying to ease his anxiety. Tom took my other hand and held it in his, twining our fingers together as he waited for the doctor.

"Everything's gonna be all right, Tom," I sympathized, resting my head on his shoulder. Tom exhaled, then leaned his head against the back of the chair.

A tall man in a white coat entered the waiting room. "Tom?" The man extended his hand when Tom stood up. "Hi, my name is Dr. Reynolds."

Before the doctor could continue, Tom interrupted, "How is he doing?"

"Your grandfather is going to be fine," Dr. Reynolds muttered. He cast a wary glance my way, then placed a hand on Tom's shoulder. "Perhaps we should step into my office and have a word," he paused, "in private." Dr. Reynolds looked me over, his expression serious and unwavering. He did not smile.

"Just tell me here," Tom stated, motioning to the relatively empty waiting room. Everyone else had already been called away to their family's rooms, except for us. "I want her to know too." Tom placed his hands on his hips, indicating that he was not going to change his mind.

"Well," the doctor huffed. "Your grandfather has extremely low blood pressure for his age, but that can be attributed to his illness." Dr. Reynolds looked down at the clipboard in his hands and scribbled a note in black ink.

"Wait a minute," Tom began, pulling the doctor's focus back to him. "What do you mean illness?" Tom tilted his head to the side. "Does he have the flu or something?" Dr. Reynolds shook his head and then flipped through the pages attached to his clipboard.

"No." Dr. Reynolds sucked his mouth into a curious expression, searching for the source of confusion. "Ah, here it is." He tapped his pen against a document on the clipboard. "Last May, your grandfather was diagnosed with Parkinson's disease." Tom sank back into the chair beside me. "It's not uncommon to experience fainting spells, stiffness, tremors, dizziness, insomnia." Doctor Reynolds gazed down at the vacant expression on Tom's face. "I'm assuming he didn't share any of this with you," he added, squatting down in front of Tom to meet him at eye level.

"No," Tom answered. "What can be done for him?" Tom braided his fingers together. He had let go of my hand.

"Unfortunately, there is no cure for the disease right now." Dr. Reynolds rose from his crouched position and continued to rifle through the papers on his clipboard. "Your grandfather never chose a treatment plan, which would help him deal with the symptoms." Dr. Reynolds looked over his shoulder into the hallway. "Why don't you take a moment to think this over? I'll go check on your grandfather." Dr. Reynolds forced a synthetic smile, then left the waiting room.

"I swear I had no idea," Tom whispered, vacantly

staring into the stretch of floor before us. "How could he not tell me this?" Tom rose from the chair and then slammed his fist into the wall. "I need to be alone," he muttered, and then walked out of the room.

Chapter 16

How are you feeling?" I sat down on the edge of Daniel's bed. He was propped up with pillows, so that it would be easier for him to sit up and eat the soup and crackers before him. Tom readjusted the serving tray over Daniel's lap, careful not to spill any of the hot chicken broth.

"All right, I suppose," Daniel said. He lifted a shaky hand and picked up a spoon from the tray, while Tom stood in the doorway. Daniel dipped the spoon into the soup bowl, and then leaned forward to bring the steaming broth to his lips. But he was trembling so badly, that the spoon fell from his grasp and into the soup bowl.

A pool of yellow liquid splashed onto the serving tray. Daniel hung his head in defeat and pushed the tray away from him. "I wasn't hungry anyway," he mumbled. Tom sulked by the door, then stormed off, slamming it behind him. I shivered at the violent sound the door had made.

"Sometimes, he doesn't handle things very well," Daniel stated. I mulled over his words, realizing that Tom had not spoken since we had gotten back from the hospital. "I'm glad you're here, Addie." Daniel smiled up at me, then grabbed my hand. His skin felt neither cold, nor hot. It just felt normal.

I returned the smile and retrieved the fallen spoon. "So," I hesitated, "Tom told me that ya'll had an intruder." I filled the spoon with broth and held it to his mouth. Daniel slurped at the yellow liquid, then licked his lips before replying.

"One of DeMilo's men," Daniel suggested. When I offered him another spoonful of soup, he gladly received it. "It had to be."

"Maybe it was DeMilo," I interjected. I was interested in catching a glimpse of my alleged grandfather, no matter how criminal he might be.

"No," Daniel insisted, shaking his head. "DeMilo would never come alone." Daniel nibbled at the edge of a saltine cracker. "It was someone else."

I thought about Ricky and the picture he had received in the mail. If anyone could make sense of what was going on right now, it was Daniel. But I couldn't let myself confide in him when he needed to rest.

"Why don't I take this out of your way, so you can get some sleep?" I removed the tray from his lap and walked towards the door. "We'll be right out here if you need anything," I announced, leaving him to the comfort of his own fireplace, which rested against the far wall. Flecks of red and orange danced throughout the flames, seamlessly mesmerizing Daniel into a peaceful lethargic state.

I gently pulled the door shut behind me, and then carried the serving tray to the kitchen. After washing my hands, I joined Tom in the main hallway, where he had begun sweeping up broken pieces of glass into a dustpan. "Hey," I whispered, keeping my voice low, so I wouldn't disturb Daniel a few rooms over. "Tom." I spoke a little louder when he wouldn't answer me. He had yet to look up from the dustpan. "Are you okay?" Tom glowered in my direction, then continued sweeping.

"How do you expect me to feel, Addie?" Tom pulled his eyebrows together and stood up straight, as if he were ready to argue. "He's my grandfather, and he can't tell me something as serious as this?" Tom gestured a hand in the air, and then exhaled through his nostrils. I noticed the rise and fall of his chest.

"Maybe," I wavered, nibbling on my lip, "he didn't want to worry you." I stepped over a painting, so that I would be closer to Tom.

"And how does he think I feel now?" Tom set the dustpan and broom against the wall. I watched him look down at the punctured paintings, full of slashes and holes.

"It's not about you," I declared. "I think you're being really selfish." Tom sank down to the floor, running a hand through his hair. "How do you think Daniel feels right now?" I sat down beside Tom and placed my hand on his shoulder, hoping that I hadn't been too harsh. "He's never going to be the same again."

A long moment passed until either of us spoke again. I studied the rubble beneath our feet, noticing the faint scribble of a signature at the bottom of one of the paintings. "I guess he won't be able to paint anymore," Tom chimed, breaking the silence between us.

"Did he paint this?" I placed my hand around the frame and pulled it towards us.

"Yep." Tom nodded, motioning the length of the hall. "All of these." Tom turned to me, making eye contact. His golden eyes looked tired. "And your grandmother's portrait?" I nodded at the question. "He did that too." I felt a wave of understanding wash over me, but then I was all the more confused. "I should take you home," he said, rising from the floor.

Tom grabbed his coat in the foyer and then opened the front door, waiting for me to cross the threshold. I slung my backpack over my shoulders and followed him into the wilderness. When we reached the fence, he helped me climb over and then walked away once my feet were firmly set on the other side.

I trudged through the forest just as the sun began to set. By the time I reached the house, darkness filled the trees. It was nice to be alone in the cool night air. I exhaled several times, watching as my breath billowed out before me in puffs of white vapor.

Headlights danced along the dirt driveway in the distance. I stood between my house and the bordering stretch of woods, wondering which way I should turn. As a black Escalade came into view, I frowned. The vehicle was unfamiliar to me.

I crept towards the edge of forest that lined the driveway, set my heavy backpack on the ground, and crouched down behind an oak tree. Just before the Escalade reached my hiding spot, a rough hand covered my mouth and muted every cry for help. I felt my stomach tighten when the stranger locked an arm around my waist and dragged me into a nearby ditch.

"Shh!" the voice whispered in my ear. "It's me." I exhaled in relief at the sight of Tom. He released me, and then held a finger to his lips. My heart started beating faster at the sound of strange voices. Tom lifted his head and peeked over the edge of the ditch. I held my breath and followed suit, unable to believe what I saw.

Two men stood at the front of the vehicle, illuminated by the glow of two headlights. The first appeared to be tall, lanky, and resilient, with piercing blue eyes and dark hair. He couldn't have been older than twenty. He held a cigarette to his lips, then tilted his head back as he exhaled, watching every cloud of smoke that escaped from his mouth. The act embellished the angular appearance of his high cheekbones and prominent jawline. I studied the pale, taut nature of his face, in case I should need to identify him later.

"It doesn't look like anybody's home," the young man said. The orange-red glow at the end of his cigarette maintained a steady burn as he let his lips blow, carrying streams of dust across the night sky.

"Let's have a look around the place," the second man stated. He dug his hands into the pockets of a long black overcoat, which was draped over his medium-sized frame.

"That's DeMilo," Tom whispered, his breath hot on my cheek. I dug my heels into the ditch, straining to get a better look at the gray-haired man and thought to myself, *so this is what my grandfather looks like.*

"C'mon, Tony," the smoker protested. "I've got a wife and kid to go home to." DeMilo snatched the cigarette from the young man's mouth and squashed the burning paper with his heel. Then, DeMilo grabbed him by the collar of his jacket and jerked him down to eye level, as the latter was just a few inches taller.

"Would you like me to pay them a visit?" DeMilo leaned over the young man, blowing hot air in his face. "Don't forget your place, Hugh," DeMilo commanded. Hugh shrugged out of DeMilo's grasp, then walked away from him and onto the front porch.

"Sorry, Tony," Hugh said as he pried the front

door open. He crossed the threshold and then motioned for DeMilo to follow him inside.

"Forget about it," DeMilo replied, shutting the door behind them.

I had heard that phrase before, and I knew what it meant.

Chapter 17

I leapt from the ditch at the sound of breaking glass. "Addie," Tom softly called. "What are you doing?" I knelt down in front of an oak tree and looked over my shoulder at Tom's head, peeking over the ditch.

"I'll be right back." I kept my voice no louder than a whisper. Creeping around the perimeter of the house, I silently stepped onto the front porch, and then ducked beneath one of the windows. Despite Tom's distant protests, I took a deep breath and peered through the glass.

To my surprise, the living room remained untouched. It looked just the way I had left it. I spotted Hugh on the staircase, trailing a few steps behind DeMilo. Before long, they were both in my room.

I rose from my crouched position by the window and walked around the front porch, careful to stay low to the ground. When I glanced through the trees in search of Tom, he was gone. I exhaled, rubbing my hands over my arms to calm myself. Where was he?

At the back of the house, I looked up through my bedroom window to find DeMilo carelessly rifling through my dresser drawers. Hugh stood by his side while they both yelled at each other, tossing my things back and forth until they ended up in a messy pile on the floor.

I retraced my steps to the front porch and quietly called to Tom in the bordering stretch of woods.

When he didn't answer, I walked over to the Escalade and looked through every window. All I could make out was a pack of Marlboros in the console and several black garbage bags that had been tied together in the back seat.

I stepped away from the vehicle with a hand held to my chest, losing my breath in a panic. The front door creaked open, sending chills along my spine.

"I told you, boss. I think it's at the old man's house," Hugh said. I ran for the woods at the sound of his voice. It sounded much closer than it should have been.

Once I passed the first row of trees, Tom tackled me to the ground to keep our presence unknown. But when he lunged towards me, I gasped in bewilderment, too startled to realize his intentions. Tom clasped a hand over my mouth to muffle the sound, but it was already too late.

"What was that?" DeMilo growled, his voice echoing across the yard. I heard a door shut and the sound of footsteps pacing the front porch.

I breathed through my nostrils, screaming at myself on the inside for making any sort of noise. Tom quietly inhaled as he hovered over me, looking through the forest at DeMilo and Hugh on the porch.

"What?" Hugh answered. It sounded like he had left the porch, but I couldn't see from the flat of my back. Tom removed his hand from my mouth and crawled across the forest floor, until he reached the nearest live oak tree.

"Thought I heard something," DeMilo mused. The sound of his voice made me shiver. I turned onto my side, searching through the crowded thickets to find Hugh climbing into the driver's side of the

Escalade. DeMilo stood in front of the vehicle, with his hands on his hips and glanced at the house one last time.

Tom grabbed my wrist and dragged me across the forest floor, until I was hidden behind the girth of the oak tree. Then, he crouched down beside me, and we both watched as DeMilo situated himself in the passenger's seat. Hugh started the Escalade and backed out of the driveway, before disappearing into the darkness.

"Are you okay?" Tom leaned his face down over mine.

"Yeah," I exhaled. "I'm fine."

Tom tugged at my wrist, flipping my palm right side up. "You're bleeding," he said. I looked down at my hand. There was a small gash in the center of my palm where blood had collected. "Let's get inside."

Tom led me into the house, nearly tripping over the broken glasses on the kitchen floor. I carefully stepped around the stray pieces of glass, understanding the noises that I had heard earlier, when DeMilo and Hugh had been lurking through the place.

"Come here," Tom called. I stood beside him at the kitchen sink, not minding when he rolled my shirt sleeve up to the elbow, and then placed my hand under the running water to wash away the blood.

For the first time, I noticed how long Tom's thick black eyelashes were. They fanned out around his honey-colored eyes in an attractive way. I scanned the length of Tom's face, studying his smooth, golden complexion and the shadow of a black beard beneath it.

"Do ya'll have any bandages?" Tom turned the faucet off and dried my hand with a paper towel.

"Yeah," I said, nodding towards the pantry. "There's a first aid kit in there." Tom knelt down in front of the pantry and retrieved a plastic rectangular box from the bottom shelf. When he placed the box on the kitchen counter, a tributary of blue veins emerged in patterns across the back of his hands.

Tom wrapped a few layers of gauze around my hand and taped the end over the gash in my palm. I continued studying Tom's aesthetic while he worked. There were so many facets of his beauty that I had never taken the time to fully appreciate.

Tom stood a few inches over six feet, with enough muscle to compliment his lean physique. I wondered if he would attend football try-outs in the fall. I had never thought Tom could have anything in common with Ricky, but as I observed his height and build, it became apparent that I was wrong.

"How does your hand feel?" Tom returned the first aid kit to the pantry, then stared at me from across the kitchen counter. "Addie," he said, as if he were repeating himself. "Are you all right?"

"Yeah." I nodded, keeping my eyes on the floor. I felt a warm, hollow feeling in the pit of my stomach. When Tom moved closer, the feeling expanded into a burst of rushing heat. But then I remembered DeMilo, and the black trash bags in the back seat, and all of those new emotions dissipated.

"When will your parents be home?" Tom lifted himself onto the counter across from me and waited for an answer. His eyes glanced down at my hand and then back to my face, in a manner that was equal parts protective and unwavering.

"I don't know." I shrugged my shoulders. "Wednesday at the earliest," I suggested. Nowadays, guessing was the only way to figure out when Mom and Dad would come home.

"I think you should stay with me and Grandpa," Tom began, "at least for tonight." I nodded, sinking my teeth into my bottom lip. "You're not safe here, Addie." Tom slid off the counter and walked through the foyer on his way to the living room.

"Tom?" I followed him into the living room, crossing my arms over my chest. "I looked in DeMilo's car when he was in the house," I muttered, bouncing my foot against the floor. "I think I saw something."

"Okay," Tom responded. "What was it?"

"A dead body."

Chapter 18

I just don't understand why DeMilo wants the necklace." I sat down on the wool rug in front of the fireplace in Daniel's room. Tom stretched out beside me, resting his head on the palm of his hand.

"It's valuable," Tom piped up. "Emeralds and diamonds. There's no telling how much it's worth."

"There's plenty of valuable jewelry in the world, Tom," I demanded, crossing my legs over each other so I could sit up straight. Tom threw a hand up in the air and shook his head in uncertainty. Daniel watched us from his bed, with a pair of folded hands resting over his lap.

"It's driving me crazy," I complained, running a hand through my hair. "Why does he want it so badly?" I pulled my legs into my chest, mulling over the events of that evening. "DeMilo's from New York isn't he?" Daniel nodded.

"How could you tell?" Daniel sipped from a red tea cup that had been cooling on the nightstand. His hands were not shaking as badly as they had been earlier today. He looked tired, yet happy, regardless.

"I recognized his accent." I played with my shoe laces until I had more to say. "I like the way he talks. But that means nothing, if he came here to kill me."

"He's not going to kill you, Addie," Daniel said. "He just wants the necklace."

"But if he murdered Antoinette, then who's to say

I'm not right?" I stared into Daniel's beady blue eyes, hoping he could see all the sense I was making. "And how do ya'll know that wasn't a dead body in the back seat?" I leaned my head over my knees and turned from one Sutton to the next, until the youngest replied.

"Because you didn't see a body," Tom protested. "You just saw a bunch of garbage bags." I closed my eyes, sighing in defeat. If Antoinette had lived, then maybe Josette would have kept me as her own, and I would have two equally-emotional women to consult with right now, instead of two plain-spoken men.

"I still think we should call the police," I insisted. Tom opened his mouth to speak, but Daniel objected first.

"No, Addie." Daniel shook his head. "Police means filing reports and reports are what lead to the newspaper articles and television shows. You can't let DeMilo know that you're onto him." I buried my head in my hands, realizing that I had never felt more vulnerable in all my life.

"Well what am I supposed to do?" I knew that I sounded like a small child whining over a new set of toys, but I was scared. I was terrified of a man that I had never even met before, whose blood was allegedly running through my veins.

"You said it yourself, Tom." I pointed my finger at him, desperate for someone to be on my side of the argument. "I'm not even safe in my own house."

"I'm not so sure that I'm safe in this house," Daniel interjected. It was no coincidence that both of our houses had been broken into on the same day. "But," he breathed, "at least we'll all be here together." I nodded in agreement, until I was struck with another surge of curiosity.

"Why did DeMilo murder her?" I looked into Daniel's eyes, searching for truth. "Why did he kill Antoinette?" I could not understand why a husband would kill his wife without cause. Something happened, and I demanded to know what it was.

"Because she didn't love him," Daniel admitted.

I assumed the most logical conclusion. "She was in love with you."

Chapter 19

The guest room sat at the end of the hall, three doors down from Daniel's room. I pushed the door open and walked inside, setting my suitcase and backpack down on the floor. A queen size bed rested against the right wall, covered in burgundy sheets and pillows. I sat down on the bed and looked around the room, noting the dresser to my left and nightstand to my right.

A beam of hazy moonlight poured through an oval-shaped window across the room. I looked through the glass and sighed. The dark forest didn't appear as frightening from here. The sound of footsteps caught my attention, as I turned to find Tom in the doorway.

"You'll need some blankets on this bed." Tom walked over to the closet by the window and opened the door. "It's supposed to get pretty cold tonight." Tom grabbed a few blankets and tossed them onto the bed. "There's more blankets in here, if those aren't enough," Tom explained, motioning to the closet first and the bed second.

"Thanks." I looked at the blankets on the bed, before glancing back at Tom in appreciation. He shut the closet door, and then trudged towards me with his hands in his pockets.

"If you need anything, Grandpa's just down the hall." Tom approached the doorway, as I silently nodded to myself. "You'll be safe here tonight,

Addie," Tom assured me. "Get some sleep."

* * *

As the night wore on, sleep became the unattainable. I tossed and turned, kicking sheets and blankets until my body was wrapped in a twisted mess of wool and cotton. Moaning in frustration, I pulled the covers back and collapsed onto the hardwood floor. The burgundy sheet was tangled around my ankles with the inhibiting force of a boa constrictor. Agitated, I crawled out of the sheet and left the guest room in search of the kitchen.

All was silent as I crept down the hallway, careful not to wake Daniel. I tiptoed in front of his room, pressing my ear to the door. He snored in a rough, stammering sort of way, like a sputtering car engine that was in desperate need of a tune-up. I smiled at the noise. At least someone was asleep.

I treaded through the house in discreet fashion and breathed a sigh of relief, once I entered the kitchen. My feet padded against the cool tile floor, as I moved forward to open the refrigerator door. Yellow light poured from the open fridge, nearly blinding me. My eyes had adjusted to the darkness hours ago.

"What are you doing?" a playful voice wondered. I flinched in alarm, slamming my elbow into the refrigerator door. A shadowy figure rose from the kitchen table and turned the light on.

"Do you enjoy scaring me?" I rubbed my hand over my elbow, exhaling in frustration. Tom grinned at me from where he stood by the kitchen counter. He was wearing gray sweatpants and a black t-shirt.

"Sorry," Tom said, ruffling a hand through his messy feathered locks.

"I couldn't sleep," I muttered.

"Yeah," Tom replied, "me either." He motioned towards the stovetop. A metal tea pot simmered over the nearest eye. "You want some?"

"I don't think caffeine is the best idea." I motioned to a clock on the wall beside the stove. My insomnia would never fade if I drank tea now, at two o'clock in the morning.

Tom opened one of the overhead cabinets and retrieved a black coffee mug. I leaned against the countertop next to the fridge and watched him fill the mug to the rim.

"It's chamomile," Tom murmured. "No caffeine." I took the mug when he offered it to me. "How's your hand?" Tom noticed that I was holding the mug with my left hand, since my right hand was still wrapped in gauze.

"Oh." I smiled, looking down at the white bandage. "Fine."

Tom stepped back and leaned into the counter across from me. "So," he began, "are your parents always like this?"

I sipped at the tea. It tasted light and flowery, much different than what I had expected. "Like what?" I kept my eyes on the steaming brew, despite Tom's steady gaze.

"Gone," he replied. But the way he answered made it sound like a question.

"Yeah." I nodded. "Usually." Tom frowned at my remark. "I'm sorry about Daniel," I sympathized, determined to change the subject. Tom pressed his hands into the countertop behind him and narrowed his eyes at the floor. I intended to offer more than condolences, but what else could I say?

"Yeah," he paused, contemplating, "me too."

I drank the tea in silence and listened to the ticking clock on the wall. Tom stared at his bare feet on the tile, lost in thought. He had never looked more mysterious.

"I was homeschooled for most of my life," Tom mentioned.

"Oh," I replied, "I didn't know that."

"Yeah," he mumbled. "At Christmas, Grandpa told me that he wouldn't be able to do it anymore," Tom trailed off, his eyes searching the floor. "Now, I understand why." Tom lifted his head to look at me. When our eyes met, I realized that some emotions were more easily expressed without words.

"How do you like Maple Creek High?" I took a sip of tea, then let the substance settle in my mouth before swallowing.

"It's all right," Tom said. "I enjoy some people more than others." His golden eyes danced around the kitchen, eventually settling on me. "I should go to bed."

"Yeah," I whispered, "me too." Tom pushed himself away from the counter, hesitating in front of the stove. "Thanks for letting me stay here tonight." I nodded to myself, cupping the mug with my good hand. "I really appreciate it."

"You're always welcome here, Addie." Tom rocked back on his heels, and then offered a final cursory glance in my direction. "Good night," he said.

I watched him walk away, until his silhouette disappeared into the shadows.

Chapter 20

I slept through the morning, eventually stirring awake in the early afternoon. As I wandered through the house, the smell of bacon filled the air. I followed the scent into the kitchen, where Tom and Daniel had been waiting for me.

"It's about time you woke up," Daniel started. He sat at the end of the kitchen table, nestling a cup of hot tea in his hands. "We thought you had slipped into a coma." I smiled at the remark. It was nice to see Daniel with a smirk on his face.

"I told him to let you sleep," Tom proclaimed. He stood in front of the stove, flipping pancakes over a cast iron skillet. I blinked at the sight of him dressed in a red-and-white striped apron. Even though the material fell over his black long-sleeved t-shirt and blue jeans in true fashion, the apron bore an uncanny resemblance to a peppermint stick. He looked like Christmas.

"Are you hungry?" Tom looked back at me, spatula in hand.

"Yes," I answered. Daniel motioned to the chair opposite him. I sat down in one swift motion and rested a hand over my stomach when it began to growl. "How are you feeling?"

"Better," Daniel said. "Some days are worse than others." He forced a smile, attempting to distract me from the trembling nature of his hands. I stared at the table, not wanting to make him feel uncomfortable.

Tom walked over with a plate of pancakes, bacon, and eggs in one hand, and a glass of orange juice in the other. I rubbed my palms together in excitement when he set the meal down in front of me. "Thank you." I beamed. Tom bowed his head in response, then removed his cooking apron and sat down at the table. I took a sip of orange juice. My jaw clenched at the sweet citrus taste.

"Why don't you stay another night?" Daniel asserted. I widened my eyes in surprise. I hadn't expected him to be so forthright. "It's nice having a woman in this house." Daniel placed a shaky hand on the table, impatiently awaiting my response. The desperate look in his eyes made me wonder how long it had been since a woman had graced the Sutton residence with her presence.

"Okay," I hesitated. I had never intended to stay the whole weekend, but when Daniel asked me to, I felt compelled to oblige him. "I brought a few of my drawings with me," I proclaimed, aiming to steer the conversation in a new direction.

"I'd love to look at your drawings, Addie." Daniel pushed his chair out and rose from the table. "After my nap," he grunted. A painful expression crossed his face, as if he had just stubbed his toe.

"Do you need some help, Grandpa?" Tom stood up and reached out, extending his hands forward. He was ready to catch Daniel, in case he should fall.

"No," Daniel objected, "I'm fine." The old man left the room in a nervous, unsteady state. Despite his stiff posture, Daniel could hold himself upright without the use of a cane. But, I believe we all knew that the mild nature of his symptoms would be short-lived.

"He's so stubborn," Tom vented. "I better go check on him." Tom marched out of the kitchen, his boots pounding against the hardwood floor.

I finished my breakfast in silence, then placed the dishes that I had used in the sink. By that point, I wanted nothing more than to take a hot shower and brush my teeth. On my way to the guest room, I overheard Tom and Daniel arguing. I stopped in front of the closed door that led to Daniel's room and listened.

"I want to take her away," Tom demanded. I recognized the timbre of his voice.

"No place is safe." I heard Daniel cough a few times, before clearing his throat.

I backed away from the door, not wanting to think about DeMilo and what he had done. Before either spoke again, I crept down the length of the hallway and entered the guest room. My suitcase sat on the floor by the window. I wrapped my hand around the handles and carried the bag with me to the bathroom.

I tried to clear my head in the shower, but a slew of muddled thoughts was all that remained. I unraveled the gauze that Tom had wrapped around my hand, pleased to find a perfectly formed scab. I wondered if it would scar.

Steam rose to the ceiling as I stepped out of the shower. I slipped into a pair of jeans and pulled a gray long-sleeved t-shirt over my head. My hair dripped down the back of my shirt, while I brushed my teeth in front of the foggy mirror. I balled my left hand into a fist and smeared it over the glass, until my reflection was visible.

When I stepped into the hallway, the hardwood floor felt cool against my bare feet. I stalled in the space between the bathroom and guest room, listening for any sign of hushed conversation.

Noting the silence, I wandered into the guest room and returned my suitcase. The view through the oval-shaped window was a sunny one. I sat down on the edge of the bed and pulled a pair of socks onto my feet. There was a knock at the door just as I began lacing up my navy blue sneakers.

"Hey," Tom droned, leaning against the doorframe. "Do you want to go for a walk?" He dug his hands into his pockets and held his shoulders in a stiff manner, as if he were about to shrug. I finished tying my shoe laces and gazed through the window pane in interest.

"Sure," I consented. Tom looked somber, as he held onto the door facing. I grabbed my jacket and followed him through the house, until we reached the foyer.

"After you," he directed, holding the front door open for me. I crossed the threshold and frowned in disappointment. The sky had turned gray in the short time it took us to walk to the front door.

I descended the porch steps and looked over my shoulder at Tom. My brow furrowed at the sight of him, because he couldn't close the door. "Need a little help there?" Tom flinched when I spoke, drawing attention to the fact that his shirt sleeve was caught in the door.

"No," he insisted, "I've got it." Tom jerked the door shut, turning his back to me.

"All right." I watched him from the bottom step as he tugged at the fabric. Tom grunted and griped, struggling to pull his sleeve free from the door. I averted my eyes and pretended not to notice when a black strip of cloth floated to the ground.

Tom rolled the torn end of his shirt sleeve up in a nonchalant manner. Then, he bounced down the front porch steps, as if nothing unusual had happened. I quietly giggled to myself, but Tom didn't mind.

And so, we strolled through the forest in silence, beneath the veil of a cloudy sky. I couldn't understand why he had invited me to walk with him, if he wasn't going to say anything. I broke the silence once we came upon a glorious live oak tree, enamored with low-hanging limbs and Spanish moss.

"Wow," I breathed, lifting my head in awe. "It's beautiful." I pressed my palm into the bark, so I could feel the rough texture for myself. Captivated by her majestic beauty, I hoisted my leg onto the lowest branch and began climbing the tree.

"Addie," Tom called from down below. I quickly moved from branch to branch, ignoring his remarks. "Be careful." When Tom realized that I wasn't listening, he pulled himself up, onto the lowest branch and climbed after me.

I crept across the highest tree limb, holding my hands out in a straight line to balance myself. Tom protested when I sat down, allowing my legs to dangle over forty feet of air. I lolled my head back in laughter. Tom had yet to learn how impulsive I could be.

I leaned back on my hands, digging them into the branch for support. Tom ascended the trunk and then stepped out, onto the tree limb, to sit down beside me. I glanced at him as he situated himself onto the branch, and then looked away when he noticed that I was staring.

"Well," I said, motioning towards the view before us. Tom took his time in observing the tree tops. I gazed across the picture perfect landscape, wishing that I had brought my sketchbook. "I haven't done this since I was a little girl," I confessed.

"Really?" I could feel Tom's eyes on me, but didn't want to look away from the forest, for fear that it might all disappear.

"Yeah," I breathed, "when I was a kid, all I wanted to do was be in the woods." A light breeze drifted through the air, calming the atmosphere. "Is that weird?"

"No," Tom answered, "I like the woods."

We sat in the tree for hours, reflecting on childhood memories. I told him about Emily and how depressed I had been when she went missing. The weekends were lonely, especially since my parents were prone to leave without so much as a word.

The sunset was beautiful from our spot in the tree, all pink and golden. I was definitely bringing my sketchbook with me the next time.

"We should head back," Tom suggested.

"Yeah." I nodded in agreement. "I'm starving." I glanced at the forest one last time, then followed him down the tree.

"Pizza?" Tom crouched onto a low-hanging limb, waiting for me to reach him.

"Yeah," I agreed. The thought of bread, tomatoes, and cheese made my stomach growl. "But I don't know if they do delivery out here." I tried to call in a large mushroom pizza one time, but when I mentioned my address, all I heard was a dial tone.

"No," Tom explained, "I make it from scratch."

"Oh, well that's even better." I steadied myself onto the next branch, careful not to lose my balance. Tom landed on the ground and then stared up at the tree, waiting for me to join him.

When I reached the last branch, I noticed that my shoe lace had come undone. Rolling my eyes, I shrugged the matter off and prepared to jump anyway. As I leapt down, the lace managed to tangle itself around my shoe, so I tripped over the branch and tackled Tom to the ground.

"I'm so sorry," I mumbled. Tom lay beneath me with a disgruntled expression on his face, as he had taken the brunt of the fall. I hoped that he wasn't hurt.

"That's okay," Tom groaned. He sat up and stretched his neck from side to side. "Are you all right?" Tom gazed up at me. His honey-colored eyes looked like they were melting.

"Yeah," I sighed. Tom picked a stray twig out of my hair and tossed it away. I laughed, slightly embarrassed at the thought of tripping into his arms.

Tom paused, staring into my eyes as he tucked a fallen strand of hair behind my ear. His hand lingered at the edge of my jaw, until he pulled my face towards his own. When our lips met, I felt a tingling, electric sensation spread across the surface of my skin. Tom buried his face in my dark blonde tresses as I kissed him back, relaxing into the weight of his body. His fingers trailed the length of my neck, before he returned his lips to mine.

A clap of thunder sounded in the distance, so we turned our heads to the sky, spotting a flash of lightning through the trees. With his hand around my waist, Tom helped me to my feet, just as rain came pouring down in a flood of liquid fury. Tom grabbed my hand and pulled me through the forest, laughing in spite of the downpour.

After jogging through the rainstorm, we left our

muddy shoes on the front porch and headed inside the house. Tom led me into the den and lit the fireplace. I shivered before the flames, feeling the dampness of my hair and clothing. Tom left the room, only to return with an oversized beach towel.

"Let's go check on Grandpa," he said. Tom wrapped the towel around my shoulders, and then dragged me into the hallway. I leaned into his tall, muscular, frame, not minding when our fingers became entwined.

"Did you kids get caught in the rain?" Daniel sat up in his bed, once he noticed us in the doorway. I felt Tom's thumb brush against the skin of my inner palm.

"Yeah," Tom chuckled. "I was thinking about making pizza for dinner." Daniel's eyes wandered between us, eventually settling on the way Tom's hand was tightly clasped around mine. "But there's leftover soup in the fridge," Tom hesitated, waiting for Daniel to respond. "I can heat some up for you on the stove, if you'd rather have that."

"That'll be fine, Tom," Daniel announced. "Just bring the soup in here." He motioned to the mattress beneath him. "I'm tired." Daniel yawned, but the action appeared too forceful to be genuine. He was distracted.

"All right." Tom nodded. We stepped into the hallway, leaving Daniel to himself. Tom closed the door behind us, and then steered me towards the kitchen.

I stood by Tom's side while he made dinner, looking on with wonder as he rolled out a large circle of pizza dough, and then began tossing it in the air. Tom was unlike anyone I had ever known before. He didn't care what was expected of him, or what people thought. I admired him for that.

"Come here," Tom beckoned. He sprinkled flour on the countertop beside him, setting a fresh heap of dough down before me. I looked up at Tom hesitantly, unsure of myself.

"Tom," I said, "I don't know how to make pizza." Tom draped his arm over my shoulder, then leaned forward, pushing my hair behind my shoulder. I felt a rush of blood color my face, revealing the nervous energy inside me.

"Well," he whispered in my ear, "that was before you met me."

Chapter 21

Tom had more patience than I could muster in a lifetime. When I accidentally knocked a bag of flour off the counter, he knelt down to clean up the mess. When I tossed a pie-shaped section of pizza dough over my head with such force that it landed on the ceiling, he merely laughed. Even when I dropped a ladleful of tomato sauce on the counter and it splattered all over his face, Tom responded with no less than a smile.

Eventually, I gravitated towards the stovetop and reheated a pot of chicken soup for Daniel. Tom finished coating the pizza with tomato sauce, then added vegetables and mozzarella cheese before placing it in the oven to bake. I stayed by the stove, not wanting to cause any more mishaps in the kitchen.

At the sound of music, I looked over my shoulder to find Tom with an outstretched hand. I placed my hand in his, letting him guide me across the tile floor, as the radio filled the room with music from an older time.

"Nat King Cole," I announced, nodding to the small silver radio on the counter. "I'm impressed."

"I'm impressed that you know who that is," Tom chuckled. I playfully nudged his shoulder for thinking that my awareness of music only delved into the past decade.

"I'm not like all those other girls," I declared.

"I know." Tom held his lips together as his golden eyes turned somber. "That's why I like you so much."

I lowered my eyelashes, turning my head in bashfulness. "I like you too," I admitted.

Tom pulled me close to him, and then lifted my chin with his hand, so that only a sliver of space remained between us. I closed my eyes once he leaned into me, brushing his lips against my own. Although my heart quivered at the slightest touch, being with Tom felt so natural and intuitive. I didn't have to try.

* * *

After dinner, I walked into Daniel's room with a handful of drawings, mostly of Tom, and set them down on the bed. Daniel picked up the sketches with a shaky hand, then began to sort through them, as I hovered by the nightstand.

"Addie," he began, all too seriously. "These are great." Daniel smiled at the sketches of Tom's honey-colored eyes. As an artist, I figured Daniel would appreciate how difficult it had been to capture them. Tom's eyes looked like magic in luster.

"Your paintings are," I hesitated, searching for the right word, "perfect." I sat down on the edge of Daniel's bed, comforted by the crackling fireplace against the wall. "Why didn't you tell me you were an artist?"

Daniel shrugged, setting my sketches aside for the moment. "I suppose it doesn't really matter anymore," he mused, watching the orange flames dance in the distance.

"But your work is fantastic," I insisted. Daniel looked down at his hands, showing me the way they trembled. I had studied Daniel's paintings in the hallway and knew that each one had been intricately detailed with shades of color and light. A steady hand was required.

"Keep drawing, Addie," Daniel advised, forcing a smile at the edge of his wrinkled lips. "I'd like to see more of these." He picked up the stack of drawings and handed them to me. A deep longing filled the pit of my stomach. I wished that I could do more for him.

"Thank you." I took the drawings from Daniel and turned on my heel. But then I lingered in the doorway, compelled by the need to say something more. "Daniel?" I approached the front of his bed, wondering if it was too much to ask.

"I'd really like to learn how to paint, but I'm only a sketch artist." I pressed my fingers against the sketches in my hand, gazing at him all the while. "I was wondering if maybe," I dawdled, stumbling over my words, "you could teach me." I paused before adding, "If you feel like it."

Daniel mulled over the thought for a moment, then turned his gaze back to the fire.

"Never mind," I faltered, stepping back into the doorway. "I should let you sleep."

"Wait a minute, Addie." Daniel looked into my eyes with a teasing smile. "I've got no problem teaching you how to paint." I beamed, clutching the sketches I had drawn to my chest. "Just try not to be so hasty."

"All right," I agreed, too delighted to be disheartened by his critique. "And thank you for inviting me to stay another night." I leaned my back into the doorframe. "My parents aren't the best..." I drifted off, unsure of what to call them.

"You're always welcome here, Addie." Daniel offered a slight nod, and then removed his reading glasses, setting them down on the nightstand beside his bed. I stepped out of the room and shut the door behind me, understanding that Daniel needed to rest.

I found Tom in the den, with his schoolwork spread out on the floor. Tom sank into the carpet, pressing his back into the couch, as if it were not intended for sitting. I joined him on the floor and rested my head on his shoulder, while looking down at the open chemistry book in his lap.

"Studying?" I locked my hands around Tom's arm. He was so warm.

"Yeah," he sighed, rifling through pages full of diagrams and charts. "We've got that quiz on Wednesday." Tom scanned the periodic table of the elements with his index finger.

"Great," I moaned. Tom laughed at my remark, and then shut the textbook with a soft thump. I lifted my chin when he turned his face towards mine, searching my eyes.

"You really don't like chemistry, do you?" Tom smirked, revealing a set of straight white teeth. His golden eyes glistened with reflections of the firelight.

"Science is just too..." I stretched the phrase out, holding my mouth in the shape of the word.

"Basic," Tom sarcastically answered.

"No." I shrugged. "I don't know how to explain it." I hesitated, feeling the presence of Tom's gaze. "It's just too exact, too linear." I watched the orange-red flames as they flickered and swayed in the fireplace. "My brain doesn't work like yours." I grew quiet, worried that I had said the wrong thing.

"Go on," Tom coaxed, lifting his arm to the seat of

the couch.

"I like the idea that there can be more than one answer to something." I braided my fingers together, slowly shifting my eyes around the room as I thought. "Two plus two will always equal four," I paused, contemplating. "But if someone asked me to describe a sunset or the rain, I could come up with a hundred different answers." I looked at Tom, who had yet to take his eyes off me. "And they'd all be right." He nodded in agreement.

Fearing that I had revealed too much, I asked, "Does that make sense?"

"Well I don't know," Tom mused. "My brain doesn't work like yours."

"Hey!" I giggled, slapping his knee in jest. "Are you mocking me?" When Tom started to laugh I added, "I meant that as a compliment."

Tom could sort through mathematical equations in a flash, while I stared into oblivion, nervously chewing on the end of my pencil. But I wasn't jealous. I was enamored.

"So did I," Tom whispered. The most genuine smile flashed across his face, charming me into a state of reverence. Sometimes, he was so beautiful that it scared me.

"Did you like the pizza?" Tom twirled a finger through the ends of my hair, anticipating my approval. I nodded, sinking my teeth into my lower lip.

"When did you learn how to cook?" I leaned my head against his chest, falling into his embrace. Tom brushed his hand against the back of my neck, as I felt a subtle shiver creep down my spine.

"When Grandpa couldn't anymore," he answered. I listened to the strong, steady rhythm of his heart and noticed how rapidly the beat increased when I stroked my fingers over the back of his hand. It sounded like drums.

"What is DeMilo gonna do to me?" I spoke into Tom's shirt, inhaling his scent. "He'll be back," I predicted. "And what will he do when he finds out that I don't have the necklace?" Tom rubbed the top of my shoulders, relieving the tension in my body.

"I can take you away from here." Tom placed his hands around my waist and pulled me into his lap. I became more aware of myself, now that Tom held his face just inches from mine.

"Where would we go?" I looked at his lips more than I should have.

"Anywhere you want," Tom murmured. I lost all concentration when he rested his hand against the side of my face, warming my skin with his own.

"What about Daniel?" I wondered, placing my hand over Tom's shoulder.

"He can come with us," Tom shrugged, devoid of second thoughts.

"And my parents?" I peeled Tom's hand from my face, trying to help him see reason. Usually, *he* was the rational one.

"They wouldn't notice," Tom assumed. I pulled away from him, taking offense in the truth. As I stood before the fireplace, Tom rose to his feet, approaching me. I kept my back to him and crossed my arms over my chest. The room felt much colder when Tom wasn't holding me.

"Addie, I'm sorry." Tom stood behind me, wrapping his arms around my stomach. "I shouldn't have said that," he whispered in my ear.

"Well then why did you?" I turned around and

pressed my palms into his chest, pushing him onto the couch. Tom looked up at me from his seated position, startled by my anger.

"I don't know." Tom gazed into my eyes, looking like a child, who had just been scolded for misbehaving.

"Tom," I began. "I'm scared." Tears brimmed along the corners of my eyes. "Even if we left," I shook my head, convincing myself, "he'd find us."

Tom tugged at my wrist, pulling me onto the couch cushion beside him. I wrapped my arms around Tom, while he cradled me in his arms. I couldn't remember anyone ever holding me so tightly.

I thought about my parents and all of the nights that I had slept alone in our house, when DeMilo could have easily broken in. They had left me in the woods, unprotected for the past four years, and never thought anything of it. Mom's only child was medicine, while Dad's was law. I had never been anything more than an item checked off a list: *Go to college. Have a Career. Get Married. Have a Child.*

Only, my parents weren't Mom and Dad anymore. They were just Jeffrey and Eleanor.

Chapter 22

The storm woke me in the night. I sat up in bed, feeling of the warm moisture behind my neck. My body ached, as if I had spent the previous day moving furniture. I pulled the covers back and slid out of the bed, walking towards the window. Rain battered against the pane. It sounded like small rocks over glass.

Lightning flashed in the forest, illuminating the black night. I stood by the window and looked out into the darkness, even as thunder shook the house. But when a shadowy figure appeared among the trees, I turned away from the window and pressed my back into the wall, helplessly sinking to the floor.

I held my breath at the sound of another lightning bolt, then cautiously returned to the window. As I lifted my eyes to look through the glass, relief swept over me. No one was there.

I rose to my feet in laughter, shaking my head. I didn't want to be paranoid. Turning on my heel, I weaved a shaky hand through my hair, attempting to calm myself. I sat down on the bed and closed my eyes, until I heard a faint scratching sound. The noise filtered through the window pane, sending chills along the length of my spine.

I crept out of the bed and approached the window, bracing myself for whatever lay on the other side. Kneeling down, I watched my breath materialize on the glass in misty fog. When the scratching subsided, I bit my lower lip, wondering if I had truly lost my mind. But then DeMilo's face appeared through the glass, and all I could do was scream.

* * *

Struggling beneath a mess of tangled covers, I jumped out of the bed and marched over to the window. "It was a dream," I whispered to myself. "It was just a dream."

The heavy rain had weakened during the night, dying down to a slight drizzle. Thunder echoed in the distance, as the storm traveled farther away. I exhaled, searching for DeMilo's silhouette among the trees, but he was gone.

Unable to sleep, I left the guest room in search of Tom. Perhaps he was in the kitchen again, experiencing a similar bout of insomnia. When I opened the refrigerator, yellow light spilled onto the tile floor. I looked around the room, expecting Tom to startle me with his presence, as he had done the night before. Instead, I found myself lurking around the kitchen table, while Tom remained out of sight.

Sauntering through the house, I reached the staircase and climbed to the top. I looked at the old wooden door on my left and thought about Antoinette's portrait hanging on the wall by the window. Stepping to the right, I stood in front of another closed door, only to discover that it was nestled at the beginning of a long corridor, which held another five rooms on either wall. I gazed down the hallway in admiration, and then twisted the doorknob on the first bedroom until it opened.

Despite the darkness, I quickly detailed the expansive layout of the bedroom. A wooden desk sat against the wall to my right, along with a blue swivel chair, though neither appeared as significant in comparison to the towering chest of drawers in the corner.

After lingering in the doorway for a moment longer, I closed the door behind me and intruded further. Double doors denoted the closet to my left. I wondered if they had been painted white to match the pale walls and carpeting. Shadows danced across the closet doors, as tree branches swayed through the bay windows on the other side of the room.

A bathroom sat snuggly within the wall that formed a perpendicular angle with the closet. I dawdled in front of the open door and looked into the spacious bathroom, complete with a walk-in shower, garden tub, double sinks, and the like.

Next to the bathroom, a king size bed lay against the wall, extending into the center of the room. I found Tom asleep on the mattress. He had kicked every blanket to the bottom of the bed. Even though he wore no more clothing than a pair of navy blue sweatpants, Tom looked warm.

I pulled the covers towards the front of the bed and slipped underneath them. Lying beside Tom in the moonlight, I felt safe from the outside world. Tom rolled onto his stomach, letting his arm dangle over the edge of the bed. I turned onto my side and studied the closet doors. The sound of Tom's steady breathing lulled me to sleep.

* * *

I felt groggy in the morning, not wanting to wake up. Rays of sunshine beamed through the bay windows across the room, as I hid beneath the covers in search of darkness. I heard running water in the bathroom and remained semi-conscious until the noise ceased.

Lethargic, I narrowed my eyes, confused by the sounds that I was hearing. For clarity's sake, I pulled the covers away and looked around the room. Opening my mouth in surprise, I realized that I was still in Tom's room. I had intended to leave before he woke up, but now that he was getting out of the shower, there was no time to hide. I buried my head in the pillow, failing to conceal my embarrassment when he opened the bathroom door and walked into the bedroom.

"Hey," he called. Looking past the pillow, I discovered Tom, dressed in warm clothes, with a towel draped over his shoulders. "Did you sneak in here last night?" Tom rubbed the towel over his damp hair, waiting for an answer.

"Yeah." I blushed. "I couldn't sleep."

Tom nodded, then walked into the bathroom to return his towel. "How bad was the storm?" I quickly combed my fingers through my hair, attempting to calm any frizzy tangles. "I was out the minute I hit the mattress."

"Not too bad," I muttered. Anxiety spread through my body like a fever. What had Tom thought when he woke up this morning and found me in his bed? I didn't want to be defined in that way, because I wasn't that kind of girl. I didn't even want to consider what Daniel would say if he knew.

"Cool," Tom said. When he walked back into the room, I couldn't understand the wave of nonchalance that preceded him. Tom opened the bottom drawer of his dresser and removed a pair of socks. He balanced on one foot as he slipped into each piece of cotton.

My eyes darted around Tom's room, searching for a diversion. I looked into his closet, noting a black leather guitar case in the corner. "You play?" I nodded to the instrument.

"A little." Tom shrugged. I bit my bottom lip, curiosity gnawing at my core.

"Could you play something for me?" I crossed my legs over each other, then glanced from Tom to the guitar and back again. He was hesitant at first, rocking back on his heels in reluctance. Eventually, Tom smiled and retrieved the guitar case from the closet.

"All right," he succumbed. Tom moved his desk chair across the floor, and then sat down in front of me. "I don't normally play for other people," he admitted.

"That's okay." I pressed my lips into a fine line. Tom glanced up at me, then rested the acoustic guitar over his knee and began to play.

All at once, Tom became someone else, with a voice I'd never heard and a face I'd never seen. I recognized the song as something I'd once heard on a Coldplay record, but never really listened to. Soon, I was singing along in my head, about all the things that were *yellow*.

I watched Tom's fingers move along the fret board in delicate fashion, even when he closed his eyes. His voice carried across the room, enveloping me in shades of light. In that moment, I could feel what Tom felt. There was a sort of haunting beauty to it. He didn't seem real.

When the song ended, Tom opened his eyes just enough to reveal thin slits of liquid amber beneath his lashes. I held my breath, waiting for him to disappear. Tom laid the guitar flat over his thighs and sighed, exhaling in accomplishment. I clapped my hands together, beaming all the while. Tom deserved applause.

"Thanks." He grinned, too modest to be proud. We shared a cursory glance, and then Tom returned the guitar to its black leather case. As he turned towards the closet, I noticed a small green notebook on the highest shelf and wondered what was written on the pages inside.

"Have you ever written any songs?" I sat on the edge of the bed, letting my feet dangle over the carpet below. Tom returned the guitar case to its spot in the closet, then hesitated, with his eyes on the green notebook.

"Yes." Tom faced the bed and began searching my eyes.

Dropping my feet to the floor, I waltzed over to the shelf in Tom's closet and reached for the notebook.

"Addie," Tom scolded, pulling me away. "What are you doing?" Tom stood in the middle of the closet, blocking me from the notebook.

"I was just wondering if any of them were about me." I leaned on one foot, and then the other. Tom shook his head from side to side.

"Addie," he moaned. "They're *all* about you."

Intrigued, I flung my arm forward and slapped the notebook down from the closet shelf. Tom grabbed my arm, jerking me away when I nearly had the notebook in my hands. Squirming out of his grasp, I lunged for the notebook, unsure why I felt so compelled to read what was inside of it. I wasn't the prying type.

I stretched my hand out and grazed my fingertips over the cover, but then Tom kicked the notebook out of my grasp. Griping in frustration, I watched the notebook slide along the white carpet, until it reached the nearest wall. The notebook crashed into the base board with a noticeable thud, and a small photograph slipped out.

"What is this?" I held the photograph in my hands. It was a picture of me.

"Addie," Tom began, placing his hand on my arm.

I couldn't have been more than eight years old in the photograph. Trees surrounded me as I smiled in the summer sun, preparing to climb another live oak. As an only child, I had grown used to entertaining myself in the forest. My parents didn't mind.

"Where did you get this?" I felt of the wrinkled creases at the edge of the picture.

"I took it," he confessed, "a long time ago." Tom shoved his hands in his pockets, nervously pacing the floor in front of me.

"Why?" I gazed up at Tom, anxious to know why he had been taking pictures of me in the forest. Tom placed a palm beneath his chin, gently stroking the stubble of his beard before responding.

"Well," he paused, swallowing. "When we were kids, I used to see you in the woods a lot." I raised my eyebrows, silently accusing him. "Don't tell me you've never jumped the fence before." Tom grinned in a juvenile way. He looked like a little boy.

"So," I contemplated. "You've been watching me this whole time?" Tom's cheeks turned scarlet red, making him look all the more cherubic. "You're a stalker!" I playfully nudged Tom's shoulder, backing him into the wall.

"Addie, it wasn't like that." Tom held his hands in the air, feigning innocence.

"Really?" I stared into his light golden eyes. Tom tucked his chin down to meet my stare, as our faces remained inches apart.

"Yes," Tom chuckled. "I liked you, and I just wanted you to be safe."

"Oh," I breathed, stepping back. "Well," I faded into the silence. We stood in front of each other, lost in thought and emotion. I liked Tom much more than I should have, but that reluctance was fading fast.

"I should go downstairs." Tom knelt down to retrieve the green notebook, and then returned it to the closet before closing the double doors. "I need to check on Grandpa and get breakfast started."

"I can check on Daniel," I offered.

"Thanks." Tom chewed at the inside of his mouth, his lips turning up at the corners. When Tom turned on his heel, I placed the photograph on his desk and then watched him walk away. Despite the absence of wings, I searched his silhouette for a halo.

Chapter 23

After walking into Daniel's bedroom, I offered him the warm cup of tea in my hand. Daniel gladly took the drink, as he lifted the cup to his mouth. I sat down on the edge of Daniel's bed, searching his face. He looked tired. I wondered if the storm had woken him during the night.

"Tom's making breakfast," I started. "Do you want me to bring yours in here?"

"No." Daniel shook his head. "I want to eat with you young folks," he declared. Daniel lifted the corners of his mouth, but the movement looked difficult for him. He was in pain.

"I should go see how much longer it will be." I smiled at Daniel, then turned to leave. But before I could slide off the bed, Daniel tugged at my shirtsleeve.

"Stay here," he begged. Daniel's eyes turned a clear shade of liquid blue. "Keep me company." I hesitated, unable to resist Daniel's requests. "Tom will tell us when breakfast is ready."

"All right," I consented. Daniel sipped at his tea, satisfied by my company. "Tell me the story," I began, catching him off guard. Daniel pulled his eyebrows together in uncertainty. "What happened back then?" I pressed my palms into the comforter, situating myself atop the bed. "Why would Antoinette marry DeMilo if she was in love with you?"

Daniel swallowed a mouthful of tea, and then placed the cup on the nightstand beside his bed. Inhaling, Daniel lifted his eyes to the ceiling, as if he were asking permission from above, before he could continue.

"Antoinette and I started dating when we were fifteen," Daniel began. "We met in high school, and soon we were spending all of our time together." Daniel tilted his head to the side, looking off in the distance. "She was so beautiful."

"What was she like?" I snapped Daniel out of his trance and returned his gaze to mine. His face fell, and for a moment, I wished that I hadn't asked him to tell me everything.

"Oh," Daniel sighed. "I don't know." I looked down at the floor and hoped that I hadn't asked the wrong question. "Antoinette was very independent for her age. She didn't like feeling restrained."

"What's wrong with that?" I placed a hand on my hip, prepared to argue.

"Nothing," Daniel answered. "You're more like her than I thought." I smiled to myself, appreciating the comparison. Daniel stared at the comforter on the bed, and then began tracing lines into the stitching with his fingers. Even though his hands were shaking, Daniel looked peaceful.

"So what happened?" I felt a space open in my chest, making room for the truth.

"Well," Daniel murmured. "During our senior year of high school, Tony DeMilo moved here with his family." Daniel took a deep breath, readjusting himself on the mattress. "They were from New York and had lived in New Jersey for a while," Daniel stated. "But Tony's mother had lived in Savannah as a child, and she wanted to come home." Daniel turned somber, as his cheeks began to turn red.

"Tony wasn't well liked at school," Daniel commented. "Kids would tease him or make fun of the way he talked." Daniel turned morose and hung his head in an unsightly manner. "I befriended him, because I thought it was the right thing to do." Daniel retrieved the tea cup from his nightstand and held it in his palms, soaking up the warmth that remained.

"After a few weeks, Tony started asking questions about Antoinette." Daniel shrugged his shoulders, as if every teenage boy had done the same. "It was rumored that Antoinette descended from a long line of French aristocracy, and that her ancestors had migrated to America, after losing everything in the Revolution."

I let my mind run away with me and imagined that the emerald necklace had been worn by Marie Antoinette, before her turn at the guillotine. But then Daniel added, "None of it was true, of course." I nodded my head in acceptance, refusing to feel any disappointment. How could I be related to a queen?

"I often caught Tony staring at her in class or in the hallway." Daniel narrowed his eyes at me, defending himself. "I wasn't possessive, or even jealous, but there was just something about Tony that seemed strange," Daniel said. "It became obvious that he wanted Antoinette for himself."

I felt woozy, growing uncomfortable at the faintest touch of light. My temples began to throb, but I ignored the pounding and focused on Daniel.

"Tony started dating Rosalyn Babbitt to make Antoinette jealous," Daniel huffed, blowing hot air through his lips. "It didn't work," he drawled. "Antoinette didn't care."

There were three knocks at the door before Tom entered the room, interrupting Daniel's story. "Breakfast is ready," he announced. I nodded to him in politeness, disappointed that Daniel couldn't finish the story now.

Daniel waited until Tom had left the room, and then leaned towards me. "I'll tell you the rest later," he promised. I knew he would.

* * *

Just before sunset, Tom and I walked through the forest, headed towards my house. I needed more clothes and wanted to make sure that DeMilo hadn't returned in my absence. Tom helped me climb over the fence, and then led me near the front porch.

Yellow light glowed through the front windows, as I realized that both of my parents were home. I caught Mom's silhouette in the living room, alongside Dad's. I silently groaned in frustration, while Tom read my mind. "I'll go back and get your bags," Tom offered.

"Thank you," I sighed. Tom kissed me in a moment that ended all too soon, and then disappeared into the trees. I held my breath, bracing myself for whatever Jeffrey and Eleanor had to offer.

"Where have you been?" Eleanor stood in the doorway with her hands on her hips. She was dressed in a formal evening gown, all black and silky. My eyes widened at the sight of her black eyes, embellished with mascara, liner, and powder. She looked like a witch.

"I went for a walk." I brushed past Eleanor, moving towards the staircase. Jeffrey dashed into the kitchen, and then ran through the rest of the house until he reached his office. I listened for Jeffrey as he pulled the door closed behind him.

"Why weren't you at school on Friday?" Eleanor jabbed a finger in my direction. Her dark hair lay twisted at the nape of her neck, within the clutching hold of a golden barrette.

"I was sick." I stepped around her, not making eye contact. "I think I had the flu or something." Eleanor grabbed my arm, pulling me back to her.

"Don't lie to me!" she exclaimed. Eleanor's skin turned bright red, hinting at the anger she felt towards me. I thought the vein on her forehead might burst.

"Well," I snarled, shriveling from her grasp. "You would know all about that. Wouldn't you, Mother?" I glared into her ebony eyes, warning her. Ultimately, Eleanor couldn't handle the way I was looking at her, so she stormed off and slammed the bedroom door behind her.

Rushing up the staircase, I walked into my bedroom and looked out the window. Tears brimmed over the edge of my eyelids, as I resisted the urge to cry. I searched the shadowy night for Tom, wishing he would appear on the tree outside my window.

I crumpled a piece of paper in the back pocket of my jeans, and then descended the staircase. Walking through the house, I stopped before the door to Jeffrey's office. I opened the door without knocking, because I knew he wouldn't mind. Jeffrey never minded anything. That was his problem.

"Hey Addie," he chirped. "Is everything okay with your mother?" Jeffrey studied the paperwork beneath him, slashing through paragraphs with a black fountain pen.

"No," I answered. "She's dead." Jeffrey looked up from his desk, paralyzed with fear. I exhaled, and then removed the crumpled birth certificate from my pocket. A wave of understanding swept over Jeffrey's face, as he came to understand what I meant.

"Your mother was supposed to fix this years ago," Jeffrey explained. He flattened the piece of paper out on his desk, though no matter of straightening could erase the creases. "How long have you known?" I eyed Jeffrey carefully, not trusting him enough to fully disclose the truth. After all, he was married to Eleanor.

"Long enough," I countered.

Jeffrey sighed to himself, running a hand through his thin blonde locks. "Addie, I'm sorry you had to find out this way." He set the black pen down on his desk, trapping the birth certificate beneath it. "Your mother and I weren't able to have children of our own." Jeffrey laced his fingers together, then tapped the edges of his thumbs against each other.

"How could ya'll keep this from me?" I stood before Jeffrey, ashamed of him. It felt like he was the teenager, and I was the parent.

"You'll always be our daughter, Addie." Jeffrey rose from his polished leather chair and leaned forward to take my hand. "We love you." I nodded to myself, remembering that Jeffrey had always been the nice one. But then he sat back down and returned to his work, as if nothing had been said.

"Dad?" I furrowed my brow in confusion. "I want to talk about this."

"I really need to work right now." Jeffrey looked up at me, forcing an artificial smile. "Can we talk about it some other time?" I staggered back in astonishment, nearly losing my balance.

"No!" I demanded. "I want to talk about it now."

"Now is not a good time for me, Addie," Jeffrey

griped. He sorted through the paperwork on his desk, ignoring my presence altogether.

I snatched my birth certificate from his desk and then marched into the open doorway. "You're just like her," I choked, unable to repress the tears.

I left Jeffrey's office with a cloud of emotions overhead. Once I reached my bedroom, I slammed the door behind me and collapsed onto the bed. I wanted nothing more than to lie there forever, immersed in my own grief.

Eventually, I forced myself out of the bed and stumbled into my bathroom. I took a shower and then brushed my teeth, thankful that my bedroom had come with a private bathroom. I didn't want to be anywhere near Jeffrey or Eleanor.

Just as I slipped into sweatpants and a baseball t-shirt, a soft thud sounded on the other side of my bathroom door. I paused, listening for the noise to reoccur. When it did, I opened the bathroom door to find Tom perched on the tree outside my window.

"You scared me," I whispered, after opening the window. Tom sat down on the tree limb, balancing my luggage in his hands. "Thanks," I said, as he tossed my backpack from his spot in the tree. I set the bag down on the floor, and then leaned out the window to catch my suitcase.

"Are you all right?" Tom stood up on the tree limb, preparing to climb through my window. I dropped my suitcase on the carpet, beside my backpack, then pushed both bags aside with the edge of my foot.

"I'm fine," I snapped. Tom studied the expression on my face, disbelief apparent on his own. "You should head back." I felt of the raw puffiness beneath my eyes. It was plain to see that I had been crying.

"Addie, what's wrong?" Tom squatted over the tree limb and gazed into my eyes. I recoiled from the window, disliking his attempt at cornering me. Regardless, I sat down on the bed and let my arms hang limply at my sides.

When Tom climbed through the window, I shivered at the hint of cold air that followed. My hair fell in loose, damp waves along my back, as I moved my hands over my arms to warm myself. Tom closed the window, and then flopped down beside me on the mattress.

"I showed Dad my birth certificate." I brushed my thumb over the curved lines of my palm. "He didn't deny it," I muttered. "They did adopt me." I rose from the bed and began to pace the floor in front of my window. "But when I wanted to talk about it," I hesitated, wrapping my arms around my ribcage. "He didn't even care." I heard Tom exhale. Even the sound of his breath felt warm.

"What did your mom say?" Tom followed me to the window. I could feel his eyes glazing over every inch of my face.

"She doesn't know yet," I grumbled. "I just told Dad." I pressed one foot on top of the other, distracted by the sound of my cracking toes.

"Well, at least he told you the truth." Tom took a step towards me, until I stood with my back against the wall. I met his gaze, repressing the onslaught of fresh tears. When I looked into Tom's eyes, he placed his hands around my waist and pulled me towards him.

Reveling in Tom's embrace, I rested my head on his shoulder, while his hands traced patterns over my back. I inhaled, forcing myself to swallow every unguarded thought and emotion. With Tom, I didn't need to seek shelter. He made me believe that there could be light in the darkness.

Tom lifted my head from his shoulder, holding my face in his hands. As he gazed into my eyes, I felt a soft, smoldering heat take hold and spread throughout my entire body. Tom leaned forward, brushing his lips over mine in a soft, delicate manner. My fingers danced across the back of his neck, tugging at the ends of his hair. Despite the warmth between us, Tom's skin felt cool to the touch.

I clung to Tom in violent desperation, gripping the fabric of his shirt. Our lips became a tennis match of sorts, constantly returning to one another, until Tom discovered the edge of my jawline. I could barely breathe, but soon realized that I didn't need to.

When Tom's hands traveled to my waistline, I trembled at the slightest caress. I fell limp in his arms, paralyzed by the way his hand slipped beneath the hem of my shirt, searching for skin. But as his fingers crept along my spine, I felt less at ease. A hollow ache formed in the pit of my stomach, willing me to resist.

"Tom," I whispered, struggling to speak. I had never felt more desired, but the feeling became too wild, too ravenous. It was something that neither of us could control.

"Hmm," Tom murmured. I pulled his arms away from my body, forcing him to take a step back and look me in the face. "I'm sorry." Tom held my hands, until our fingers became entwined. "It's just that," he paused, "I've waited so long." Tom studied the floor, then glanced up at me.

"I know." I smiled. Now that I knew Tom had been watching me for nearly ten years in the forest, I understood the intensity of each smoldering gaze and affectionate touch. I wrapped my arms around Tom, hugging him tightly. It felt good to be wanted.

"Addie," he moaned. "Not helping."

"Sorry." I stepped back, resisting the desire to tempt him further.

"I should go," Tom said. He trudged towards the window with a pair of reluctant feet, shoving his hands into his pockets. "I need to check on Grandpa anyway."

"Okay." I stretched out the sleeves of my shirt, until the fabric was long enough to cover my hands.

Tom climbed through my bedroom window, and then jumped onto the nearest tree limb. I watched him scale the length of the great oak, and then plant his feet on the ground, once he reached the bottom. My eyes danced across the wilderness as I leaned against the windowsill, ignoring the rush of cold air. I followed Tom's figure in the darkness, until it became nothing more than a silhouette.

Chapter 24

When my alarm went off the next morning, I groaned in frustration and buried my head beneath the covers. I had only fallen asleep two hours prior, as most of the night had been dedicated to homework. Dreading another week at Maple Creek High, I stomped down the staircase and walked into the kitchen.

"Dad?" My brow furrowed at the sight of him. I blinked twice, to make sure that I wasn't hallucinating, but Jeffrey remained. "What are you doing here?"

Jeffrey sat at the kitchen table with a newspaper spread across his lap. "Well, after what happened last night, I thought that we should start spending more time together." He took a sip of coffee, while I noted the blue housecoat and gray slippers.

"Okay," I exhaled. With a hand held to my head, I moved towards the refrigerator.

"What do you want to do today?" Jeffrey crossed one leg over the other, waiting for me to respond.

"What?" I leaned against the refrigerator door, overcome by the throbbing sensation in my head. I must have been dreaming.

"I took the day off from work," Jeffrey droned, annoyed that I wasn't catching on.

"Okay," I reiterated. Jeffrey grinned, but he looked more like the Cheshire cat than a middle-aged attorney.

"So we could spend time together." Jeffrey motioned his hand in the air as he extended the length of each word. At that moment, I realized how much I wanted to climb inside the refrigerator and shut the door.

"Dad, it's Monday," I announced. Jeffrey blinked, as if I had just delivered the weather forecast. "I have school."

"Oh, that's right." His face shriveled in disappointment, highlighting the wrinkles on his forehead. For the first time in my life, I actually pitied Eleanor. "Well," he sighed, "maybe this afternoon."

I placed a pot on the stove and boiled enough water for a cup of tea. But if Jeffrey kept talking, I would need something stronger than that.

"Where's Mom?" I sat down beside Jeffrey at the table.

"Hospital," he answered. I nibbled at the edge of a blueberry muffin, waiting for the tea to cool. If Eleanor was gone, then I definitely wasn't dreaming.

After five minutes of the most silent, awkward, non-family breakfast I had ever had, I pushed my chair back and said, "I should get ready for school." I rose from the table in a rush, desperately seeking the solace of my own bedroom. Jeffrey simply nodded, then reverted to the thin gray pages of his newspaper.

When I returned, Jeffrey stopped me in the foyer, studying the backpack over my shoulder. "Come here," he beckoned, leading me back into the kitchen. Jeffrey opened one of the drawers beneath the kitchen counter, revealing a pair of shiny silver keys.

"Have those been there this whole time?" I glared at the keys to my Volkswagen Beetle, unable to believe that Eleanor had hidden them within reach.

"Yeah, I'm pretty sure." Jeffrey nodded. I grabbed my car keys, and then balled my hand into a fist to secure them.

"Thanks Dad," I murmured.

"You're welcome." Jeffrey shut the drawer with a smile. "You better get going," he advised, pointing to the clock on the wall. "I don't want you to be late." A fleck of green twinkled in Jeffrey's hazel eyes, illuminating the pool of colors.

Without thinking, I wrapped my arms around him. Jeffrey held me as I sank into his chest. He smelled of coffee and aftershave. Jeffrey stroked the ends of my hair, like he had when I was a little girl. "I love you, Dad."

I pulled away, resisting the urge to cry, but the tears came anyway. I felt Jeffrey's eyes on me as I turned to walk away. "Hey Addie," he called after me. I stalled before the front door and looked over my shoulder. "I love you too."

Those short, simple words stayed on my mind as I walked down the dirt driveway, leading to the gate. Tom's black Mustang glimmered in the distance, reflecting sunlight through the trees. I rapped my knuckles against the passenger's side window, then opened the door and climbed inside.

After last night, I had not been able to stop thinking about the way Tom had held my body so closely to his. Even now, I wanted him, but in the right way.

"I got my car keys back." I jingled the silver key chain in the air for him to see. Tom turned his head, looking to the keys, and then my eyes, before returning his focus to driving.

"Oh." Tom kept both hands on the wheel,

constantly scanning the road before him. "That's great," he coughed. "I guess you don't need a ride to school anymore."

"Yeah," I agreed. "I guess not." My eyes became fixed on Tom's cold, impassive expression. He had grown distant and reserved overnight, too rigid to be welcoming. Sighing, I rested my head against the window and closed my eyes.

* * *

The day dragged on in a tortuous manner. I couldn't even glance at a textbook without yawning. Every teacher grated on my nerves, tormenting me with useless information that had no value in the real world. I had a tyrannical mother, an erratic father, a frustrated boyfriend, and an estranged, potentially lethal grandfather to worry about. I didn't have time for Pythagoras and his stupid theorem.

At the end of the day, I stood before my locker in a state of exhaustion. I wanted nothing more than to climb into bed and fall asleep beneath the soft, warm covers. But then I caught a glimpse of Ricky's figure approaching in the distance, and my eyes widened with apprehension.

"Hey," Ricky murmured. "Did you find out anything yet?"

Ricky leaned against the locker beside mine, then folded his arms to expose the prominent musculature of his chest. He wore a form-fitting athletic shirt. I could easily see the contours of his upper body through the thin black fabric.

"About what?" I averted my eyes, looking into my locker to return a textbook.

"The picture I gave you," Ricky goaded. "The lady

that looks like you."

"Oh," I pondered, "no." I grabbed a spiral notebook and slipped it into my backpack, while Ricky watched me, evaluating every move I made.

"Well, let me know when you do." His steady gaze never faltered.

"Yeah, sure," I retorted.

A moment passed, as I began to wonder why Ricky was still standing there, gawking at me. I shut my locker door, then clasped the combination lock in place.

"So..." Ricky mused. "How have you been?" I turned to face him, overcome with bewilderment. "You weren't in class on Friday, and Jeanine told me you were out sick. Are you feeling better?"

"Excuse me?" I closed my eyes, and then opened them again. When Ricky shrugged his shoulders, feigning innocence, I asked another question. "Am I supposed to think it's normal that you're being nice to me all of a sudden?"

"Addie," he sympathized. "That's in the past." Ricky rested his hand against my shoulder and squeezed my arm. "Can't we just get along?" He brushed his thumb against my cheek, sending ripples of heat across the surface of my skin. I took a deep breath when he walked away, confused by it all. "I'm not a bad guy, Addie," he yelled down the hallway. Ricky pushed through the double doors, and then headed towards his shiny BMW in the parking lot.

"What was that about?" Tom appeared before me, disconcerted.

"Oh," I started. "He was just asking about Antoinette's portrait again." I shook my head, brushing the matter off as nothing of importance.

"I thought I told you to stay away from him," Tom barked. He turned red, boiling over with anger.

"Who do you think you are?" I jabbed my finger into his chest. "You don't own me!" I stormed off, enjoying the sound my boots made as they clicked against the ground.

"Well, you must like him then," Tom accused. I clenched my teeth together, balling my hand into a fist. When I turned on my heel, Tom took a few steps forward, meeting me in the middle of the hallway.

"Ricky? You think I like Ricky?" I cackled. "Are you insane?"

"Why do you keep talking to him then?" Tom crossed his arms over his chest, revealing the strength of his forearms. I looked into his eyes, searching for flecks of golden honey, but there were none.

"If you think, for one second, that I would ever be interested in Ricky," I trailed off, letting the phrase hang idly in the air. "Do you know me at all?" I backed away from him, and then scampered across campus in time to catch the bus.

When I got home, Jeffrey sat in the living room with paperwork scattered all over the floor. I closed the front door, and then approached the recliner, where he ruminated over a three-ringed binder. I noted countless pieces of paper strewn over the couch and the wooden table beside it.

"I thought you had the day off." I moved towards the couch, then pushed the scattered pages aside, so I could sit down on one of the cushions.

"Yeah," Jeffrey sighed. "I know." He looked up from his binder, and then waved a hand over the mess. "I was looking for something," he explained.

"Well, I hope you found it." I smiled. Jeffrey set

his work aside and laughed. I couldn't remember the last time he had done that.

"How was school?" I shuddered at the question, which made Jeffrey smirk. "That bad, huh?" Jeffrey leaned forward to stretch his back, as he rested his elbows against his knees. "Hey, how did you get to school? Your car's been sitting here all day."

"Oh," I hesitated, then confessed, "I already had a ride."

"Really?" Jeffrey relaxed into the recliner. "With who?" I bit my bottom lip, anxious about Jeffrey's sudden interest in Tom.

"A boy from school," I admitted. It wasn't the farthest thing from the truth.

"Oh, I didn't realize you had a boyfriend." Jeffrey looked me over with a pair of worried eyes. I began to fidget, nervously shifting on the couch. Had he heard Tom climb through my bedroom window last night?

"Why don't you invite him over for dinner on Friday?" Dad rose from the recliner and knelt down to collect his scattered pages on the floor. "Your mother and I will both be home and-"

"Dad," I interrupted. "I don't know if that's such a good idea."

"Listen Addie," Jeffrey crowed, acting like a true patriarch for once. "I talked to your mother last night, and she wants us to have a nice family dinner on Friday." I rolled my eyes, blowing hot air through my nostrils. "Maybe that will give the two of you a chance to," he paused, searching the floor for papers, "understand each other."

"Dad," I griped. "Mom and I are never going to understand each other." I lifted my chin in defiance, failing to meet his gaze.

Jeffrey fell to his knees and began crawling on the floor. "Yeah, I know," he replied.

"Dad, what are you doing?" I stood in front of the couch with my hands on my hips. Why was I always the parent and Jeffrey the child?

"Have you seen my blue pen?" Jeffrey looked underneath the recliner, before pawing at the rest of the furniture.

"Okay." I held my hands up in surrender. "I'm going upstairs."

"Hey Addie," Jeffrey called after me. I stood at the foot of the staircase and looked back at him. "Don't forget about Friday. It'll be fun!" Jeffrey was definitely the child. No adult would ever equate Eleanor with fun.

I climbed the stairs in a hurry, desperately seeking the comfort of my own bedroom, but then Jeffrey spoke up again. "And Addie," he pleaded, "bring the boy."

Chapter 25

B y Thursday, I slouched at the lunch table with my head in my hands, devoid of hunger and thirst. Jeanine sat across from me, finishing off a peanut butter and jelly sandwich. Tom and I hadn't spoken in three days.

"Where's Tom?" Jeanine cut an apple into five slices, then handed me one.

"I don't know," I sighed, refusing the fruit, once I spotted a package of frosted animal crackers on her lunch tray. As a child, I had squealed at the sight of those pink giraffes and white elephants, all covered in sprinkles. I would have eaten an entire jar of those colorful confections back then. But now, they just looked pretty.

"Did ya'll break up?" She slipped the first wedge of apple into her mouth, and then swallowed. The red peel matched the color of her lips.

"I don't know," I repeated. "We had a fight, and now he won't talk to me." I scanned the cafeteria, searching for jet black hair and muscle tone.

"What was the fight about?" Jeanine lifted her bright blue eyes in concern, searching my face. I nodded my head towards a nearby table, where Ricky sat with a group of football players. "Leave it to my brother." Jeanine sipped at a plastic cup, filled with lemon water.

"Are you doing anything after school?" I tapped

my fingers against the table, growing restless. When Jeanine shook her head, I smiled. "Can you help me with math homework? Tom usually does, but..." I drifted off. She already knew the rest.

"I'm only a freshman," Jeanine said. "You don't want to ask someone else?"

I raised my eyebrows in disapproval. "Jeanine, I know you're already in Advanced Calculus." Crimson flooded Jeanine's cheeks, betraying her inner emotions.

"Who told you?" Jeanine folded her arms in secrecy and looked over her shoulder. When she did, Ricky turned towards us and smiled.

"Let's face it, Jeanine." I rose from the table in a sluggish state. "Someone has to make up for the acumen deficit in your family." My eyes darted across the cafeteria, returning to Ricky. Jeanine followed my vacant gaze, as we watched him stuff an entire hamburger down his throat, despite the heavy blobs of ketchup streaming down his arm.

"You're right!" Jeanine stood up, fueled by my words of empowerment.

I nodded to Jeanine, then walked with her to the kitchen, where she returned her lunch tray. I searched for Tom among the crowd of bustling students, but he never appeared. I didn't like not knowing where he was.

Jeanine led me out of the congested building, until we emerged upon a deserted walkway that led to the other side of campus. Before long, the levee broke, and Jeanine relayed countless bits of salacious gossip regarding her dear, older brother. I listened intently, as Jeanine described Ricky's blatant lack of responsibility.

"He's complacent, deceitful, self-centered, and

vain," she droned. "And don't even get me started on all the girls." Jeanine swayed her hips as she walked, emphasizing the youthful slenderness of her petite frame.

"Wait." I stopped in my tracks, and then tugged at Jeanine's sleeve until she did the same. "What girls?"

"Trust me," she whispered, leaning in closely. "You don't want to know." Jeanine continued down the breezeway, and then stopped in front of the high school building. "Are you coming?" She opened one of the double doors that led to the locker-filled hallway.

"Yeah," I answered. Jeanine waited until I reached the door, and then we both walked inside. I approached my locker, while Jeanine trailed behind me. "Let's meet in the library after school," I suggested. "No one's ever in there."

"Okay," Jeanine agreed. "Can you drive me home when we're done?"

"Sure." I twisted the locker dial, entering the numbers of my combination until it opened. Jeanine ran off at the sound of the bell, frantically scampering to class. I grabbed my history book and shoved it into my backpack, not caring that I was late. Mr. Robinson already loathed me anyway.

Just as I began to close my locker door, an unfamiliar object caught the corner of my eye. I looked down at a yellow #2 pencil that sat on the bottom shelf. There was a tattered sheet of notebook paper beneath it, with a handful of words scrawled in graphite.

Sorry I forgot to give it back.

Ricky

Two years ago, I let Ricky borrow a spare pencil in math class. But when he failed to return it, I refused to lend him anything else. Now, every time Ricky came to class unprepared, he knew not to ask me for anything. I grumbled at the memory, then squashed the note in my hand.

After stuffing the pencil into my backpack, I shut my locker door and tossed the note into a nearby trash can. Then, I walked the length of the hallway, stopping once I reached the staircase that led to my next class. Just as I arrived at the top, an oblivious student appeared out of thin air and crashed into me.

I stumbled backwards, dropping my backpack, as I fell down the first three steps. My knees dug into the rigid surface of the third step, while I winced in pain. I lifted my head in discomfort, surprised to find Tom jerking me upright.

"Addie, I'm so sorry." Tom tugged at my arms, until I was standing on my own two feet. "Are you okay?" I nodded, hardly noticing when Tom collected my backpack from the floor and slipped one of the straps over my shoulder.

"I'm fine," I proclaimed, holding my chin taut. Tom pushed a strand of fallen hair out of my eyes, then loosely tucked it behind my ear. When he turned away and began walking down the steps, I said, "You're not coming to class?"

Tom looked back at me from where he stood at the bottom of the staircase. I watched his face harden into a mask of subdued emotion. "No," he answered. I raised my eyebrows in concern, as Tom turned on his heel and left me standing in the stairwell.

* * *

Later that afternoon, Jeanine sat beside me in the car, chattering on incessantly about the thoughtless demeanor of her absent parents. Jeanine's father had been a professional quarterback in the NFL, eventually retiring after his last season with the Atlanta Falcons. When I heard the name Lawton Travis, I only thought of the alcoholic playboy who had taken the bulk of his earnings to start an international corporation that was currently worth $1.2 billion. I wondered what the name meant to Jeanine.

Her mother, Candy Travis, had been crowned Miss Georgia in 1989, after conquering every local beauty pageant across the state. Despite the fifteen year age difference, Candy had married Lawton on her twenty-first birthday, and then quickly settled into the role of suburban housewife. I couldn't remember ever seeing Mrs. Travis with a nail unpolished or hair out of place. After twenty years of marriage and two children, she hadn't aged a day past twenty-nine.

"Turn here," Jeanine instructed. I pulled up to a gated entrance and rolled my window down, while Jeanine leaned over the steering wheel and yelled into a gray speaker box, until the gate opened. "Sorry about that." Jeanine sat back in the passenger's seat. "Ricky has the gate opener."

I drove through the open gate, noting the iron arch overhead, adorned with the words *Château Rouge*. The affluent neighborhood looked like something I had seen in a magazine once, but never had the privilege to enter on my own accord. Every mansion appeared more extravagant than the last, with refined architecture, stunning grounds, and lavish swimming pools.

"Great," Jeanine sighed. "Lucifer's home." I slowed the car down, while Jeanine turned to me with an irritated look on her face. When she unbuckled her seatbelt, I gazed out the window at the nearest mansion and found Ricky's BMW in the driveway. My mouth fell open, because the Travis residence most closely resembled the elaborate framework of a French castle.

"You live here?" I exhaled in disbelief, nearly forgetting to place my foot on the brake before shifting into park. Jeanine snatched her backpack from the floorboard and opened the car door, glancing to the mansion in dismay.

"Yeah," Jeanine said. "It's not like you haven't been here before." She stepped onto the curb, and then shut the door behind her.

"Hey Jeanine!" I rolled the window down, calling after her. "When was I here before?" A look of confusion fell over her face, while she held her backpack by the handle.

"After the dance," Jeanine began, only adding to the phrase when I offered no words of remembrance. "You dropped me off," she explained. "Don't you remember?"

"Oh yeah," I said, even though I didn't.

* * *

When I finally got home, empty silence filled the house. Jeffrey's attempt at spending more time with me had been short-lived, as I hadn't seen him since Monday.

Eleanor had become even more difficult to reach in recent days, even though she was allegedly hosting a family dinner the next night. I contemplated another evening of solitude, and then left for the woods.

Fallen twigs cracked beneath my feet, as I trudged through the forest. Before long, I reached the fence that separated our land from Sutton territory and climbed over. I wasn't looking for Tom. I just wanted to talk to Daniel.

After sunset, the sky darkened and an icy chill fell over me as the temperature began to drop. I folded my arms over each other, seeking comfort in my own embrace. Suddenly, I had the eerie feeling that someone was watching me.

"What are you doing here?" The voice surrounded me, descending from some point of elevation. I lifted my head to the trees, where Tom sat with his legs dangling at the top of a live oak.

"I just wanted to see how Daniel was doing." My voice carried through the forest, as I waited for Tom to respond. He scanned the surrounding territory, searching in silence.

"He's resting," Tom hissed. I stepped back, watching Tom from where I stood.

"Why are you doing this?" I felt blood rushing to my cheeks, as they turned warm and pink. When Tom gazed down at me, my heart skipped a beat. "Why weren't you in class this afternoon?"

"I wasn't feeling very well," he snarled. I looked at the forest floor beneath my feet, then shifted my eyes to Tom.

"You look fine to me," I countered. Tom kept his eyes on me, as I moved towards the base of the tree. With my hands against the bark, I prepared to climb up. Tom looked like a predator, carefully stalking his prey.

"Go home, Addie," he commanded. I lifted my hands from the bark and took a few steps back.

Scowling, I glared up at Tom, though he refused to look my way.

"You can't just shut me out!" Wind rippled through the trees, while I waited for Tom to say something. "Talk to me," I begged, holding my chin high in determination. When Tom wouldn't budge, I turned my back to him and walked away.

"Addie," he called after me. Tom quickly scaled the length of the tree, before landing on the ground. As Tom approached, I studied his face. The light in his eyes was gone.

"I don't care about Ricky," I pleaded. Tom crossed his arms over his chest, briefly considering me before turning his head away. Displeased, I placed my hands on either side of his face, until Tom had no other choice but to look at me.

"I. Want. You." Each word became a sentence all on its own. I stared into the depths of his eyes, searching for belief. Tom rested his hands over mine, then slowly peeled my fingers away from his skin. I narrowed my eyes at Tom, wounded by the resistance of my affection.

"I want you too," Tom admitted. He leaned towards me, until no more than a sliver of space remained between our faces. I quivered in anticipation, preparing to be kissed, but then Tom brushed his cheek against the side of my face instead. I felt his warm breath in my ear, as he whispered, "But I'm not the only one."

I furrowed my brow in concern and frowned at Tom. I didn't know what to say. So, I changed the subject to avoid discussing Ricky any further. "We're having a family dinner tomorrow night." I rolled my eyes, feigning displeasure. "You're invited," I paused, searching Tom's face. "If you want to come." I watched his lips until they curved into a smile.

"Really?" Tom chuckled, then cupped the side of my face in his hand.

"Yeah," I answered. "Dad wants to meet you." I held my breath, too unsettled to move. Tom traced the edge of my jawline with his thumb, upsetting my concentration further. I tilted my head at an angle, so that my cheek fell perfectly into the center of his palm.

"What about your mother?" Tom pressed his lips into a fine line.

"You know how she is," I admitted. Tom leaned into me, and then planted his mouth against the side of my throat, trailing the skin beneath my ear. "But I can handle her," I breathed. Tom chuckled, while I marveled at the return of his warmth.

Chapter 26

When I woke up on Friday morning, a deep nausea spread through my stomach, as I willed my body to relax. For the first time, I actually wanted school to last as long as possible, because that would prolong the inevitable family dinner. I wasn't worried about Jeffrey. In fact, I felt more at ease, knowing he would be there.

But I couldn't gauge how Eleanor would react to Tom, because I had never brought a boy home before. Despite her impeccable bedside manner, Eleanor's temperament tended to turn sour when there wasn't a patient in sight. If she couldn't even be respectful towards her husband and daughter, what hope did that leave for Tom?

I lurked towards my locker after school, dragging my feet in reluctance. Tom had to stay behind, in order to make up the quizzes and other assignments he had missed the day before, so I had no time to prepare him for Eleanor.

As I shuffled through the books in my locker, Jeanine ran down the hallway, then came to an abrupt halt once she reached me. "Please tell me you're free tonight," she gasped, struggling to catch her breath. I looked over at Jeanine and smiled.

"Family dinner," I sighed. Jeanine's eyes widened, as the color drained from her face. "Why?" I dropped a notebook into my locker. "What's going on tonight?"

"Ricky's having a party," she grumbled. Jeanine placed her hands over her elbows, then leaned her head against one of the lockers next to mine.

"Your parents don't care?" I wondered.

"They just left this morning for a week-long cruise in the Bahamas." Jeanine lifted two black eyebrows in disapproval. "Can we do something tomorrow?" She leaned towards me, her deep blue eyes begging. "I can't stay in that house all weekend!"

"Sure," I agreed. "Let's have lunch and then go see a movie." I leaned against my locker door, spotting Ricky in the distance. "I'll pick you up at noon."

"YES!" Jeanine threw her hands in the air, jumping up in excitement. After celebrating, Jeanine encircled me in her arms. She had a tight grip to be such a little thing.

Ricky walked up behind Jeanine, tapping two fingers on her shoulder. Jeanine looked back in surprise, then curled her lip. "Oh." She shrugged. "It's just you." Jeanine widened her eyes before turning on her heel to walk away. "See you tomorrow, Addie!" she yelled over her shoulder.

"Well," Ricky murmured. "How is it that my little sister likes you more than she likes me?" Ricky placed his hands in his pockets, then casually leaned into a nearby locker.

"What do you want, Ricky?" I slammed my locker door shut, intending to ward him off. My hands moved deftly, as I returned the combination lock and clicked it in place.

"Sorry," he apologized. "I just wanted to let you know that I'm having a party tonight, at my place." Ricky's eyes glazed over my mouth first and eyes second. "My parents are out of town," he explained. I crossed my arms over the textbook in my hands and narrowed my eyes at him.

"Come on, Addie," he coaxed. "It'll be fun, and Jeanine will be there." I looked over his shoulder to find Jeanine in the hallway, talking to another student. When she realized that I was staring at her, Jeanine looked from Ricky to me, then slashed her fingers in a horizontal line across her throat, gesturing for me to stop talking to her brother.

"I'm not going," I retorted. "Have fun at your brothel." I left Ricky standing in front of my locker with his mouth ajar. When I passed Jeanine in the hallway, she lifted her hand in the air and I slapped it with mine. As we laughed together, Jeanine and I watched Ricky storm down the hallway in a fit of rage, until he disappeared through the double doors.

* * *

By four o'clock, campus grew quiet, with every hallway cleared and free of students. A few teachers lurked behind, grading papers and making lesson plans, but for the most part, the building was empty.

Tired from the long week, I wandered the campus alone, not minding that I had to wait for Tom. Now that the two us had reconciled, we saw no need in taking two cars to school, when we were both driving to the same place anyway. But with Tom making up schoolwork and Jeanine gone, I found myself heading upstairs to the library, where I could be alone with my thoughts, for the time being.

My mind flooded with worry, as the evening's family dinner approached. Eleanor's cooking skills began and ended with the trifling task of boiling water. I wondered if she would order take-out from a restaurant, and then serve it as her own. It wouldn't be the first time. But then I spotted Nicki Caldwell in the staircase, and all thoughts of Eleanor Jacobs dissolved.

"Hello Addie." Nicki began her slow descent down the staircase, her dark eyes ablaze with every downward step. Despite the closing distance between us, Nicki's high-heeled boots left her towering over me, just the same.

"Hi?" I furrowed my brow, looking over Nicki in confusion.

"I noticed that you've been talking to Ricky," she accused. I quietly surveyed her elaborate wardrobe, complete with a gray fur coat and black leather gloves. Nicki was dressed for New York, not Georgia.

"More like the other way around." I rolled my eyes, aggravated that Nicki thought I actually wanted to have a conversation with her ex-beau.

"I just wanted to warn you," Nicki whispered. After looking over her shoulder, Nicki placed her hand on my arm. I took a step back, doubting the tone of her voice.

"I don't need to be warned," I snapped. Nicki eyed me carefully, before crossing her arms in frustration. I noted the flawless cork-screw shape of each blonde ringlet that fell over her shoulders and wondered how long that had taken with a curling iron.

"Ricky's not what you think," Nicki offered. I searched her bronze-colored face, never fooled by the artificial nature of her radiant complexion.

"And how do you know what I think?" I raised my eyebrows, refusing to pretend that we could ever actually be nice to each other.

"Ricky chooses girls," Nicki confessed. I glanced at the purple scarf around her neck, in an attempt to

164

distract myself. It reminded me of violets and lavender.

"What do you mean?" I cocked my head to the side. "Ricky chooses girls," I repeated. "I don't understand." I rested a hand over my shoulder, nervously fidgeting.

"I mean he *chooses* them," Nicki explained. I felt dizzy, as my head began to spin. The staircase looked smaller. "He picks girls out." Nicki stared down at me, growing more insistent with each passing second. "He picks them out," she paused, averting her eyes to search for words, "like I pick shoes out of a catalogue."

"But what does that mean?" I felt my heart rate increase, while I grew hot all over.

"Just beware." The way Nicki spoke reminded me of Eleanor, and the rare instances when she had actually tried to be a mother. "As a girl, I'm obligated to let you know." Nicki finished walking down the staircase, while I stood in confusion, trying to make sense of her vague explanation.

"Oh, and Addie?" Nicki turned back to me, clutching the zebra-striped handbag over her shoulder. "Ricky prefers the ones who haven't been touched."

Chapter 27

I entered the library in a rush, overcome by emotions that only Tom could suppress. What had Nicki meant, and how could I trust her anyway? Nicki had loathed me for years, and now that Ricky Travis was no longer interested in her company, she wanted nothing more than to pester her replacement. I rolled my eyes at the thought. If Ricky were the last man on Earth, I would gladly die a spinster.

Wandering through the vacant room, I noted the tables to my left and bookshelves to my right. Countless shelves lined every wall, complete with almanacs, dictionaries, and encyclopedias, all the books that no one ever used, but the school was required to supply, regardless. I trudged towards the back of the library, where I could bury myself in a pile of dusty books and think in peace.

Mrs. Chapman slept restlessly at the check-out desk, with a palm pressed to one of her rouge-laden cheeks. I paused before the librarian, silently regarding her sleeping presence. She looked exactly like Lucille Ball, though she had never made me laugh, and I highly doubted that anyone would care to watch her perform in Technicolor. Rolling my eyes, I continued past Mrs. Chapman's desk and weaved my way through stacks of classical literature, contemplating why, of all the librarians in Georgia, Maple Creek High had chosen to employ Mary Chapman.

Sinking to the floor, I sat down between two rows of bookshelves, content to be sandwiched among the stacks. My thoughts drifted to Tom, as I wondered how much longer he would be. At this point, I wanted nothing more than for the day, and night, to be over.

I tilted my head back for a moment, closing my eyes to quiet my mind. After a brief minute of silence, a strange, disturbing noise startled me. Rising to my feet, I followed the sound, only to discover that Mrs. Chapman snored like a thousand pound grizzly bear.

Once I returned to my spot between the bookshelves, I listened to the clock that ticked decisively on the wall beside me. I glared at the time, taunted by the lengthening day, and the inevitable night that awaited me. Surely, Nicki's behavior was no less than hinting at what Eleanor had planned for Tom tonight. Sighing, I scanned the bookcase before me, soon spotting a row of Maple Creek High yearbooks from the 1950s. Unable to contain the seething curiosity that rippled through me, I grabbed the first one I saw off the shelf and began flipping pages.

Unfamiliar faces caught my eye, each equally gray in color. I leafed through the black-and-white photographs, wondering what Maple Creek High had been like all those years ago, what Savannah had been like, what life had been like. I noted the flowery poodle skirts, cat-eye glasses, slim jeans, and leather jackets, though observed no real difference in the students, apart from how they dressed. They were still teenagers.

They drove cars, drank Coke, watched movies, went on dates, fell in (and out) of love, broke the rules, obeyed the rules, loved (and hated) their parents, laughed, cried, and eventually, grew up. I brushed my fingers over a double-page spread of candid photos and wondered where each student had ended up, who they had married, and if they ever felt as happy (or sad) as they had been in high school.

I carelessly browsed through the rest of the book, before discovering a section of pages that had been dedicated to Homecoming Week. Widening my eyes in surprise, I blinked twice at the oval-shaped image in the center of the page. "Wow," I breathed.

The caption beneath the photo read:

Daniel Sutton and Antoinette Beaumont –
1959 King and Queen

Glancing suspiciously over the picture and the pages that followed, I spotted a candid shot of a handsome high school boy, nearly too striking for the camera. I didn't have to read the caption to know that the boy in the picture was Tony DeMilo.

Frustrated, I shook my head and relaxed into the bookshelf behind me. Daniel and Antoinette had undoubtedly been the most beautiful, well-matched couple of high school sweethearts that I had ever seen, so why had she chosen to marry DeMilo instead?

I shut the yearbook, then tapped my fingers over the hard-bound cover, thinking. Had DeMilo come from a wealthy family? Or been able to offer her something else that Daniel couldn't? I couldn't envision Daniel ever hurting Antoinette. He loved her.

So what was it then?

Stumbling to my feet, I walked the length of the library, until I reached the table of computers just past the entrance, and sat down. After logging on to one of the computers, I clicked on the Internet Explorer icon, then stared at the bright white screen in silence. It wasn't like I could just Google her name, so I decided to search the town archives instead.

Thirty minutes later, I felt my entire body sag into the back of the chair. Every bit of blood, oxygen, and life drained out of me, as I tried to make sense of the words before me. In an attempt to disprove the truth, I clicked on the "Print" icon at the top of the screen. The truth didn't look any better on paper.

~The Savannah Times~

December 21, 1963

The body of twenty-one-year-old Antoinette Beaumont Sutton was found floating in the Savannah River on Tuesday morning, by local law enforcement. Police believe the young woman drowned, due to the sudden, yet severe torrential downpour, that caused flooding the night before. Antoinette was the wife of artist, Daniel Sutton, as well as mother of their two children, Josette and Wesley. Funeral services will be held this Saturday morning, at nine o'clock, preceded by an honorary memorial service at Glenview Baptist Church.

~ ~

Heat rushed over me, as my insides turned to mush. I realized the truth and accepted the fact that I had been lied to once again, by someone I truly cared about. There was only one question left to answer. I just didn't want to be the one asking it.

"Hey," Tom breathed, appearing behind me. "Sorry that took me so long." I sensed his hand on my back, though felt too paralyzed to move. "What are you working on?"

I closed the open window on the computer screen and stuffed the article into my backpack, before Tom could notice either. "Homework," I replied, forcing the word out in one syllable.

"Are you okay?" Tom's golden eyes glazed over me, disbelieving.

"Yeah," I answered, quickly moving the cursor to shut the computer down. "I'm just tired." Tom sat down in the chair beside me, placing a palm over my hand. I cringed at the slightest touch. Everything that had been so right, now felt so wrong.

"You look like you've seen a ghost," Tom continued. I felt his eyes on me and reluctantly allowed him to pull my gaze towards his own. I held my breath, nearly ready to tell him everything. But then I noticed that golden, glowing flicker in his eyes and knew that I had to make the dream seem real for just a little bit longer.

"I guess I'm just worried about dinner tonight," I offered. Tom placed his hand against my face, running his thumb along the edge of my cheekbone. I felt my heart swell with pleasurable pain, as I contemplated the duration of this delicate torture. I had to tell him soon.

"I'm ready to go," I declared, my tone icier than I

had intended.

Tom drew back, as if I had splashed cold water on his face. "Okay," he said.

As Tom drove me home, I melted into the passenger's side door, concealing my tears beneath a pair of cheap sunglasses that I hardly ever wore. If we were related, then how? Was Tom a cousin? A brother? I felt bile creep along the edge of my throat, while I swallowed to keep the liquid down.

"Addie, are you sure you're okay?" Tom broke the silence, before pulling up to my gated driveway. "You've been so quiet." I felt a numb, hollow feeling in my chest that spread like wildfire.

"I think I just need to lie down." I unfastened my seatbelt, preparing to bolt. "I haven't been feeling very well." Tom frowned, then lifted my sunglasses and saw that I was crying. "Tom, please," I begged. He pulled me into his lap anyway, quickly wrapping his arms around my waist. I rested my head on Tom's shoulder and closed my eyes, remembering how perfect everything had been before I read that article.

"What's wrong?" Tom cupped my chin in his hand, forcing me to stare into his glistening honey-colored eyes. "Come on, baby. What is it?" I turned away, ashamed of each choking sob. Tom splayed his fingers along my neck, sending hot desire all over my body.

"Please don't kiss me," I pleaded. Tom narrowed his eyes at me, then removed his hands from my waist. "I could be contagious," I backpedaled. "I don't want you to get sick." Tom pressed his lips together, nodding. I opened the driver's side door and climbed out of his lap, before setting my feet on the ground.

"What about tonight?" Tom called after me, while

I climbed over the gate. "Should I even come now?" Tom jerked his head to the side. I knew he was angry.

"If you want to," I muttered, looking over my shoulder at him. After all, it was a *family* dinner. "I really don't feel well, Tom." I leaned against the gate, peering at him through the open spaces. "Please believe me."

Tom twisted his mouth into a sideways smirk, then sank his top row of teeth into his bottom lip. "Feel better, Addie," he said.

I watched him drive away.

Chapter 28

An hour later, I found myself at Tom's door, hoping to be let out of the cold. I knocked five times, and then turned away, realizing how much Tom must despise me. But when he came to the door, I froze in place, unable to find the right words to say.

"Are you coming in or not?" Tom lingered in the doorway, causing my heart to skip a beat. Why did reality have to be so cruel? Of all the guys in town, I had chosen the one that I couldn't have.

"Yeah," I whispered, slowly lugging my feet across the threshold. My entire body felt sluggish, weak, and dejected, as if I had just competed in an Olympic decathlon and lost. Tom shut the door behind me. The rush of outdoor air sent a cool shiver along my spine.

"Are you feeling better?" Tom crossed his arms over his chest, daring me to speak.

"Not really," I admitted. My throat felt dry, but I wasn't about to ask him for a glass of water. Tom glanced down at my still, silent figure in the foyer, his eyes antagonizing.

"You look fine to me," he countered. I shoved both hands into my jacket pockets, despite the slight perspiration that had gathered in the slits of each palm.

"I just came by to see Daniel." I averted my eyes, talking to the hardwood floor.

"Of course you did," Tom snapped.

"I need to talk to him about something." I took a step forward, then tilted my head back to gauge the level of resentment in Tom's eyes. He looked more guarded than angry.

"You know where to find him." Tom uncrossed his arms, then jerked his head in the direction of Daniel's room. I swallowed, forcing a nod before cutting through the spacious den that led to the other side of the house.

I hesitated before Daniel's open door, too afraid of the inevitable truth. Surely, he would confirm what I already knew. Tom and I could never be together. But then, why had Daniel never said anything? Had he failed to recognize the romantic nature of our relationship?

"Come in, Addie," Daniel beckoned. I lingered in the doorway, before crossing the threshold and closing the door behind me. "How have you been?"

"Fine," I remarked, making my way towards the window. Daniel rested in the bed, with pillows propped behind his neck. I wondered how ill he actually was. "How about you?" I turned around, leaning into the windowsill for support.

"Fine," Daniel echoed. I gazed into his eyes from where I stood across the room, realizing that he had already pinpointed the deception in mine. Perhaps Tom had mentioned something when he got home, though Daniel shouldn't have been surprised. He already knew that our relationship had been doomed from the start. He had to know.

"Are you my grandfather?" The words left me, just as I thought of them. I saw no purpose in thinking before I spoke. Where had that gotten me so far?

Daniel pressed his lips into a fine line, readjusting

174

his reclined posture beneath the covers. I searched his ice-blue eyes, anticipating the explanation to follow. When he didn't speak, I fished the newspaper article regarding Antoinette's death out of my pocket and handed it to him. Daniel unfolded the paper in his hands, and then lifted his eyes to me.

"Addie," Daniel implored, shamefully shaking his head from side to side. "I never meant for you to find out like this." I turned my back to him and stared through the glass.

So it was true.

"You lied to me," I accused, too overcome with disappointment to raise my voice. "Why does everyone keep lying to me?" I closed my eyes, and then ran my fingers through my hair. I didn't know who I was anymore.

"Addie, please," Daniel softly spoke, coaxing me. "If everything weren't so complicated," he paused, waiting for me to say something. "I didn't think you were ready."

"Ready for what?" I paced the floor in front of his bed. "The truth? I'm not a child." On the verge of tears, I sat down by the fireplace and pulled my knees into my chest. "I thought I could trust you."

"You can trust me, Addie," Daniel exhaled, searching my face. "I just thought it would be easier for you, if you got to know me first, before I told you who I really was."

I buried my head in my hands, too overwhelmed to feel any one emotion. "This is too much," I admitted. "It's all too much." I gazed around the room, unsettled by the fact that, once again, my grandfather was somebody else.

"Sometimes, it's better, not knowing the truth." I

glanced up at Daniel, noting the blatant sincerity in his voice. "DeMilo was never married to Antoinette," he clarified. "I was." Daniel glanced at me from across the room, claiming me with his eyes. "You are my granddaughter, not his."

"Then why would you tell me anything different?" I felt very sick and began to rock myself in front of the fireplace. I had longed for Daniel to tell me the truth, as long as it contradicted the newspaper article. But now that he had, and the article was right, I only felt worse.

"Was it not enough to learn that you were adopted, that Jeffrey and Eleanor weren't your real parents?" Daniel gestured with his hands, allowing me to see how much they were trembling. I turned my head and stared at the wool rug beneath my feet, spotting shades of yellow in the fabric.

"What about Tom?" I sighed, failing to calm my rapidly beating heart.

"What do you mean?" Daniel pulled the covers up to his shoulders, burying his shaking hands beneath the blankets. I wondered whether or not he was cold.

"How are we related?" I let my body weight sag, and then listened for Daniel to hammer the last nail in the coffin. "Is Tom my cousin, my brother?"

"What are you talking about?" Daniel practically laughed at me. "Tom's not related to us." Daniel studied the evolving expressions on my face, as I caught my breath. I didn't know whether to smile or cry.

"Tom's not your grandson?" I asked.

"Not biologically," Daniel explained. "I'm his legal guardian and godfather, but there is no blood relation."

"What?" I snapped, jerking my chin in his direction. "Why didn't Tom ever say anything to me?" I felt my lips turn downward, into an unwelcome frown.

"Tom doesn't know yet." Daniel darted his eyes across the room, sensing my disapproval. I rose to my feet, awakened by a surge of repressed aggression.

"What?" I placed my hands on my hips, preparing to scold him. "You never told him?" Heat spread through me as I returned to pacing the floor. "How could you do that?"

"Think about it Addie," Daniel began, looking me squarely in the eyes, in an attempt to steer me in his direction. "How did you feel about Jeffrey and Eleanor when you thought they were blood, compared to how you feel about them now?"

"That's sick and twisted, and you know it." I pointed my finger at Daniel, eyeing him suspiciously. "What happened to Tom's parents anyway? He never told me."

"They died in a car accident when Tom was two." Daniel took a deep breath. I wondered how badly his hands were shaking. "There was no one else, Addie. That's why I raised him. That's why he was placed in my care."

"What about me?" I scoffed at his remark. "You'll raise Tom, but won't raise your own grandchild?" I felt my lower lip quiver, but didn't care. "I needed you."

"By the time I discovered what Josette had done, it was too late. You had already been given away." Daniel looked lovingly over me, sincerity placating his appearance. "I did everything I could to find you."

"But you didn't." I shook my head in disbelief, wiping away tears.

"Addie, do you think it's a coincidence that your closest neighbor is me?" Something inside my head clicked, compelling me to stop discarding his statements as false and just listen. "I wanted to be nearby, to feel that you were safe."

A long silent moment passed, in which neither of us said a word. I tried to organize all of these new pieces of information in my head, but no more than a migraine resulted. Eventually, I settled down enough to think rationally.

"Who's Wesley?" I gazed into the fireplace, searching for solace in the dancing flames. "The article said that ya'll had two children, not one."

"We did," Daniel murmured. His voice felt far away. "Wesley was born with a rare disease that attacks the blood." I turned my head to look back at Daniel, noticing that the fire had captivated him as well. "He didn't live past five."

"Oh," I began, as feelings of loss and sorrow washed over me. "Daniel, I'm so sorry. I had no idea." Despite his deception, I empathized with Daniel. How could it be that he had lost a wife, a son, and a daughter within a lifetime?

I was the only one left.

Chewing at the edge of my lip, I tried to make sense of it all. Daniel lay motionless in the bed, and for the first time, I understood why. "If Tom really isn't related to us, then what was his name, before the adoption?"

"Thomas O'Brien," he answered. I tilted my head to the side, repeating the name over and over again in my head. It didn't sound right. Then again, I didn't entirely feel like a Beaumont.

"Listen Addie," Daniel coughed. "I love Tom like

my own flesh and blood. I've raised him as my own, and I've never done anything to harm that boy."

"Tom deserves to know the truth." I stood up in front of the fireplace and ambled towards the door, intent on finding Tom and telling him everything.

"Addie," Daniel beckoned. "What good would it do, telling him now? He's gone this long without knowing." I placed my hand on the doorknob to leave, but then Daniel called after me. "Addie, promise me that you won't tell Tom." Daniel held his mouth ajar, desperate for my compliance.

"Fine," I consented, sighing in reluctance. "I promise."

Chapter 29

I stood in front of Tom's bedroom door, wondering if I had been too forthright to knock. Excitement overwhelmed me, because Tom could truly be mine, if he would still have me. Sighing, I rapped my knuckles against the wooden surface and braced myself.

When the door opened, I had no more than loving smiles to offer. Yet Tom glowered at me, his face a smoldering blaze. My face fell, as I thought of the best way to convince him that everything between us was fine.

"Can I come in?" I leaned back on my heels, never losing eye contact with Tom.

Although he didn't say anything, Tom took a few steps back, making room for me to enter. I shut the door behind me and exhaled.

"Tom, I'm sorry," I began. "I don't know what got into me today, but," I babbled on, searching for words. "I wasn't myself." Tom leaned into the edge of his desk, carefully studying me. "I'm sorry," I repeated. "I don't know what else to say."

Tom pulled his eyebrows together, as he slouched over the desk, with his arms crossed over his chest. If I had only told Tom everything, then he would have been able to understand. Defeated, I watched Tom stare at me, until he nearly turned to stone. He never even blinked.

"Aren't you going to say something?" I rubbed my

palms together and waited.

"What do you want me to say?" Tom's voice sounded deeper than I remembered.

"I don't know," I whispered. Tom walked towards me, seamlessly backing me into the wall by his closet. I swallowed, embarrassed by the sound each of my quickening breaths made.

"You told me not to kiss you." Tom leaned into me, stilling his face just inches from mine. I searched those sultry, honey-colored eyes and wondered what he was thinking.

"That wasn't because I didn't want you to." I bit my lower lip, while Tom gazed from my mouth to my eyes. Desire coursed through my veins, as he placed his hands against the wall, on either side of my face, consequently trapping me.

With his lips nearly touching mine, I couldn't help but quiver, unable to stand the closing distance between us. Tom spread his fingers at the base of my throat, tempting me, teasing me. Just as I felt myself begin to unravel, Tom released me and moved towards his closet.

"Are you ready to go?" Tom opened the closet door, retrieved a black leather jacket, and slowly slid his arms through the sleeves, with a seductive smirk on his face. I stood with my back against the wall, still heated and panting. Of all the times Tom had held me so close, I had never expected to be hoodwinked.

"Go where?" I breathed, still regaining oxygen.

"Your house." Tom grabbed my hand and led me out of his bedroom. "Dinner with your parents?" He raised his eyebrows in a questioning manner, as we climbed down the staircase.

"Oh," I sighed, struggling to keep up with Tom's

hurrying pace. "Right."

* * *

When Tom and I arrived, Jeffrey greeted us at the door, happily introducing himself to Tom and shaking his hand. I found Eleanor in the kitchen, stirring a large pot of vegetable soup with a wooden spoon. A sudden bout of dizziness came over me, because she was wearing a cooking apron. Was I dreaming?

"Hello darling," she chimed, pecking my cheek with a kiss. "How was school?"

"Fine," I softly answered, too overcome with shock to add anything else.

When Tom followed me into the kitchen, Eleanor's face lit up. "Oh, hello there," she beamed. "I'm Addie's mother."

"Tom," he modestly stated, shaking her hand when it was offered.

"Well, why don't you all have a seat in the dining room? Dinner is almost ready." Eleanor retrieved a pan of thickly sliced French bread from the oven and set it down on the stovetop to cool. "Go on, Addie," she commanded. "I'll join you all in a moment."

Tom tugged at my wrist, motioning for the two of us to follow Jeffrey into the dining room. I felt stock-still, unable to move. Tom searched my face, furrowing his brow at my sluggishness. Shaking my head, I walked with him into the dining room, surprised to find that the table had been set with sterling silver and fine china, objects that had been housed in the attic for the entirety of my existence.

I blinked twice and then pinched myself, causing Tom to scrunch his face in confusion. Even Jeffrey looked up at me before sitting down at the head of the table. Sighing, I sat down in the chair closest to Jeffrey, while Tom took a seat to my right.

Jeffrey took a sip from his water glass, and then drummed his fingers against the tablecloth. Anxious, I spread a cloth napkin over my lap and nodded to Tom. He quickly followed suit. After encountering Eleanor in the kitchen, I knew that we would all have to be on our best behavior tonight.

"Darling?" Eleanor peered through the dining room doorway. "Could you help me with the salads?" I looked to the ceiling and began counting to fifty.

"Yeah, of course." Jeffrey rose from the table and followed Eleanor into the kitchen.

"You okay?" Tom grabbed my wrist, pressing our palms together beneath the table.

"I don't know what has gotten into her," I griped, reaching for my water glass with my free hand. After taking a sip, I felt no more relaxed than I had been before.

"What do you mean?" Tom searched my eyes.

"Mom," I mouthed, nudging my head towards the kitchen.

"She doesn't seem so bad," Tom said, trying to make the best of everything.

"You should see what she's like when she's not acting," I boldly declared.

Just then, Eleanor and Jeffrey entered the dining room and set a bowl of soup at each placemat, with a smaller bowl of salad to the left. I readjusted, straightening my posture in the stiff, wooden chair. We never ate meals in the dining room. The furniture had been purchased for aesthetic value, not comfort.

Eleanor returned to the kitchen one last time, to remove her apron and collect the bread. I slouched into the back of my chair, dreading the torture that would surely follow. If Eleanor offended Tom in anyway, the evening would certainly end in bloodshed.

"So Tom," Jeffrey began. "Tell us about yourself."

"What do you want to know?" Tom placed a spoonful of soup in his mouth and swallowed. I turned my head to Tom, noting the hint of a smile at the edge of his lips.

"Anything," Eleanor answered, batting her lashes ever so coquettishly. I felt the desire to speak for Tom, in order to spare him from Eleanor's belligerent inquisition. But then I realized who that sounded like and held my tongue. Emasculation was Eleanor's forte, not mine.

"Well," Tom started. "I'm sixteen. I'm a junior, and I go to school with Addie."

"You're sixteen?" I interjected, wincing once I heard the tone of my voice.

"Yeah," Tom shrugged, irritated by my interruption.

"I'm older than you." I didn't know that.

"Does that matter?" Tom hesitated, waiting for my approval.

"No." I shook my head, embarrassed by the look on Eleanor's face.

"When's your birthday?" Tom kept his eyes on me.

"October," I murmured.

"April," Tom similarly stated. It sounded like we were quizzing each other.

"Are you from Savannah?" Eleanor eyed Tom, occasionally flicking her eyes in my direction. I reached for a slice of French bread and began tearing off small chunks, before popping each piece into my mouth.

"Yes ma'am," Tom nobly replied. "I've lived in Savannah my whole life, with my grandfather." I dunked a piece of bread into my soup bowl, glancing to Jeffrey when Eleanor wasn't looking. He knew how I felt.

"Where are your parents?" Eleanor stabbed a shred of lettuce with her fork, never taking her eyes off Tom. I grabbed his hand beneath the table, rubbing my thumb over his knuckles. Tom glanced at me, while we communicated without speaking. I gently widened my eyes, letting him know what I meant. Tom didn't have to answer the question, if he didn't want to.

"They died when I was a boy," Tom admitted. I studied the reaction on Eleanor's face, but she was no more than feigning sympathy. I could tell the difference.

"Oh Tom, I'm so sorry. That's awful." Eleanor knitted her eyebrows together, pulling her mouth into a pouty smirk. I glared at Jeffrey, willing him to say something.

"I've tried to make the best of it." Tom squeezed my hand beneath the table. "I'm really close to my grandfather. He's practically my best friend."

"Nothing wrong with that," Jeffrey commented. Eleanor rolled her eyes, before taking a sip of red wine. Was Jeffrey not allowed to speak?

"What are your plans after high school? Have you applied to any colleges yet?" I glared at Eleanor from my seat across the table. What was she doing? Interviewing him for a job?

"I do plan on attending college, Mrs. Smith." Tom held Eleanor's gaze, never breaking eye contact. "And I'll go wherever Addie goes." I smiled with delight, realizing the spine it had taken to say that in front of Eleanor.

"Well," Jeffrey proclaimed, breaking the tension among us. "Who would like dessert?" I breathed a sigh of relief. Eleanor rose and made her way towards the kitchen.

* * *

After Tom left, I strolled into the kitchen, blankly staring at Eleanor's figure by the sink. Jeffrey stood nearby at the counter, lazily sipping at the last of his wine. When I cleared my throat, they both looked back at me and smiled.

"Addie." Eleanor beamed. "I like him."

"You do?" I cocked my head to the side, unable to tell if she was being honest.

"Yes," she insisted with three overly enthusiastic nods. "Why?"

"It was hard to tell." I shrugged. Jeffrey nodded to himself while I moved closer, lifting myself onto the counter across from him.

"Your father told me that Tom lives in the lot next to us, with his grandfather." Eleanor placed the dishes and silverware in the sink, before running hot water over them.

"Yeah." I looked to Jeffrey in disappointment. "That's right."

Jeffrey had asked me about Tom two days ago, merely curious, or so I had thought. Since Tom and I weren't speaking at the time, I had told Jeffrey whatever he wanted to hear, not realizing that he was taking notes for Eleanor. Why did he always have to listen to her?

"Did you know that the grandfather is just some

obscure painter, who inherited millions when his parents died?" Eleanor widened her smile, revealing a straight, sharp set of pearly whites.

"So that's it," I decided. "That's why you like Tom so much?"

"Addie," Eleanor chattered, attempting to coax me. "We just want you to be taken care of." I slid off the kitchen counter, not caring when I accidentally nudged Jeffrey.

"I can't believe this! All you care about is the fact that he's got a lot of money? You're ridiculous!" I stormed out of the kitchen, with Eleanor following closely behind.

"Why are you so mad, Addie?" Eleanor grabbed my elbow. "This is great news!"

"Mom," I snarled, pulling my arm out of her grasp. "Tom's not like all those other boys!" I walked through the foyer in a fit of rage. "I know we haven't been together that long, but Tom actually cares about me. Can't you see that?"

"Of course we can sweetheart," Eleanor cheered, looking back at Jeffrey's lingering presence in the kitchen. He joined us in the foyer, popping almonds into his mouth.

"Yeah," he agreed. "Tom seems like a nice kid."

"And what if Tom were poor?" I noted the childish grin on Eleanor's face.

"But Tom's not poor," she giggled, as if I were the foolish one.

"But what if he were?" I waited in silence, while Eleanor and Jeffrey exchanged a pair of looks, none of which were directed at me.

"I have to pack and get ready to go out of town in the morning." Eleanor turned to Jeffrey. "And so does your father," she added. I crossed my arms over my chest, scoffing at her remarks with bitterness. "Why don't you be a doll and do the dishes?"

Eleanor left the room, with Jeffrey slowly trailing behind her. I trudged into the kitchen and rolled up my sleeves, looking down at the sink full of dirty dishes. Neither fine china nor sterling silver was dishwasher safe. I sighed aloud, closing my eyes.

Had she just called me a doll?

Chapter 30

Later that night, I stood in front of the bathroom sink, brushing my teeth. A glass bowl, filled with potpourri, sat at the back of the counter, near the mirror. After rinsing my mouth out with water, I returned my toothbrush to the cabinet on the wall, and then lowered my head over the bowl, to inhale the scent of jasmine, juniper, and cloves.

I never wanted the bowl of potpourri, but Eleanor rarely considered what others wanted. Five years ago, I came home from school to find the strange mixture of dried flowers and plant shavings on my bathroom counter. When I confronted Eleanor, she merely smiled, then relayed the punishment that would result if I removed the potpourri. I scowled at the memory, wondering how Eleanor had become so cold.

Brushing the matter off, I pulled my hair back into a loose ponytail, and then placed a headband along my hairline. With a quick gesture, I turned the faucet on and waited for the water to warm. Clear liquid poured into the sink, while I retrieved a fresh bar of soap from the bathroom cabinet. Just as I started to wash my face, a soft thud landed on my bedroom window.

I walked into the room, quickly realizing that someone was tossing rocks. Smiling, I returned to the sink and rinsed my hands off with water, then patted them dry before walking towards the window. Tom stood on the ground below like a mirage through the glass. I opened the window and ducked my head into the cold night air.

"Hey," I gently yelled.

"Can I come up?" When I nodded, he began scaling the oak tree outside my bedroom. I moved away from the window, deftly combing a hand through the ends of my ponytail. As I turned my head, Tom climbed into my bedroom and closed the window behind him.

"What are you doing here?" I kept my voice low, no louder than a whisper.

"I wanted to see you." Tom grinned in the darness, his white teeth glowing in the moonlight. "What's on your face?"

"Oh." I froze, and then rushed into the bathroom. "I was just washing my face." I turned on the faucet and cupped my palms beneath the water. Closing my eyes, I splashed the liquid all over my face, until all remaining traces of the soap were gone. Afterwards, I turned the water off and grabbed a clean washcloth to dry my face with.

"Dinner wasn't so bad." I opened my eyes to find Tom's reflection in the mirror. "Your parents are actually kind of great," he softly spoke, leaning against the wall by the door.

"I think they both really liked you." I studied him through the glass, not mentioning why Eleanor had approved of him so easily. Maybe Daniel was right. Sometimes, it is better, not knowing the truth.

"And thanks for saying all that at dinner, about college." I turned around to face Tom and tossed the washcloth on the counter. "I think you made quite an impression on my mother." I looked up at him in admiration, spotting flecks of honey in his eyes.

"That's not why I said it, Addie." Tom shoved his hands into the pockets of his jeans, holding his jaw taut. I rested my palms along the bathroom counter behind me, gauging Tom's reaction.

"Then why did you?" I held my breath, waiting for an answer.

"Because I meant it." Tom stepped forward, shortening the distance between us. I hesitated, not knowing how else to respond, while Tom's eyes stayed on mine. Tom looked at me through his lashes, charming me without any effort at all.

I gazed into his eyes, failing to blink when Tom placed his hand at the base of my throat. He leaned into me slowly, gently placing kisses along my jawline. My hands trailed the length of his chest, until our mouths met in a moment of mutual desire. In haste, Tom brushed his lips against mine, before clutching my waist and lifting me onto the counter.

I felt Tom's hands at the small of my back, as his fingers pressed into my skin. Breathless, I let my fingers dance along the back of Tom's neck, until he drew in a quick breath and pushed me back farther, along the counter. Giggling, I playfully nipped at the edge of his lip, not realizing how profoundly my touch would affect him. Tom leaned over me with a smile and forced my back into the mirror, before returning his lips to mine. Neither of us was expecting the sound of shattering glass that inevitably followed.

Tom and I froze, slowly turning our heads to find the potpourri bowl in pieces on the floor. Flower extracts lay scattered across the tile, like a rainbow broken into bits. Tom released me, then stepped back to look at what we had done.

"Addie," Tom whispered. "I'm so sorry." He knelt

down before the mess, picking up and inspecting a piece of jagged glass. "I'll replace it," he offered, setting the broken glass aside.

Without warning, I burst into laughter, alarming Tom as he rose to his feet. "Addie?" He stood in front of me, with his hands on his hips. "Are you okay?" I nodded, though my giggling never ceased. "Addie," he called, placing his hands on my shoulders.

"Sorry," I murmured, still catching my breath. "It's just that," I paused, attempting to suppress my cackling for the time being. "I hate potpourri."

"What's that?" Tom wondered.

I lolled my head back in laughter, while Tom stared, raising his eyebrows in concern, as if I had just inhaled nitrous oxide. When he covered my mouth with his hand, my eyes widened in surprise, until I heard her voice.

"Addie!" Eleanor called from downstairs. "What are you doing up there?" I felt my heartbeat quicken, anxiety rippling through me. "Did you break something?" I pulled Tom's hand away from my mouth and bolted into my bedroom, closing the bathroom door behind me. "Addie!"

I met Eleanor at the top of the staircase, just outside my bedroom door. She wore a silver silk nightgown, trimmed with black lace and chiffon. I paled at the sight of Eleanor, as she slipped her arms through the matching gray wrap, loosely knotting the waist tie around her stomach.

"Sorry, Mom," I started. "I just," I stumbled over my words, backing my way into the closed bedroom door before continuing, "dropped the soap." When Eleanor eyed me suspiciously, I added, "and the shampoo!" She jerked her chin to the side. "Actually, I knocked a bunch of stuff over in the bathroom," I explained. "But everything's fine." Eleanor looked into my eyes, searching for deceit, then changed the subject.

"Your father and I are leaving at five thirty in the morning," she proclaimed. "Could you try *not* to destroy the house while we're gone?" Eleanor jabbed a pointed finger in my direction.

"Yes," I hissed back at her. Eleanor turned on her heel and crept down the staircase, until her figure dissipated into the darkness. I breathed a sigh of relief, opened my bedroom door, and then locked it behind me.

I found Tom pacing in the bathroom, his hands behind his back. "What happened?" he asked, approaching me. I turned to the mirror and removed my headband.

"Nothing," I mumbled. "She's fine." I waved a hand in the air, and then let my hair down, tossing the ponytail holder onto the counter. When I turned off the light and walked into the bedroom, Tom followed me.

I sat down on the edge of my bed and motioned for Tom to do the same. He joined me on the mattress, sitting ever so closely. I noted the fact that our arms were touching. As I yawned, exhaustion set in, reminding me of the long day behind me. I rested my head on Tom's shoulder and wrapped my hands around his arm, feeling his warmth, his strength.

"I should take off," he offered, "let you sleep." Tom shifted, preparing to stand up.

"No." I clung to his arm. "Don't go." I stared into his eyes, as glistening as molten honey, and willed him to stay.

Tom glanced over me and smiled. "Okay."

We stayed awake for hours, talking about Daniel, Savannah, and Maple Creek High. Tom told me stories of his childhood with Daniel, reflecting on the way things had been before the disease invaded his body. I listened, thinking about the fact that Daniel was my grandfather, not Tom's, and wondered how he would feel if he knew the truth.

As the night wore on, I crawled underneath the covers, unable to stay awake any longer. Lying back on my pillow, I relaxed into the mattress and closed my eyes, even though Tom was still talking. Exhausted, I stifled my last yawn of the night and drifted off to the sound of Tom's chattering voice.

Chapter 31

When I woke up the next morning, Tom lay beside me in the bed, his breaths a patterned rhythm of inhales and exhales. I grinned at the sight of Tom. He was still dressed in yesterday's clothes, lying on his back, atop the many covers. I spotted his boots on the floor by the window, then looked back at his sleeping body, restful in the daylight.

Beside Tom, the clock on my nightstand glared 11:00 in electric blue numbers. I pulled the covers back and climbed out of bed, silently tiptoeing towards the closet, where I swiftly assembled an outfit for the day. With my wardrobe in hand, I sauntered over to the bathroom and gently closed the door behind me.

In the shower, I thought about what I had told Eleanor last night. Tom wasn't like all those other boys. He was kind, smart, and good. Every other male adolescent merely paled in comparison, because Tom was the type of guy that a girl wanted to grow old with.

I stepped out of the shower and wrapped a towel around my body, noting the broken potpourri dish on the floor. For years, I had longed for the day when Eleanor's precious bowl of scented shavings reached an untimely end. Dressing myself, I glanced at the foggy mirror, then smiled at the open space on the countertop, where the potpourri used to be.

After towel drying my hair, I opened the bathroom door to find an empty bed. Frowning, I walked towards the closet and slipped into a pair of gray sneakers, noticing that Tom's pair of boots by the window was gone.

As I descended the staircase, the smell of bacon wafted through the air, leading me into the kitchen. Tom stood in front of the stove, scrambling eggs in a skillet. Even though we were in my house, he looked at home.

"Hey." He beamed, placing a soft kiss on my lips.

"I thought you left," I admitted. Tom shook his head, then pushed a plateful of eggs, bacon, and toast towards me. "I have to pick Jeanine up at noon." I scarfed down the bacon, retrieving a fork from the silverware drawer for my eggs. "We're having lunch and then going to see a movie." I bit into a piece of toast, then gladly accepted the glass of orange juice that Tom offered me. "She needs to get out of the house." Tom watched me as I ate, nodding in agreement. "I think Ricky's driving her crazy," I added, stabbing the eggs with my fork.

"So, Ricky won't be there?" Tom narrowed his eyes at me, contemplating.

"No," I asserted. "It's just me and Jeanine."

Tom scraped the remaining eggs from the skillet and onto his plate. I caught the faintest hint of disappointment in his eyes and wished that I had told him about my plans earlier. But with everything that had happened yesterday, it was no wonder that the thought had slipped my mind.

"I should go," I said, eyeing the clock on the wall. I didn't want Jeanine waiting for me to rescue her from Ricky any longer than she already had to. "Don't worry about all of this." I motioned towards the dishes before he could start washing them. "I'll clean it up later."

Tom kept quiet, following me onto the front porch. I locked the door behind me, then turned to Tom. "Do you want me to drive you home?" Tom shook his head from side to side, as I became overwhelmed with the feeling that I should have invited him to come along. "Do you want to go to lunch with us and see a movie?"

"No." Tom shrugged. "You girls go have fun."

"Are you sure?" I searched his eyes as they fluttered away from me, scanning the nearby trees instead. "Jeanine won't mind."

"Yeah, I'm sure." Tom smiled, feigning happiness. When I furrowed my brow in disbelief, Tom wrapped his arm around my shoulder and walked me down the front porch steps. As we neared my car, I felt the need to say more than I already had.

"I should have told you that we had already made plans, but with everything-" Tom held a finger over my lips, silencing me before I could explain further.

"Addie," Tom coaxed. "It's fine. Really." Tom traced my lower lip with his thumb, and then kissed me. I felt my knees weaken as sweet desire coursed through me, sending a soft ache throughout my body. When Tom released me, I nearly forgot how to breathe. "I'll call you later." He smirked, and then walked off into the woods.

* * *

Jeanine sat on the front doorstep of the Travis residence, impatiently twiddling her thumbs. When I pulled into the driveway, she jumped up in delight and quickly scurried over to my car. Unlocking the doors, I gazed at the mansion in shock, as my jaw dropped to the floor.

"What happened to your house?" I stared into Jeanine's eyes, while she climbed into the passenger's seat and shut the car door behind her.

For starters, the entire house had been covered with toilet paper. Beer bottles and soda cans lay scattered in the grass, accompanied by the bodies of three shirtless teenage boys. The driveway was lined with confetti, popcorn, and candy wrappers. I furrowed my brow at the sight of lingerie hanging from the power lines. It hung like Spanish moss in an oak tree.

"Ricky, the football team, the cheerleading squad, the entire senior class, and a few guys from Walmart," Jeanine whined, counting each one on her fingers. "I spent the whole night locked in my room with a chair against the door!"

"Walmart?" I gazed at her in confusion, unsure if I had heard her correctly.

"Yeah." She nodded, then turned her head towards the window and pointed. "Look! There's one of them right there." I widened my eyes at the sight of a young blonde man lying on his stomach, on top of the roof. He was naked.

Cupping my hands over my mouth, I tried not to laugh, but could not help myself. "Jeanine," I started, failing to suppress my cackling. "You should have called last night. You could have spent the night with me." Jeanine fastened her seatbelt, then looked through the windshield at the power lines.

"Is that," she paused, on the verge of laughter, "what I think it is?"

"I'm afraid so," I said, as we pulled out of the driveway.

Jeanine looked back at the man on the roof. "I

guess it is kind of funny," she realized. "Where are his clothes?" Jeanine turned to me, suddenly animated.

"I don't know," I chuckled. "But if he can't find them, he won't have to look too far." I pointed to the lingerie overhead, until we drove off like a pair of giggling fools.

We dined at an Italian restaurant for lunch, where Jeanine relayed the events of the previous night. She had slept with cotton in her ears, securely buried beneath the weight of five blankets. Jeanine's parents would not return from their Bahamian cruise until the following Friday, which meant she would be stuck with Ricky's partying antics for another six nights. I didn't want to think about how damaged the house would be by then.

After lunch, we drove to the theatre, where the new Leonardo DiCaprio movie was playing. I had never seen Jeanine run so fast. She bolted for the ticket booth, and then raced inside to snag a pair of front row seats. I sat down beside her, observing the genuine way she was grinning from ear to ear, like a small child.

As the movie trailers began, Jeanine squealed with delight, clapping her hands together in elation. I smiled at her beaming presence, too adorable to miss. Within a few minutes, I settled into my seat and sighed. I couldn't stop thinking about Tom.

Chapter 32

When I pulled up to the Travis residence, to drop Jeanine off, we spotted Ricky in the driveway, leaning his head through the window of a shiny, red Mercedes Benz. I recognized the driver as Jane Dorsey, fellow Maple Creek High student and athlete. She was a senior, volleyball captain, yearbook editor, and future prom queen.

All the boys loved Jane, because she looked like a supermodel: long legs, slender frame, soaring height, olive skin. Her long, brunette hair fell in soft, smooth waves, nearly spanning the length of her back. She should have been in a shampoo commercial. The guys took notice too, always talking in the hallway about how beautiful her big, brown eyes were.

Jeanine watched in silence, as Ricky leaned into Jane, kissing her on the mouth. I unfastened my seatbelt, looking on in perplexity. "I thought she was dating Garrett Dunne," I said, recalling the senior running back. When Jeanine didn't reply, I pushed the matter further. "Isn't Garrett friends with Ricky?"

"Yeah," Jeanine retorted. "Some friend, huh?"

Ricky backed away from the Mercedes, as Jane rolled the window up and started her car. I narrowed my eyes at Ricky's figure. He raised an index finger in the air and pointed at Jane. "We're having another party tonight!" he yelled at her through the glass. "And you better be there!" Jane waved to Ricky, laughing, then drove away.

"That's it!" Jeanine scoffed in the seat beside me. "I'm not staying here another night." I stiffened my posture, while Jeanine unfastened her seatbelt and opened the car door. "Could you drive me to my grandmother's?" Jeanine looked back at me, desperation evident in her pleading blue eyes. "She only lives a few minutes away."

"Sure," I agreed. Ricky began walking over to us, as I cringed in aggravation.

"Wait right here." Jeanine shut the car door, but kept talking. I rolled the window down to hear her. "Let me grab my bags and I'll be right back!"

"Okay." I took my keys out of the ignition, prepared to wait. Just as Jeanine left, Ricky approached my car and leaned into the passenger's side window.

"Why didn't you come to my party last night?" Ricky's arms dangled over the car door, while I recoiled at the strong scent of alcohol on his breath. Blue veins traveled along either of his forearms, reminding me of slithering snakes and vines.

"Because I have a brain," I crowed, talking down to him. "You're the one without a heart." I turned my head away from Ricky and placed my hands on the wheel, ready to depart as soon as Jeanine returned from inside the house.

"I never liked *The Wizard of Oz*," Ricky droned, sliding his tongue along his top row of teeth. I thought to myself: *If this is how Ricky flirts, then Jane Dorsey and Nicki Caldwell must be dumber than I thought.*

"I'm surprised you know what it is." I buckled my seatbelt and honked the horn, anxious to leave. Ricky merely grinned, making me feel even more uncomfortable.

"You really don't like me, do you?" Ricky stared into my eyes, never blinking.

"No, Ricky! I really don't." I jerked my chin at Ricky, resenting the idea of arguing with him while Jeanine was packing her suitcase. Was he that thick-headed?

"Is there anything I can do to change that?" Ricky scanned the length of my body with lustful eyes. He watched me the way an animal would, the way a lover would.

"I have a boyfriend," I informed him. "You know this."

"So," Ricky drawled, shrugging his shoulders. A wicked smile crossed his face. I rolled my eyes, looking through the windshield with a sour expression. "But what if you didn't?" I shook my head from side to side, my blood boiling.

"Ricky," I demanded. "It's NEVER. GONNA. HAPPEN." Ricky straightened his slouchy posture, feigning sadness with his eyes. "Get over it."

"And what if I can't?" Ricky pouted.

"Tell me something," I commanded. Ricky nodded, elated at my interest. "Do you choose girls who love you or hate you?"

"Depends," he muttered. I heard a door slam and spotted Jeanine running towards us from the house. She carried a pillow, two suitcases, and a backpack.

"On what?" I pressed a button on my car keys that popped the trunk, anticipating Jeanine. Half-heartedly listening, I started the ignition and glanced back at Ricky.

"On how much she hates me." Ricky clicked his teeth together, then turned his head to observe

Jeanine's approaching figure. She stowed her luggage in the back, then shut the trunk and walked around to the passenger's side door.

"What did you do? Pack the whole house?" Ricky glowered down at her, blocking access to the car door. How did Jeanine put up with him every day?

"The better half," she snapped. "Now move!" Ricky stepped aside, while Jeanine opened the door and climbed into the car. She fastened her seat belt and began rolling the window up, until Ricky leaned his head through.

"Wait!" He panicked, reaching for Jeanine's arm. "You're actually leaving with her?"

"It's better than staying here with you!" Jeanine peeled his hand away in defiance.

"What about this mess?" Ricky pointed at the house behind him. "Who's gonna clean it up before Mom and Dad get back?" He gazed into Jeanine's eyes, imploring her.

"Not me." Jeanine looked her brother over impassively, then pushed him away so she could finish rolling the window up. "Bye," she chimed through the glass, waving.

As I drove away, Ricky's image appeared in the rearview mirror. In all the time I had known Ricky, he had never looked so stunned before. I turned to Jeanine, watching her look through the window, a victorious smile on her face.

Chapter 33

By the time I headed home, the sky had already darkened around me. Jeanine's grandmother had been pleasant, offering milk and cookies. The three of us talked for hours about Ricky's salacious party from the night before. Jeanine's grandmother despised Ricky and repeatedly declared how many lashings he would have received after pulling a stunt like that, if Ricky had been her son. She recalled disciplining Lawton when he was a young boy, though could not understand why her son would not do the same, as Ricky had been stepping out of line for years.

The minute I dropped Jeanine off, I noticed the overwhelming sense of relief in her eyes. As an only child, I had never been subject to the inevitable turmoil of having an older brother as hedonistic as Ricky. Jeanine promptly decided that she would not return home until her parents were no longer floating in the Atlantic.

When I finally made it home, I parked in the garage and headed inside, glad to have the house to myself. Jeffrey and Eleanor may not have been the best parents in the world, but they had yet to turn the house into a brothel. I couldn't begin to fathom how Jeanine would be able to continue living in the same house with Ricky. He wouldn't leave for college for over a year.

Sighing, I headed upstairs and changed into a

button-down long-sleeved flannel shirt, then kicked my shoes onto the floor. I hadn't eaten dinner yet, though felt satisfied enough, after munching on the chocolate chip cookies that Jeanine's grandmother had given me. Shrugging the matter off, I headed back downstairs and flopped onto the couch, where I began aimlessly flipping through channels on TV. I could eat later.

As I relaxed into the sofa, with a blanket atop my sprawling figure, the phone rang. I snatched the cordless receiver from its cradle on the end table next to the couch and answered. I didn't bother checking the caller ID, too engrossed in channel surfing.

"Hey," Tom began. "I called earlier and never heard back. I was getting worried."

"Sorry," I exhaled. "I just got home." I tossed the remote onto the couch and left the TV on an infomercial for food processors, overcome by a sudden craving for hummus.

"How was the movie?" Tom inquired, slowly clearing his throat.

"Good," I said. "We saw the new one with Leonardo DiCaprio."

"Oh," Tom drawled, knowing where the conversation would lead.

"Jeanine went out of her mind," I blurted, recalling her overzealous reaction to Leonardo's presence on the big screen. "You know how she is about him."

"Yeah," Tom chuckled. "I remember."

Every week, Jeanine spent at least one lunch hour relishing in every detail of her celebrity crush. Tom and I always kept quiet, letting her prattle away carelessly. Jeanine was a single lady, and with a brother like Ricky, there wasn't much hope of finding a good man in Savannah. Before I met Tom, I had figured as much. Regardless, Jeanine's obsessive fandom was beginning to cross the border of Infatuation Isle and head straight for Stalker City. If Leonardo DiCaprio were ever in Georgia, Jeanine would surely be able to track his scent for miles.

"Anyway, when I took Jeanine home, after the movie," I paused, resting my head on one of the couch's many plush pillows, "she just couldn't take it anymore." I laid flat on my back and stared at the ceiling. "You should have seen their house, Tom. It was so trashed, because Ricky's having parties every night until their parents get back."

"Where are they?" Tom demanded, an edge of irritation to his voice.

"The Bahamas," I answered, matching his tone of disapproval. "Anyway," I continued, "when we got there, Ricky said that he was having another party tonight and-"

"Wait a minute," Tom interrupted, silencing me. "You saw Ricky?"

"Not by choice," I admitted. "He was in the driveway when we pulled up."

"I thought you said that he wasn't going to be there," Tom scolded. I rolled my eyes, loudly exhaling in frustration. How many times were we going to have the same argument?

"Tom," I reasoned, "Jeanine is my friend." Tom moaned over the phone line, nearly interrupting me again. "And I'm not going to stop seeing her, just because she lives in the same house as Ricky." I waited for Tom to say something, until the silence became unbearable. "I don't want to fight," I pleaded. "I missed you today."

"I missed you too," Tom conceded, his voice

husky. "Can I come over?"

I nearly melted at the sound of his words, as aching warmth spread through me like wildfire. Feeling sultry, I caressed the phone with my breath and smiled.

"How fast can you run?" I hung up and placed the phone on the end table beside me, wondering how quickly Tom would arrive at my front door, fervently knocking until I let him inside. Excitement surged through my veins, as I lay back on the sofa, stretching my arms in anticipation.

Within minutes, I heard a car door slam, followed by the sound of heavy footsteps across the front porch. "Cheater," I snickered before waltzing into the foyer. Impatiently yearning, I placed my hand on the doorknob and peeked through the curtained window. My body stiffened as I backed away, retreating in terror. Tony DeMilo was standing outside my front door.

I froze in place, falling to the floor as I held my head in my hands. When I heard a second pair of footsteps, my heart nearly stopped. I prayed that they didn't belong to Tom. Relief swept through me once I recognized Hugh's voice. The feeling didn't last long.

My eyes widened as the doorknob began to twist back and forth. Fleeing to the kitchen, I flung the silverware drawer open and grabbed a sharp butcher knife. A soft gleam traveled along the edge of the blade, sending a cold shiver through my body.

With no time to think, I turned on my heel and ran through the house, quickly reaching the staircase. I could still hear the doorknob rattling in the distance, as I hurried upstairs and into the guest bedroom at the end of the hallway. Just as I locked the door behind me, an abrupt crash startled me from down below.

They were in the house.

Scanning the guest room, I retreated into the connecting bathroom, then shut and locked the door behind me. When I turned around, the blonde girl in the mirror scared me. I hadn't recognized my own reflection.

Taking a deep breath, I looked around, eyeing the window on the far wall, between the bathroom sink and shower. I set the butcher knife down on the counter, then stilled at the sound of DeMilo and Hugh in the adjoining bedroom. In an instant, they were banging on the bathroom door, while I slid the window open and extended my feet through.

As I stepped onto the roof, the door flew open and Hugh burst through, latching his arm around my stomach. I yelled in defiance, kicking and screaming all the while. Hugh jerked my legs from the window, then slammed it shut, obliterating any chance of escape.

"LET GO OF ME!" I screamed, clawing at the side of Hugh's face with my fingernails. He tossed me onto the bathroom floor, where I hit my head against the wall, before collapsing onto the cool tile. I groaned, holding a hand to my head.

My vision blurred, as I noticed Hugh squatting down before me, a glass bottle in his hand. I blinked twice, then watched him retrieve a white handkerchief from his pocket. I felt nauseous, growing dizzy at the sight of him saturating the cloth with clear liquid from the bottle. When Hugh lunged towards me, I slapped him, horrified by the icy-blue coldness in his eyes. He wanted to hurt me.

Hugh grabbed my wrist, while I stretched my other hand out, reaching for the knife by the sink. As I leaned towards the bathroom counter, Hugh clasped my other wrist and pinned me to the ground, beneath the weight of his body. "NO!" I cried, yet Hugh pressed his arm over my shoulders, forcing my back deeper into the tile. "PLEASE!" I begged, my eyes brimming over with tears. Hugh gazed down at me, then held the handkerchief over my mouth.

"Just let it happen," he whispered, mercilessly sedating me.

I felt myself drift away like a wilting flower.

There was no more pain, no more light. And just before everything went black, I detected the faintest silhouette of Tony DeMilo in the doorway, looking on with a smile.

Chapter 34

I woke, surrounded by darkness. Voices echoed in the distance, murmuring violent, yet inaudible commands. I swallowed, wincing at the terrible pain in my head. My temples throbbed relentlessly, though I silently pleaded for relief.

"Is she conscious?" My heartbeat quickened at the sound of his voice.

"Yes." Hugh spoke near my ear, his breath caressing the side of my face. I felt his hands at the back of my head, tugging and fidgeting until a thick strip of cloth fell away from my eyes.

"Hello Addie," DeMilo snarled. I jerked my arms forward to no avail, then looked down at my figure in horror. DeMilo merely snickered, as I observed the rope tied around my wrists and ankles. Lifting my head in alarm, I scanned the cold rock interior of a cave, where I sat with my back against the wall.

"What do you want?" I mumbled, unable to disguise my trembling voice.

"You know what I want." DeMilo paced the floor in front of a small fire. The flames cast shadows of him upon the opposite wall. Hugh stood in the corner, leaning against another wall of weathered rock.

"The necklace," I answered, eyeing DeMilo from my spot on the floor. When he smiled, I felt a terrifying chill creep through my skin. Despite the soft lighting, I could see how handsome, alluring, and seductive he must have been. Antoinette never stood a chance.

"I don't have it," I confessed. Hugh marched towards me and struck his hand across the side of my face. I closed my eyes, absorbing the harsh, stinging sensation, as warm blood rushed to the surface of my cheek.

"Would you like to try that question again?" DeMilo pressed his lips together. I looked him over carefully, studying the black liquid luster of his eyes. Hugh hovered nearby, never taking his eyes off me. He looked like a male model that I had once seen in a magazine, too beautiful to forget.

"I'm telling you the truth," I spoke, gazing into the fire. "I've never seen it before, in my entire life." Hugh slapped the other side of my face, sending me to the ground, as my shoulder dug into the rough, rocky floor.

"Does Daniel have it?" DeMilo leaned over me, as I tried to ignore the pain.

"I don't know," I cried, widening my eyes in terror. Hugh slammed the heel of his boot into my abdomen, then began to pound at the side of my rib cage.

"I DON'T KNOW!" I screamed, unable to stifle the choking sobs.

"PLEASE!" I moaned, "I DON'T KNOW!"

"STOP!" I wailed, cringing at the sight of Hugh. He held still, feigning mercy for a moment, and then balled his hand into a fist. I shut my eyes, bracing myself for the next blow. When it didn't come, I looked up at DeMilo, who had grabbed Hugh's wrist.

"Not the face," DeMilo ordered, staring into Hugh's cold, clear eyes. "Don't touch her face anymore. Do you understand me?" Hugh nodded, then sauntered over to the far wall. I spotted claw marks across his cheekbone, where I had scratched him earlier.

My breathing grew shallow, as I noticed how badly I was shaking. Tears streamed down my face, slowly falling to the ground like rain. DeMilo knelt down before me and set his fingers beneath my chin. I flinched at the touch of his cold, rough hands, then lifted my eyes to meet his own.

"Did you kill my grandmother?" I took a ragged breath and clenched my jaw. DeMilo ran his thumb beneath my right eye, wiping tears away in a delicate manner.

"You look just like her." DeMilo smiled. My throat tightened, as I pressed my back into the wall, growing increasingly uncomfortable. "Those green eyes." He parted his lips, then dug his fingers into my scalp, tugging at my tresses. "This blonde hair," he inhaled.

"Did you kill her?" I asked, relaxing as DeMilo released my hair and stood up.

"No Addie," he denied. "I didn't kill her." DeMilo walked over to the fire and gazed into the flames, searching. "I loved her," he murmured, as my eyes darted to Hugh, and then back to DeMilo. "I loved her more than anything," he stopped, shifting his eyes carefully, then added, "or anyone." I furrowed my brow in confusion, contemplating.

"Then what happened to her?" I thought about what I had read in the newspaper article about the night Antoinette drowned. Had a rainstorm really killed her? Or had Daniel lied to me again?

"She drowned in the river, Addie." DeMilo hung his head, mournfully gazing at me. "But she knew what she was doing." I didn't know who to believe anymore.

"Why would Antoinette kill herself?" I remembered the yearbook picture of Daniel and Antoinette as Homecoming King and Queen. "That doesn't make any sense." I shook my head, ignoring the throbbing ache that had yet to subside. I had never known Antoinette, yet intuitively doubted that she had been suicidal.

"What does?" DeMilo gestured to the cave walls that surrounded us.

"Why do you want it so much?" I gazed into the depths of his dark, motionless eyes. DeMilo lifted his lips into a quirky smile, regarding me playfully.

"What?" DeMilo inquired, shrugging his shoulders in curiosity.

"The necklace," I explained. "Why do you want it so much?"

"Because it's mine," DeMilo claimed, widening his lips into a wolf-like grin. In that moment, I realized how much it terrified me, the way his mood shifted like mercury.

"What do you want me to do?" I asked, feigning compliance. DeMilo smirked in my direction, tilting his chin upward, rejoicing at my submission.

"Go to Daniel's house, find the necklace, and take it," DeMilo commanded. I shifted the angle of my body, uncomfortably seated atop the jagged floor.

"Even if the necklace were at Daniel's house," I began, narrowing my eyes.

"It is," DeMilo replied, interrupting me. I felt the burning rope, tightly laced around my ankles and wrists. My ribs ached, as I tried to mask the discomfort that permeated the entirety of my body. Even my fingertips hurt.

"I'm not a thief," I proclaimed. Despite his threatening demeanor, I held my chin taut, unwilling to succumb without reason.

"Oh, but you will be," DeMilo assured, twisting his mouth ruthlessly.

"I can't do that." I shook my head, shivering from the cold cavern air. My eyes searched the ground, studying each rough, etched groove of rock. "I won't do that."

"Oh yes, you will," DeMilo softly spoke, predicting the future. I gazed into his eyes, resenting the power they held over me. It was nearly impossible to look away.

"You can't make me," I whispered, knowing the opposite was true. I felt like a child.

"I think you'll find my methods of motivation to be very," DeMilo grew silent, carefully regarding me, then continued, "effective."

DeMilo turned towards Hugh, gesturing his hand in the air. I cringed, desperate to prolong the harsh treatment that would inevitably follow. "Why me?" I felt my throat constrict and blushed in embarrassment.

"Isn't it obvious?" DeMilo shifted, momentarily distracted. "You're his granddaughter." He tilted his head, examining me. "And he trusts you."

"If the necklace is yours, then why does Daniel have it?" I asked, stalling. DeMilo merely smiled, ignoring my question, then moved so that he was standing directly in front of Hugh, blocking his tall, slender figure.

"You have sixty days to find the necklace," DeMilo began. "You won't tell anyone about anything that we have discussed, or involve any police." I recoiled into the wall, my heart pounding as DeMilo stepped towards me. Hugh remained out of sight.

"You will not send anyone looking for me or any of my men." DeMilo tipped his head back, indicating Hugh's obscured presence on the wall, but my eyes remained on his. "You will give the necklace to me at the end of the sixty days." Before I could ask when and where, DeMilo spoke again, seamlessly reading my mind. "We'll find you."

"And if I don't?" I tried to blink, but his eyes were like a snake's, charming me, enchanting me. Within his presence, my willpower crumbled like ice beneath a pick.

"We'll kill him." DeMilo slipped his hands into the pockets of his jacket, as a shudder crept along the back of my neck. He spoke of murder much too casually, like it was some mindless, reoccurring task that must be dealt with, that could not be avoided.

"Who?" I panicked, mentally flipping through faces of the men in my life.

Jeffrey... Daniel... "Tom?" I felt the quickening pulse along the side of my throat.

"No," DeMilo chuckled, clapping his hands together, as if I had just delivered the punch line of a good joke. My back stiffened in response, while I came apart at the seams, cursing myself inwardly. I never should have uttered his name.

"We'll kill Daniel," DeMilo clarified. I widened my eyes, embracing the dull, deadening emotions that sifted through me. An image of Daniel's lifeless corpse came to mind, as warm liquid drops sprung from my tearstained eyes.

I already knew my answer. Of course I would not let them harm Daniel. But the prospect of his death rattled my senses to such a degree, that the simple task of saying *yes* became arduous. I felt numb to the core.

"Having trouble deciding?" DeMilo glanced at me for no more than an instant, then stepped aside, flicking his eyes in Hugh's direction. I cleared my throat, willing myself to speak, but there were no words to delay Hugh's threatening demeanor. A black strip of cloth lay across the flat of his hand. It was the same material that I had been blindfolded with.

Before I could flinch, Hugh shoved the fabric between my top and bottom teeth, then tied the ends of the cloth into a knot at the back of my head. I sobbed aloud, attempting to free myself from Hugh's grasp, but every attempt proved futile. No matter how I resisted, Hugh remained in control. He was a man devoid of empathy.

DeMilo watched nearby, as Hugh wrapped a smaller piece of rope around my tethered hands, then jerked me forward with the newly fashioned leash. I fell to my knees before him, wincing in pain. It felt like he owned me.

Lifting my chin, I gazed into his piercing blue eyes, pitifully begging for mercy. Hugh brushed his thumb along my lower lip, smoldering all the while. Privy to his response, I clamped my teeth around the black cloth in my mouth and pressed my cheek into the palm of his hand, relinquishing the only card that I had yet to play.

Hugh inhaled at the touch of my skin, his senses awakening. I closed my eyes and sighed aloud, visualizing Tom for the sake of my own sanity. Somehow, I managed to appease the lump in my throat enough to lessen the onslaught of fresh tears.

When I opened my eyes, Hugh began to trace a line from the side of my mouth to the space just below my ear, his lips slightly parted. In my mind, I could imagine Tom's hand on my face, his fingertips caressing the length of my throat. He was the only one that I ever wanted to touch me like this. Regardless, I played along, nearly gaining the upper hand, until a lonesome teardrop fell from the corner of my eye, betraying me.

Hugh pressed his thumb over my cheek, trapping the tear, as his face grew red with rage at the discovery of my deception. Slouching, I fell limp, my plans foiled. If I couldn't beguile, seduce, or placate him into submission, then there was no guarantee that I would survive the night. I looked to DeMilo, imploring him with my eyes, before Hugh knocked me onto the flat of my back and began dragging me across the jagged cave floor.

I kicked my heels against the weathered rock, struggling in vain, until Hugh jabbed my stomach with such force that no more than silence could cope with the pain. An aching throb traveled through my body, reaching every bone, tendon, and muscle. Hopeless, I closed my eyes, conjuring an image of Tom in my mind, as Hugh pulled me behind him like a wounded deer that had just been slaughtered in the forest.

I imagined the curve of Tom's smile, the hint of yellow in his honey-colored eyes, and the rough stubble of his beard in the morning. I tasted the rich, soft texture of his lips on mine, before I had left to pick Jeanine up earlier in the day.

Funny, that seemed like a long time ago.

The temperature shifted around me, as I felt cooler air spread across my face. Cringing in discomfort, I opened my eyes to the moonlit sky above me, watching the stars form glimmering specks of white against the flat, black tapestry. My ears perked up at the sound of rushing water, as I realized how thirsty I was, desperate for a drink.

DeMilo walked past my outstretched body, casually slipping on a pair of black leather gloves. I craned my neck to follow his fading figure, then dipped my head back to gauge the treachery that lay ahead. It was far worse than I could have imagined.

Hugh was dragging my body towards the Savannah River.

Chapter 35

anicking in fear, I jerked my hands out of Hugh's grasp and leapt to my feet. If not for the rope around my ankles, I might have garnered a decent chance at running away. Instead, I lost my balance and fell forward, stumbling to the ground in a moment of wasted opportunity. As my hip bone dug into the solid forest floor, I cried out in anguish. For the slightest moment, I had actually believed that I could get away.

Hugh crouched down beside me, chuckling all the while. I gazed into his piercing blue eyes, unable to understand how someone so beautiful could be so cruel. He pulled a pair of black leather gloves over his hands, identical in style to the ones that DeMilo was wearing. I shrieked in terror, because nothing could have prepared me for what they had planned next.

Each man grabbed an elbow, callously flipping me onto my back. I cried out in pain, though my voice could hardly be heard, trapped behind the cloth in my mouth. Hugh tugged at the rope around my wrists, then continued dragging me towards the water.

My arms grew weak above my head, aching relentlessly. I didn't want to do this anymore. I felt helpless and exhausted, slowly losing the strength to fight back. Warm tears flooded my cheeks. They were the only comfort that remained.

When Hugh reached the edge of the river, he placed my body on the ground and removed the black cloth around my mouth. Then, he cut the rope binding my ankles and wrists. I furrowed my brow in confusion, feeling the ends of my hair dampen from the cool river water at my back. Was Hugh releasing me?

DeMilo caught the corner of my eye, as he leaned against a nearby tree to light a cigarette. I flicked my eyes back to Hugh, watching him toss the rope onto the ground, and then slip the black cloth into the pocket of his pants. I must have looked like a puppy, innocently observing its owner, because Hugh smoothed his face into an angelic grin, amused by my silent surrender.

"Don't scream," he whispered, leaning over me. "It's not like anyone is going to hear you." I opened my mouth to protest, but no words came out, as Hugh placed his hands around my waist, picking me up in his arms. I remained voiceless, unable to speak, until he dunked my body into the river.

I screamed beneath the water, overcome by the sharpest sensation of fine needles prickling every inch of my skin. It felt like suffocating beneath an overturned glass of liquid ice. I flailed around in a fit of panic, longing for the use of my limbs. Then, after what seemed like an eternity, Hugh pulled me out of the river, violently tugging at my hair.

"Well," Hugh taunted, gripping the fabric of my shirt. "Have you decided yet?"

Before I could catch my breath, Hugh slammed his hands into my shoulders, effortlessly submerging me into the river again. My fingernails dug into the flesh of his forearm, as I held on for dear life. When he lifted me above water again, I screamed.

"YES!" I clung to Hugh's chest, as he knelt down

at the riverbank.

"Yes what?" Hugh shouted into my face, his breath hot on my skin.

"I'll do whatever you want," I acquiesced, coughing up water.

"You'll find the necklace?" Hugh confirmed, his fingers digging into the flesh beneath my arms. I moaned, squirming beneath him like a fish caught in a net.

"YES!" I nodded until my neck began to hurt.

"And give it to us?" Hugh's breath smelled of coffee and cigarettes.

"YES!" I repeated, desperate to escape the biting cold.

"And you won't tell anyone about anything that has happened here tonight?"

"No," I agreed, violently shivering.

"Good." Hugh smiled, pulling my body out of the water.

I crawled onto the riverbank, gasping for air on all fours. Two bright lights beamed in the darkness, nearly blinding me as DeMilo's black Escalade came into view. Hugh grabbed my arm, walking me towards the nearest oak tree, while DeMilo wandered off, tossing his cigarette onto the ground.

"Hurry up, Hugh," DeMilo ordered, returning to us with a bundle of rope. He tossed it onto the ground before Hugh's feet, then rushed towards the Escalade and climbed into the back seat.

Hugh pushed my back into the tree trunk, pinned my arms to my sides, and then began wrapping the rope around my torso. When he pulled tightly, knotting the rope at my left hip, I moaned in protest. Hugh circled the base of the tree twice, eventually stopping to my right, where he knotted the last of the rope beneath my breast.

"Don't worry, Addie," Hugh coaxed, stepping back to admire his work. "We'll make sure Tom finds you." He removed a package of Marlboros from his pocket, then pulled out a cigarette with his long, pointed fingers, and wedged it between his teeth.

"Leave him alone," I whimpered, pulling against the rope. "Please."

"Why wouldn't we?" Hugh grinned, deftly lighting the end of his cigarette. I felt the rope burning against my skin, confused by his question. Hugh took a deep drag, slowly pulling on the skinny, cylinder-shaped stick, then placed his lips over mine and blew. "You're the one we want."

I began coughing the minute Hugh pulled away, exhaling to force the toxic vapor from my lungs. Ice cold droplets spanned the length of my body, trickling down from my wet hair. I stood shivering against the tree, unable to move, while Hugh climbed into the black Escalade and slammed the car door behind him. The vehicle sped away without a moment's hesitation, swiftly disappearing into the dark forest.

My body shivered violently, worsening the aching nature of my bones. I thought about Jeanine's giddy playfulness at the movie theatre and Tom's lingering question on the phone. *Can I come over?* Oh, how I wished he had spoken sooner.

Lifting my head to the sky, I spotted the perfect, pearly center of the moon, as it cast shadows among the trees. Time leisurely passed, slowly dragging on, while I kept my eyes on the ball in the sky. It was the only clock I had.

My teeth chattered incessantly, as foggy breaths

billowed from my mouth like cigarette smoke. Hugh's poisonous kiss lingered on my tongue, filling my throat with bile. In disgust, I closed my eyes and willed the night to disappear, longing for warmth.

Bright lights interrupted my silent reverie, as I looked ahead. A car door flung open, and a young man stepped out, impatiently running towards me. When he said my name, I nearly convulsed with relief. I knew that voice.

"Addie." Tom inhaled at the sight of me. His breath had never been sharper. He held my face in his hands, carefully inspecting the state of my body. A flood of emotions danced across his face: fear, panic, rage, disbelief.

I closed my eyes as he cut the rope attached to my waist and chest, hurriedly freeing my body from the tree. Tom let out a gasp of air when I collapsed, no longer able to hold myself upright. He caught me before I hit the ground, before everything turned black.

Chapter 36

I heard the distinct sound of a key clicking into place, metal against metal. My temples throbbed violently, reaffirming the pain in my body, as I stirred awake. Tom had me cradled in his arms, warm and protected, though my ribs ached in agony. I recognized Daniel's paintings in the foyer, as Tom carried me across the threshold, gently closing the front door behind us with the heel of his shoe.

My eyelids fluttered, though I resisted the urge to sleep. Tom walked into the den and slowly placed my body on the couch, then left for a moment, swiftly returning with several blankets and a pillow. He lifted my head, carefully wedging the pillow between the couch and my neck, before covering my body with warm wool layers of blanket.

I parted my lips to speak, just as Tom rose from the couch and left again. Disgruntled, I turned onto my side, watching the lively amber flames dance in the fireplace. A moment later, Tom returned with a glass of water in one hand and two small, round tablets in the other.

"Aspirin," he offered, lifting his palm towards me. I swallowed the pills without thinking twice, then drained the glass of water until no more than a drop remained. Tom took the empty glass in his hand, then sat down on the couch, pulling my blanket-covered feet into his lap.

"How did you know where to find me?" I grumbled, my throat dry and hoarse.

"I got a phone call," Tom started, distantly gazing into the fire. "The number was blocked," he droned, still exasperated. "But I knew it was him." Tom draped his arm over the couch, his eyes ablaze with fury. I had never seen him like this before; it scared me.

"Where's Daniel?" I felt frantic, desperate to know that he was safe.

"Asleep," Tom answered. His quick, cold response startled me; it felt like ice.

"Does he know about-?"

"No," Tom snapped, cutting me off. "And I'd like to keep it that way, if you don't mind." I felt small, shrinking beneath the covers. Had I touched a nerve?

"Are you mad at me?" I searched Tom's face, longing to read his thoughts. After everything I had been through today, couldn't he show a little more sympathy?

"Mad at you?" Tom tilted his head to the side, gaping at me in confusion. I nodded, wanting to know the truth. "Mad? Yes. At you? No." Tom smoldered, his golden eyes softly burning. I remembered what Daniel had told me about Tom, after returning home from the hospital. *Sometimes, he doesn't handle things very well.*

"If DeMilo ever touches you again..." Tom leveled his eyes at me, clenching his jaw. I leaned forward, despite the aching discomfort and placed my hand on Tom's arm. He relaxed at my touch, but even I couldn't keep him from saying, "I'll kill him."

"Tom, don't say that," I begged, eyeing him carefully.

"Why not?" Tom touched the small of my back,

pulling me towards him, until I was seated in his lap. "It's how I feel." He brushed his fingers against my jawline, then rested his chin on my shoulder, embracing me. "If anything ever happened to you, Addie..." he faded, unwilling to finish.

"Tom?" I wrapped my arms around him, while he traced soft patterns over my back. "You have to promise me that you won't tell anyone about what happened tonight."

"What?" Tom pulled back, holding me at arm's length. "We need to call the police, Addie," he asserted, squeezing my elbow. "The only reason why I haven't yet is because I wanted to give you a chance to breathe." Tom sank into the couch, releasing me.

"Promise me, Tom," I commanded. "Promise me that you won't say a word about the phone call, or where you found me, or what they did to me." I held his gaze, steadying myself with my hands over his shoulders.

"If you think I'm going to sit here for another minute without calling the police, you're insane." Tom slid off the couch and left the room, while I moaned in frustration.

"Tom," I pleaded, painfully following him through the house. "You can't call the police." When he stopped in the kitchen, I sighed in relief. My muscles ached as if I had just championed an Ironman Triathlon.

"And why not?" Tom lingered near the phone on the wall, impatient.

"I can't tell you." I folded my arms across my abdomen, as a way of easing my own discomfort. Tom glared down at me, gritting his teeth in frustration. "You're just going to have to trust me," I offered, unable to think of a better explanation. "Okay?"

"Fine," Tom barked, letting it go for now. He placed the back of his hand to my forehead, reminding me of the way Eleanor had doted over me as a child, frantically rushing to my side at the first sign of illness. For the first time, I realized how much I had missed being cared for and how frequently Tom filled my desire to be nurtured. He was there when she wasn't.

"Are you hungry?" Tom asked, disrupting my daydream. "I could make some soup." Tom brushed his fingers against my temple, though the throbbing remained.

"Yes," I nodded, recalling that I hadn't eaten dinner yet. "Thank you." Tom silently stared, tucking a piece of fallen hair behind my ear. "I'd like to take a shower," I announced, still feeling the icy-cold river water on my skin.

"Okay." Tom twisted his mouth into a crooked smile, amused. "Let me get you some clothes," he suggested, before turning on his heel and heading upstairs. On my way to the bathroom, I spotted Daniel's closed door and froze. I needed to see him for myself.

Gently twisting the doorknob, I peered inside the bedroom, relieved to find Daniel asleep. He looked peaceful, his light snoring like music to my ears. Satisfied, I shut the door and continued down the hallway, until I reached the bathroom.

My stomach growled with ravenous hunger, as I leaned against the bathroom counter, eyeing my reflection in the mirror. A narrow gash marked the side of my forehead, but for the most part, my face remained unaltered.

As I weaved my fingers through my hair, Tom

stepped into the doorway, startling me with his presence. "Here," Tom breathed, handing me a fresh set of clothes. The edge of his fingers grazed my stomach in the process, making me wince.

"Let me see," Tom commanded, holding his jaw taut. Cringing, I accepted the clothes and then folded my arms across my stomach. "Addie," Tom scowled, tugging at my wrist. I couldn't hide from him. Exhaling in frustration, I set the clothes down by the sink and let my arms dangle limply at my sides.

Tom scanned the length of my torso, brazenly unfastening each button of my long-sleeved flannel shirt. Plagued by his disarming touch, I kept my eyes down, searching the tile floor desperately. When his fingertips lightly skimmed the space between my breasts, I blushed scarlet. No more than a bra lay beneath my shirt.

"What have they done to you?" Tom released the last button, freely exposing my upper body. I recoiled at the touch of his cool fingers against my ribcage, examining every inch of skin. "I'm taking you to the hospital," he abruptly declared, dragging me towards the door.

"No," I resisted, glaring into Tom's eyes. I pulled my hand from his grasp and stepped back, unwilling to succumb.

"I think you need to see a doctor, Addie." Tom placed his hands on his hips, hovering before me in dramatic fashion. "You could have a cracked rib, for all I know."

"I don't!" I began buttoning my shirt, chastened and exposed. I wasn't a child.

"Just look, Addie," Tom begged. He turned my body towards the mirror, then opened the front of my shirt. I swallowed, feigning indifference. "Look," he pleaded.

My entire stomach was covered in red, swollen bruises, attributed to Hugh's violent temper, no doubt. Tom placed his hands over either side of my ribcage, drawing attention to the most significant bruises, which had already begun to turn dark and blue. They looked as painful as they felt.

"Tom," I breathed, "I'm fine." I didn't want to look at the damage Hugh had done.

"No, you're not!" Tom splayed his hands at my throat, pulling me towards him. "You need to go to the hospital," Tom growled, gritting his teeth. "Let me take you." I hesitated, unable to turn away. "Please," he whined, pressing his forehead to mine.

"No!" I pushed him away long enough to button my shirt.

"Addie," Tom scolded, his hand on my shoulder. I wrapped my arms over my stomach and then turned around to face him. "There are doctors who can help you."

"And what will you tell them, Tom? That I fell off my bicycle? They don't exactly treat bruises like these without asking questions first!" I hated the sharp, acrid bite to my voice. But in the moment, I didn't know of any other way to communicate.

"Please, Addie," Tom badgered, relentless as ever. "Let me call somebody."

"I can't!" I snapped back at him, my blood boiling.

"Why not?" Tom softly spoke, lowering his voice.

"Because if you do, something terrible will happen," I admitted, immediately wondering if I had disclosed too much. Tom pursed his lips together, regarding me quietly.

"I'll let you take a shower," Tom sulked, lingering in the doorway. "Let me know if you need anything," he offered wistfully, before closing the door behind him.

I stood in the bathroom, staring at the place where Tom had been. Couldn't he see that I had no choice in the matter? That my hands were tied?

Moaning in frustration, I quickly undressed, before stepping into the warm, welcoming shower. A wave of steam rushed over me, relaxing every aching muscle, though I knew the sensation wouldn't last. When I turned the water off and stepped out of the shower, exhaustion descended, reaffirming how weak and ragged I felt. I hurriedly wrapped my body in a large blue towel, then stepped towards the mirror.

Struggling to keep my balance, I slipped into a pair of loose athletic pants and tugged at the drawstrings, until the fabric clung tightly to my waist. I felt a shiver crawl up the length of my spine, causing my teeth to shudder. Searching for warmth, I snagged a sleeveless white undershirt from the bathroom counter, as well as a navy blue long-sleeved t-shirt, and pulled both over my head.

My stomach rumbled violently, as I hung my towel up to dry and headed towards the other side of the house. I felt comfortable in Tom's clothes, more relaxed than I had ever been, in fact. Although his sweatpants were much too long for me, I wasn't about to complain. After wading in the Savannah River, with Hugh's hands at my throat, all that I desired most in the world was food, clothing, and shelter.

I found Tom in the kitchen, stirring a pot of soup over the stove. My feet padded across the hardwood floor, as I trudged towards the table in silence. Taking a seat, I exhaled aloud, reveling in the heavenly, mouthwatering aroma that wafted through the air.

Tom noted the sound, turning his head towards me in acknowledgement. He looked different, older somehow, and had yet to say a word. I wondered at the silence. It wasn't like either of us to keep quiet in front of the other.

Clearing his throat, Tom walked over to the table and placed a bowl of soup in front of me, along with a silver spoon and a small package of saltine crackers. Before I could ask, Tom waltzed into the kitchen and filled a glass with water, then swiftly returned to me.

"Tom," I mumbled, catching his eye. "Thank you." Tom stood next to me, lifting the side of his mouth into a crooked smile. I wondered if he knew how much I was *indebted* to him, how much I *appreciated* him, how much I *loved* him.

"Not a problem," Tom replied.

I wanted him to know that I had meant for more than just the meal, but no longer possessed the strength to say so. I felt so tired and knew that my knees would begin to buckle if I stayed awake any longer.

Tom watched me quietly, leaning over the back of the nearest chair. I took a sip of water, noting the way he held his body in a surly, reticent manner, further accentuating the tall, muscular nature of his physique. If I hadn't known Tom, I would have been afraid of him. He looked like a wolf ready to strike, his golden eyes blazing with fury.

Famished, I devoured the soup in minutes, adoring every tomato, carrot, and mushroom that slid down my throat, as well as the red, rich, flavorful broth. The saltine crackers curbed any hunger that remained, though increased my level of thirst. Tom took note, promptly refilling my glass with water. I thanked him with a smile, then gulped the remaining liquid down, in an eager attempt to ease the dry feeling in my throat.

"I'm really tired," I mused, pressing my palms into the table as I rose to my feet. "Really tired," I repeated, feeling shaky. My entire body felt strange, like pieces of wobbly, pliable gelatin that had been sliced into small, square-like chunks. I wanted to lie down and drift off into a dream-like trance, escaping all that had happened.

Sleep would bring comfort and peace, two sentiments that I longed for desperately. Yet, as I treaded across the cool hardwood floor, my thoughts proved distracting. I furrowed my brow in confusion, unable to step forward as I lost my footing and stumbled towards the ground.

Tom lunged forward and latched his arms around my waist, catching me before I had the chance to fall. Drowsy, I closed my eyes, snuggling into Tom's chest. He picked me up in his arms and carried me out of the kitchen, while my feet dangled in the air, slowly swaying from side to side.

Tom gently placed my body on a soft, firm mattress, carefully tucking me in beneath the warm, inviting covers. I lolled my head back on the pillow and yawned, stretching my legs out like a sluggish housecat. Dozing off, I heard the bedroom door shut and rolled onto my side, hardly noticing when the weight of the mattress shifted beneath me.

"I'm staying in here with you," Tom whispered, his breath tickling my ear. I opened my eyes to find him lying beside me in the bed, close enough to touch.

Smiling, I leaned towards Tom and rested my head on his chest, listening to the strong, steady sound of his heartbeat. He wrapped his arm around my waist, careful not to touch my bruised torso.

"Okay," I murmured, relaxing in his embrace.

I had never felt more relieved.

Chapter 37

On Sunday morning, I woke to an empty bed, though the space where Tom had slept remained warm. My head hurt and my ribs ached, compelling me to search through the house until I had found Tom and a bottle of aspirin. We ate breakfast together in quiet solitude, neither of us willing to reiterate the events of the previous evening.

Tom loaded the dishwasher, thoroughly cleaning the kitchen countertop before redirecting his attention to me. Had Tom grown up like this? Always taking care of Daniel?

"I don't understand," Tom started, gazing at me from across the room. I rose from the table and joined him in front of the kitchen sink. Tom looked exhausted, his eyes swollen and bloodshot. I wondered if he had slept at all last night.

"What do you mean?" I stepped in front of Tom, while he crossed his arms over his chest, pressing his back into the edge of the countertop. Tom's eyes drifted downward, eventually settling on my waistline. I tilted my head to the side, perplexed by his behavior.

"If DeMilo is your grandfather, then how could he do this?" Tom took my hands in his, then flipped them both over, so that each palm was facing up. I bit my lip, not knowing how to respond when Tom pressed his thumb against my wrist, tracing the visible marks that Hugh's rope had left behind.

"I don't know, Tom." I recoiled, pulling my hands away from him. "I don't know."

"Didn't you tell him that you were Josette's daughter?" Tom searched my face, desperate for answers that I couldn't give. "You're his flesh and blood, Addie." I kept quiet, averting my gaze to the tile floor. "Doesn't he know?"

"No," I admitted. After last night, I couldn't keep Tom in the dark anymore.

"What? How could he not know?" Tom stared into my eyes, willing me to answer.

"Because he's not my grandfather." I watched the truth take hold, realizing that I had broken my promise to Daniel. Images of Eleanor and Jeffrey came to mind, as I held my head in my hands, wishing that I were still asleep. Hadn't we all lied to each other?

"What?" Tom's face fell, as his lower lip began to twitch. He didn't look happy.

"No," I denied, "he's not." Taking a deep breath, I swallowed before divulging the harshest piece of the truth. "Daniel is." I couldn't have been more abrupt.

Tom's burning gaze felt like fire on my skin. Once again, I was plagued by Daniel's words: *Sometimes, he doesn't handle things very well.* I cringed at the thought, pondering whether or not there would have been a better way to tell him.

"What did you just say?" Tom stepped forward, leaning towards me.

"Daniel is my grandfather," I clarified. "DeMilo was never married to Antoinette. Daniel was." I felt cold all of a sudden, terrified that I had just created an irreparable rift between Tom and Daniel. "He is Josette's father," I paused, feeling detached from my own voice, as if these words were coming out of someone else's mouth. "My grandfather."

Tom widened his eyes, obviously understanding that I was being honest. I wanted to cry, because I knew that Tom would withdraw from me. It was the way he dealt with pain.

"Does that mean that we're...?" Tom held his hand in the air, wildly gesturing between our two bodies. All the color drained from his face, as he waited for an answer.

"No," I reassured him, jerking my head from side to side. "We're not related."

"I don't understand what you're saying, Addie." Tom took a step back, distancing himself from me. "Daniel is my grandfather too." I leaned forward, but my desire to be near Tom only made him retreat further. "You must know what that means."

Sighing, I gazed at the face of the man I loved, though he didn't know it. Tom looked like a boy when he felt alienated. I resented myself for making him feel that way.

"Daniel is your godfather," I graciously confessed. Tom deserved an explanation. "He was friends with your parents, and he adopted you when they died." Tom turned his head away, not letting me see the reaction on his face. "But Daniel does love you, Tom," I continued, placing my hand over the stiff muscle in his arm. "Like a son."

"How long have you known about this?" Tom pulled away, though his eyes remained steadily fixed on my face. He was watching me, judging me.

"Not long," I replied, bracing myself for his reaction.

"I can't believe this!" Tom shouted. I stiffened at

the sound of his angry voice. "How could you not tell me about this? How could Grandpa-" Tom cut himself off, realizing that he had been deceived by the man he loved most.

"Daniel hadn't thought of the right way to tell you yet," I offered, feeling as if I were reciting the next line in a play. When Tom wouldn't respond, I added more dialogue.

"The only reason I didn't tell you is because Daniel made me promise not to," I blubbered, sounding like a child. Tom clenched his jaw decisively. I knew that it was over.

"How can I trust you?" Tom accused, glowering at my very presence. I felt him slipping away, even as he stood before me.

"Tom," I breathed, pressing my hand to the side of his face.

"Either of you?" Tom pushed my hand away, then fled the room, leaving me alone in the kitchen. My body jolted when he slammed the front door. I didn't know what to do.

Sauntering through the house, I stopped by Daniel's bedroom and let myself inside. Daniel lay awake in bed. I wondered if our argument had disturbed him.

"Addie," Daniel beckoned, extending his hand towards me. "Has the world ended?" I smiled and sat down on the edge of Daniel's bed, taking his hand in mine.

"Tom and I had a fight." Daniel's palm felt warm and wrinkled. I noticed that his hands weren't shaking, but the calm was disheartening. Something was wrong.

"Oh, I see," Daniel exhaled, turning his gaze to the ceiling. "Tom won't stay mad at you for long," he assured me, squeezing my hand with his. I wasn't so certain.

"How do you know?" I leaned over Daniel's bed, digging my elbows into the mattress. When Daniel spoke again, I listened, hanging on his every word.

"Because he loves you." Daniel twisted his mouth into a playful smirk. I tilted my head to the side, feeling my cheeks blush scarlet. Bright, glowing warmth rippled through me, as I failed to repress a face-splitting grin. It felt so good to hear those words.

"How do you know? Did Tom-?"

"Tom doesn't have to tell me," Daniel interrupted. I held my breath, longing for an explanation. Daniel lifted his hand to my cheek, then murmured, "I just know."

Hesitating, I looked down at the mattress before me, pondering carefully. The confession that I was about to make could not be taken back.

"I love him too." I smiled at the sound of my own voice. It was the most honest form of liberation that I had ever experienced... admitting that I was in love with Tom.

"Go look in my closet," Daniel advised, curtly changing the subject. I fluttered my eyelashes in confusion, studying the expression on Daniel's face. "Go on." He nudged my shoulder, further piquing my interest.

Rising from the bed, I walked towards the closet in anticipation and opened the door. Clothing racks lined either wall, complete with flannel shirts and pleated pants. I found the light switch by a collection of smooth silk ties along the wall and flipped it on.

A wooden easel sat in the middle of the closet with a blank canvas in tow, eagerly awaiting a painter's touch. I turned back to Daniel and shook my head in surprise.

"Tom picked that out for you last week." Daniel raised his eyebrows, enjoying my reaction. "You can use my palette and brushes to get started." When I hesitated, Daniel's mouth turned into a downward arch. "Didn't you want to learn how to paint?"

"Yes, I do." Daniel shrugged his shoulders, imploring me to explain. "It's just that," I paused, lingering near the foot of Daniel's bed. "My parents aren't so keen on the idea of me being an artist." I crossed my arms over my chest, then stepped closer to him.

"There's this art program at the institute in Atlanta this summer. I really want to go, but a school administrator's signature is required on the application." Daniel stuck his lower lip out, as if that were no problem. "And let's just say that I'm not Principal Caldwell's favorite student."

"You're a natural-born artist, Addie. You couldn't help it if you tried." Daniel folded his hands together, as his eyes shifted across my face. "Do what you want, Addie. It's your life, and you only get one." Daniel relaxed into the pillow behind his head, though his eyes remained on me.

"How much were the canvas and easel?" I pointed towards the closet. Daniel stilled, as irritation reshaped his face.

"It's a gift, Addie," Daniel grumbled, "from both of us."

"Thank you, Daniel," I said with a smile, reaching over the mattress to give him a hug. Daniel placed his arms at the top of my back and pulled me close. I noted the loose way Daniel held his body. He looked relaxed, too relaxed.

"Can you get my pills? It's time for me to take my medicine," Daniel announced, an edge of desperation to his voice. I had no idea what he was talking about.

"Sure." I pulled out of his embrace, masking my ignorance. "Where are they?"

"Open this drawer over here." Daniel pointed to the nightstand by his bed. I opened the first drawer and fished out an orange translucent bottle of medicine.

"That's them," Daniel acknowledged. "I take two every four hours."

"That seems like a lot," I managed, deftly twisting the cap off the bottle. "I didn't realize you were on a prescription." Daniel's eyes glazed over, revealing his state of fatigue.

"Just had it filled a few days ago," Daniel mentioned, nonchalant as ever.

"Oh," I replied, feigning indifference. I didn't like feeling so out of the loop.

"Dr. Reynolds said that it would help with the symptoms." Daniel picked up the glass of water that sat on a coaster atop the nightstand. "Didn't Tom tell you?"

"No," I curtly responded, shaking two red pills out of the bottle and handing them to Daniel. "He didn't."

Daniel placed the pills on his tongue, comfortably swallowing them with a few mouthfuls of water. I took the glass from Daniel when he was done and returned it to the nightstand, along with the bottle of pills.

"I'll let you rest," I said, turning to walk away.

"How did you hurt your head?" I froze at the sound of Daniel's words, unable to speak. I had forgotten the gash in my forehead, mindlessly standing before him, as if I were unchanged. What else had he discovered?

"Addie," Daniel called, holding onto my arm. Blood rushed to my cheeks, as I grew heated and nervous. I wanted to hide. "Some secrets aren't meant to be shared."

My breathing stalled.

Did Daniel know about what happened last night? I didn't think Tom would have told him, especially after demanding that I keep my mouth shut. These Sutton men loved to keep things from each other.

Daniel released me, then closed his eyes and fell into a calm, tranquil slumber. I left him in peace, gently closing the door behind me, all the while plagued by the uncanny feeling that Daniel knew a great deal more than he was letting on.

Feeling drowsy, I continued down the hallway and walked into the guest bedroom, shutting the door behind me. As I collapsed onto the bed, my racing thoughts diminished. All I wanted to do was sleep.

Beneath the covers, I felt warm, safe, and protected, the exact way Tom made me feel. I closed my eyes with him in mind and drifted off, gladly succumbing to exhaustion.

Chapter 38

I t's a large emerald stone surrounded with small white diamonds. The pendant hangs from a silver chain. You wouldn't mistake it for anything else," DeMilo repeated.

I searched his rough, handsome face, while keeping a close eye on Hugh in the corner. I couldn't believe that I had actually let them into my house, my bedroom, my life. DeMilo sat in the chair by the window, Tom's chair.

"Where do I look for it?" I let my legs dangle off the edge of my bed. I never thought I'd feel so comfortable around them.

"We already searched the whole house," Hugh started, pacing the floor in front of my closet. "It's nowhere obvious, that's for sure." Hugh's piercing blue eyes met mine, sending cool shivers through my body.

"Daniel has hidden the necklace in a place where no one would ever find it, especially someone who's looking for it." DeMilo leaned forward in the chair, his elbows propped up against his knees.

"Then how am I supposed to find it?" I watched DeMilo rise to his feet, then join Hugh by the door. They always left me hanging, with more questions than answers.

"You'll figure something out," DeMilo grinned, bearing his white gleaming teeth.

"What if I can't?" I pressed my palm into the bed sheet, hanging on DeMilo's every word. I felt lost. DeMilo cocked his head to the side and patted Hugh on the back, seamlessly ignoring me. After DeMilo left the room and pulled the door closed behind him, a strange feeling crept through me, alarming my senses. I was alone with Hugh.

My body tensed, anticipating the swelling discomfort in the pit of my stomach. Hugh moved without hesitation, immediately lunging for my throat. His hand had already covered my mouth by the time I started screaming.

"Hey," a silky voice spoke.

I felt someone's hands on my shoulders, shaking me.

"Addie, come on. Wake up."

When I opened my eyes, Tom sat in front of me on the mattress, running his hands through my hair. I cooled down from the horrid nightmare, as my pulse and heartbeat returned to normal. Tom's eyes looked like honey, glistening and golden as ever.

"You're back," I noted, catching my breath. Tom smoothed his fingers along my jawline, tipping my chin up to reach the edge of his thumb. I took a short, shallow breath, eyeing him ardently. Tom had never been more enchanting.

Unable to resist the seductive spell that Tom had cast upon me, I fell limp in his arms, sighing as his face stilled no more than an inch from mine. Tom parted his lips, wantonly gazing from my eyes to my mouth. I felt his breath on my neck, while his fierce, golden eyes traveled the length of my face, searching.

Heated desire coursed through me, nearly tearing me to pieces, until Tom finally leaned forward and brushed his lips against my own. I gladly returned the favor, sacrificing oxygen for the sweet, soul-stirring taste of his mouth. Tom's hands slid along my waistline before moving to the small of my back, where they supported my weakening posture.

I quickly grew breathless, wrapping my hands around the back of Tom's neck to steady myself. Tom planted soft kisses along the length of my jawline, anxiously drifting to the space above my clavicle. I had never felt so alive with longing and passion. A mixture of the two swept through me like wildfire, threatening to disarm me completely.

"You look good in my clothes," Tom mumbled between breaths. I twisted my fingers through his hair, awakened by the touch of his palm beneath the undershirt I was wearing. As Tom's hands splayed across my ribcage, I winced in pain, still tender from the bruising. Tom recoiled immediately, as if I were too fragile to be touched.

"I'm sorry." Tom sat on the edge of the bed, gasping for air.

"No," I begged, "don't stop." I reached out to Tom, placing my hand on his shoulder. "I don't want you to." Tom turned his head towards me, his jaw clenched.

I held Tom's gaze, willing him to touch me. Tom exhaled, painfully lost in thought, before pressing my back into the mattress. I reveled in glorious anticipation, glad that Tom had succumbed. But then he caught me by surprise and pulled the covers over my body, innocently tucking me in. "Not like this," Tom said. I knew the conversation was over.

"I'm sorry I yelled at you," he muttered, while I lay in bed, disappointment present on my face. I watched

Tom knead his hands together in frustration and wondered what it felt like to be touched in that way.

"Tom, I should have told you about Daniel," I confessed. Tom shook his head in exasperation, as if he were angry with himself. I could not take my eyes off him.

"You didn't have to," Tom droned. I gazed at the side of his face, confused. Tom ran a hand through his hair in frustration, before turning his body towards me. "I think I already knew," he continued, his golden eyes solemn. "I think I've known for a while."

I parted my lips to speak, but no words came out. Tom held my gaze, never faltering. I couldn't blink when he stared at me like that. I couldn't breathe.

"It's the way Daniel looks at you," Tom explained.

"How does he look at me?" I sat up in bed, pulling the covers into my lap. Tom mulled over the question, as his mouth set into a hard line. I longed to flatten that line.

"Like he's been waiting," Tom said, regarding me passively. I shifted my eyes to the mattress beneath me, while my mind raced with questions. Did Tom resent me? Had I stolen the role of grandchild, ultimately weakening his relationship with Daniel?

"Everything's been so strange," I reasoned, trying to steer the conversation into neutral territory. "Sometimes, I feel like I don't even know who I am anymore," I paused, studying Tom's handsome, chiseled face, "or where I've come from."

Tom looked me over precariously, his eyes shifting ever so slightly. I leaned my head back to avoid his stern, scrutinizing demeanor. When he opened his mouth again, I was surprised by the words that came out of it.

"Maybe we are perfect for each other," Tom mused, stifling a thin smile.

"What do you mean?" I narrowed my eyes at him, curious. Tom stared at me in silence, deepening my degree of frustration. It was strangely beguiling.

"Who else would understand how I feel but you?" Tom stood up to leave, while I pondered quietly, examining every word he had said. It didn't take long for me to realize how right he was.

Tom and I had both been raised to believe that our family members were just that. I never doubted that Jeffrey and Eleanor were anything less than flesh and blood, until the moment I discovered that they weren't. Now, Tom felt the same way towards Daniel, like he was just as much of a stranger as he was a good liar.

"Tom?" I stopped him on his way to the door.

"Yeah," Tom answered, turning back to me. He looked empty.

"Thank you for the easel and canvas." I smiled. Tom's mouth fell open in surprise. "Daniel showed them to me," I added, merely to clarify. Tom rolled his eyes, then shook his head from side to side. "What?" I wondered.

"How could I not have known?" Tom started, walking back over to the bed. "You and Daniel are the only artists I know." I kept still, unable to respond. Tom placed his hand against the side of my face, while I closed my eyes and sighed, affected by his touch.

"Get some sleep," Tom commanded, abruptly pulling away. He trudged towards the door and then pulled it closed behind him, leaving me angry and alone.

Chapter 39

S ix weeks later, I found myself at a local drugstore, casually perusing an aisle of cough drops and chewing gum. Tom stood in line at the pharmacy, just a few aisles over, ready to pick up Daniel's prescription. Just as I rounded the end of the aisle, a familiar face caught my eye. Nicki Caldwell had just passed through the sliding glass doors.

Cringing in panic, I stepped back, desperate to avoid an undesirable run-in. As I peeked around the corner, Nicki headed towards the makeup department, her blonde cork-screw curls bouncing with every step. Before I could blink, Ricky Travis appeared as well, swiftly following Nicki through the store.

When Nicki firmly planted her feet before a rack of liquid foundation, Ricky whispered something in her ear. She nodded without smiling, then flicked her wrist at him, as if he had just been given permission to stroll through the aisles without her. Ricky shoved his hands into his pockets, regarding her amicably before walking off.

Ready to bolt, I took advantage of the moment and made for the exit. Tom would be done any minute now, and I could wait for him by the car in the parking lot. I felt like a coward, running at the first sight of Nicki Caldwell. But we had nothing nice to say to each other, so what was the point in staying?

"Addie?" Nicki called, stopping me before the

sliding glass doors. The surprise in her voice was as heavy as the dread in mine.

"Hey," I managed, lingering near the exit. Until Tom arrived, I would have to endure the superficial chatter of Principal Caldwell's favorite daughter.

"How are you?" Nicki stepped towards me, clutching her handbag.

"Fine," I curtly replied. "Tom and I were just running a few errands."

"Oh," Nicki squeaked, then moved closer. "Where is he?"

"In the back," I answered. Nicki looked over her shoulder, scanning the store.

"Ricky came with me too," Nicki mentioned with a shy smile. I couldn't understand why she was being so polite, just like the day in the stairwell at school.

"So, are ya'll back together?" I inquired. It seemed like a fair question. Nicki glowered at me, recognizing the tone of disapproval in my voice. I shook my head and sighed. "What are you doing with him, Nicki?"

"I love him," she whined, "and we're right for each other." Nicki looked hopeless and weak, pitifully gazing at me. Where was the girl who had tainted my locker with cherry red lipstick, for the sole purpose of exposing my secret virtue, and then blamed her boyfriend's sister for it?

"Nicki, I know he's hurt you," I paused, recalling her bloody lip, our conversation in the stairwell, and Ricky's encounter with Jane Dorsey, then spoke again, "in more ways than one." I gauged Nicki's evasive response, as her eyes dropped to the floor. Loving Ricky must have been a tangled, toxic nightmare, yet Nicki couldn't stay away.

"You're really lucky, Addie." Nicki scanned the

linoleum beneath her feet.

"Lucky?" I scowled. Nicki obviously knew nothing about my personal life.

"We don't all get to end up with someone like Tom." Nicki weakly shrugged, lifting her eyes to my own. I didn't know whether to be flattered or irate. Did Nicki like Tom? Or had she just banished all hope of finding a guy that wasn't like Ricky?

"Nicki, I've seen what Ricky's like. You don't have to put up with that," I said, trying to make her see reason. But Nicki simply shook her head, as if I didn't understand.

"Everyone has a cross to bear," Nicki claimed, acting more serious than I had ever known her to be. "Ricky is mine." I twisted my face into a sour expression, realizing that Nicki would stay with him no matter what, even if they both went down in flames. For the first time in all the years I had known Nicki, I felt sorry for her.

"Addie?" Ricky approached the two of us, carrying a liter of soda and two bags of popcorn. I coldly regarded him with disdain. Ricky knew how I felt about him.

"Ricky," I nodded, merely for the sake of Southern hospitality.

"Tom?" Nicki practically squealed at the sight of him. Tom rushed to my side, placing an arm over my shoulder. He carried a small plastic bag with the name of the drug store written on the front.

"What's going on?" Tom quickly darted his eyes among the three of us, paying particular attention to Ricky. Nicki and I shared an awkward glance, as the boys glared at one another. If we stayed a minute longer, one of them would throw the first punch.

"We were just leaving," Nicki brusquely replied. "Bye Addie." She tugged at Ricky's sleeve, dragging him towards the opposite side of the store, as far away as possible.

"Bye," I echoed, before they disappeared into a distant aisle.

"What was that all about?" Tom fished his keys out of the front pocket of his jeans, as we passed through the sliding glass doors. I avoided eye contact, still contemplating over all the things that Nicki had just said to me.

"Nothing," I said. Tom had enough to worry about.

Chapter 40

I like this one," Jeanine chirped. She ran her fingers along the hem of a yellow strapless gown, carefully eyeing the fabric. We had been at the mall for hours, on the hunt for a prom dress. I hated shopping, but Jeanine loved it. My chore was her pastime.

"Wanna try it on?" Jeanine batted her thick black lashes.

"Sure," I grumbled, unable to resist rolling my eyes.

"Yay!" Jeanine clapped her hands together in delight, jumping up and down. I extended my hand out for the dress, but Jeanine held her index finger in the air. "Just a few more," she insisted, hurriedly scanning any clothing racks that remained.

"Jeanine, I don't want to be here all day," I protested. Jeanine threw gowns over her shoulder in haste, picking out anything else that she thought I ought to try on. Her fashion sense surely surpassed that of most teenage girls. It was like having my own personal stylist.

"We've already been here all day," Jeanine noted. "Here," she said, nearly knocking me over with the plethora of gowns she had chosen for me. I grasped the bundle of fine fabrics in my arms, careful not to drop anything.

"Thanks," I droned, then wandered towards the dressing room. Jeanine stood on the other side of the door, ready and waiting to critique each gown that I tried on.

"I saw Ricky at the drug store yesterday," I chattered, making small talk while I slipped into the first dress that Jeanine had chosen. It was as comfortable as barbed wire.

"Really?" Jeanine sounded less surprised than I thought she would.

"Yeah," I continued, "and Nicki was with him." I waited for Jeanine to volunteer her opinion. When she didn't, I added, "I guess they're back together."

"Wouldn't be the first time," Jeanine scoffed. I opened the dressing room door to reveal the yellow gown. She shook her head in disapproval, mirroring my own reaction.

"What do you mean?" I shut the door and shrugged out of the dress, more interested in what Jeanine had to say than the next gown I had to try on.

"Nicki and my brother are the epitome of on-again, off-again relationships," Jeanine reported. My ears perked up at her every word. I never knew that Ricky and Nicki had broken up multiple times. What else did Jeanine know?

"But every time they break up, it doesn't last," Jeanine continued, scowling at the thought. "She always goes back to him." I stood in silence, forgetting all the dresses that I had left to try on. Why would Nicki keep going back to Ricky? Did she really love him? Or had he forced her into a situation that ultimately meant she could never leave?

"Hey." Jeanine banged on the dressing room door. "How's it going in there? Don't leave me in suspense." I reached for the next dress in reluctance, then smiled. Jeanine may have been bossy, but at least she was a straight shooter. I wondered who she had gotten that from.

* * *

After trying on five more dresses, my shoulders sank in defeat. The chiffon was too scratchy, the color too bright, the length too short. I didn't like any of the gowns for the same reason that I loathed shopping in the first place. I was unapologetically picky.

"What about this one?" Jeanine grabbed a green satin gown from the return rack and raised her eyebrows in delight. I stood in the entryway to the dressing room, already dressed in my own clothes and ready to leave.

"Fine," I groaned. Jeanine handed me the gown and then closed the door to the dressing room. I scowled in aggravation, tugging my clothes off for the hundredth time today.

"I wish I could go," Jeanine yelled through the door.

"You will," I offered, stepping into the dress.

"Only if my date looks like Leo," she retorted, making me laugh.

"Well, maybe he will," I encouraged.

By the time Jeanine was a junior, I would have already graduated with Tom and left Maple Creek High behind forever. But when the moment arrived, if Jeanine actually managed to snag a DiCaprio look-a-like for prom, I would find a way to be there.

"Well? How does it look?" Jeanine probed. I could feel her impatience seeping through the dressing room door, as I took a moment to decide for myself.

I turned to my side in the full-length mirror, evaluating the soft, silky texture of the formal gown.

The deep green satin draped over my skin in a flattering manner, drawing particular attention to the emerald hue of my eyes. Thick one-inch straps ran parallel to one another, extending from the back of my shoulder blades to the space beneath my collarbone, and then connecting to the gown's sleek, fitted bodice. I blushed at the plunging neckline, where the rich satin fabric dipped into the shape of a V, exposing the length of my sternum. A ribbon of silky, green cloth sat farther down, along my waistline, while the remainder of the luxurious gown skirted outward, skimming the dressing room floor in true, elegant fashion.

"Good," I answered, listening for Jeanine's audible gasp.

"Let me see!" Jeanine busted through the dressing room door the minute I unfastened the lock. Her mouth fell open in awe, as her bright blue eyes widened before me.

"Well? What do you think?" I inquired, pleased that I had rendered her momentarily speechless. Jeanine quickly came out of her reverie, delightfully bouncing from foot to foot like an insatiable child who had just spotted the ice cream man.

"IT'S GORGEOUS!" Jeanine exclaimed, insisting that I turn in full, slow circles to provide her with a panoramic view. "You have to get it, Addie! You just have to!"

"Don't worry. I am," I declared, holding my hand in the air to calm her excited spirits. Turning back to the full-length mirror, I spun around in the dressing room, the green silk fabric cascading beneath me. "Do you think Tom will like it?"

"The question isn't will he like it, Addie," Jeanine

sassed, a hand at her hip.

"Then what is?" I looked over my shoulder and into the glass, noting the sensual, skin-revealing nature of the backless gown. I could have walked the red carpet in this dress.

"When Tom sees you in that dress, what is he going to do to you?" Jeanine winked, curving her lips into a teasing smirk. My cheeks blushed crimson in response.   "Jeanine," I scolded, playfully punching the side of her shoulder.

"What?" Jeanine coaxed, feigning innocence. "Isn't it obvious?"

"Isn't *what* obvious?" I countered, though my tone remained cool.

"How crazy he is about you," Jeanine stressed, turning serious all of a sudden.

"Is that a bad thing?" I raised my eyebrows, confused by her belligerent concern.

"No," Jeanine answered. "But I'd hate to be the person standing in his way." Jeanine moved a fallen strand of hair over my shoulder, then gazed down at my dress again, before turning her blue eyes on me. "There's no telling what Tom would do to him."

I didn't have to ask.

I knew she meant Ricky.

Chapter 41

When I got home that night, I was surprised to find Jeffrey in the kitchen. He stood in front of the stove, nibbling on a piece of burnt toast, still dressed in work clothes. For a brief moment, I wondered where Eleanor was, but then decided that I didn't care. I could never have a real conversation with Jeffrey when she was around anyway.

"You're home," I commented. It was a rare occurrence.

"Yeah." Jeffrey nodded, offering the faintest of smiles. He placed the half-eaten toast on a napkin, then rinsed his hands off in the sink. "What's that you've got there?"

"Prom dress," I gushed, slinging the plastic garment bag over my shoulder.

"Let me see," Jeffrey implored, curious. I pulled the protective covering back and revealed a bit of soft green satin. "It's very nice, Addie," he mentioned, flattering me.

"Thanks," I replied, astonished at Jeffrey's sudden interest in my fashion sense.

"When is that, by the way?" Jeffrey crossed his arms over his chest and pressed his back into the counter. He hadn't been this inquisitive in months.

"In a couple weeks," I vaguely responded, regarding him impassively.

"Are you going with Tom?" Jeffrey asked. His eyes

remained cool, hazel.

"Yeah," I murmured, gnawing at the edge of my lip. What did he want?

"Well," Jeffrey exhaled, darting his eyes to the tile floor. "I'm sure ya'll will have a good time." I narrowed my eyes at him, deep in thought. *Why wouldn't we?*

"Yeah, I think so too," I retorted, growing uneasy.

"Addie, I know that I haven't been the best father," Jeffrey started, catching me off guard. Of all the days that we had lived under the same roof, Jeffrey had chosen this one to have a heart-to-heart with me. I couldn't imagine why.

"Dad," I coaxed, not wanting him to apologize. It was too late for that.

"No, I want to say this," Jeffrey demanded, holding his hand up in the air. "You're mother and I wanted a child for years. And when..." he drifted off, lost in the past. Jeffrey chewed the edge of his thumbnail. I'd never seen him so nervous before.

"After a while," he continued, "your mother gave up on the idea of children, altogether." I found that odd, since Eleanor delivered babies for a living, but gave her the benefit of the doubt, for the time being.

"She threw herself into her work, and so did I." Jeffrey pressed his palms into either side of the countertop behind him. His eyes remained on the tile, scanning, searching.

"And then, one day at the hospital, Eleanor delivered a baby to this sixteen-year-old girl." Jeffrey grimaced in the way one regarded a painful memory. "She was so pale and thin. I think she'd run away from home and didn't know where the baby's father was, or something like that."

I twisted my mouth into a rueful expression. Josette was gone, but at least I knew something about her, at least I knew her name. For my father, I couldn't say the same.

"She decided to give the baby up for adoption." Jeffrey smiled, lifting his face from the floor to look at me. "So we brought you home, so excited to have this child that we had wanted for so long." Jeffrey's face darkened, then turned forbearing.

"But both of us had become so focused on work, wanting so badly to distract ourselves from the fact that we couldn't have a child, that when we finally did, we didn't know what to do," Jeffrey fussed, lifting his hands from the countertop in a range of swift, gestured motions. "I didn't know how to react," he confessed. "And you were so different from Eleanor, not all rigid and domineering," Jeffrey exhaled. "You looked like that girl."

I didn't know how to respond. Jeffrey had just revealed more about my past, about my origin, about my mother, than anyone else ever had before, even Daniel.

"Why are you telling me all of this now?" I inquired, utterly confounded.

"Because you'll have children one day, and I don't want you to make the same mistake," he proclaimed, showing more interest in my future than he ever had before.

Oh *Jeffrey*, I thought to myself. He could be so wholly earnest and kind one minute, then dismissive and abrupt the next. How long had he been like this?

"Do you know what happened to her? To my mother? Josette, right?" I stared into Jeffrey's eyes, realizing that the levee had broken. Now was the time to ask questions.

"Yes, that was her name." Jeffrey nodded. "Are you sure you want to hear this?" His eyes glazed over me, cautious and observant. After seventeen years of being carelessly tossed aside, I finally had his undivided attention.

"Tell me," I demanded, keeping steady eye contact with Jeffrey. He took a deep breath, bracing himself, then shrugged his shoulders and began.

"A couple months after you were born, we got a phone call from the hospital." Jeffrey pressed his lips together, momentarily hesitating. "Your mother and I didn't know it at the time, but Josette had been living on the streets," he paused, then clarified, "homeless, essentially." Jeffrey took a step towards me. I didn't like where this was headed.

"Someone found Josette on the side of the road and took her to the hospital. She had pneumonia." Jeffrey moved even closer and rested his hands on my shoulders. "We promised Josette that we would bring you by the hospital once she got well, so she could see you again," Jeffrey coaxed. "But when we came back a few days later, she had died."

I pushed Jeffrey away from me and turned my back to him, sauntering towards the kitchen table. Tears rolled down my face like morning dew, calming me, saturating me.

I longed for Josette, Antoinette, and all of the other Beaumont women in my hidden ancestral line. All I could feel was the pain that rippled through me in waves of mournful sorrow. How could something I had never known hurt so terribly?

I wanted my mother.

I wanted my father.

I wanted my grandmother.

I wanted Daniel.

"Your mother never forgave herself for not letting Josette see you one last time," Jeffrey said, wakening me from my tortuous daydream. "That's why her name is still on your birth certificate," he admitted. "Neither one of us could bring ourselves to change it."

Silently sobbing, I left my belongings in the kitchen and headed for the front door. I wanted out of the life that had been chosen for me and into the one that I had created.

"Addie," Jeffrey called after me. "I'm sorry. I didn't mean to upset you." He kept at my heels, following me into the foyer. "I just thought you should know the truth."

Shaking my head, I opened the door and walked outside, too detached from these poor, self-absorbing replacements to feel like staying. Jeffrey and Eleanor had nothing to offer me but neglect and credit cards. I had never felt any deep emotion, any strong bond to either of them. And if they could leave without any notice, then I could too.

I belonged on Sutton territory, because I was a Sutton myself.

* * *

I knocked on Daniel's front door with tears in my eyes, longing for my own blood, or what remained of it. Tom opened the door and pulled me across the threshold, swiftly closing the door behind him. I fell into his arms, rested my head on his chest, and sighed. If I could count on anything in this world, it was that Tom was always warm.

"What's wrong?" Tom pressed his hand against

my cheek and wiped my tears away. I gazed into his eyes, so pure that they glistened like honey, grateful that I had a man like this, a man who listened.

"I want Daniel," I whimpered, embarrassed for sounding like a child.

"Okay," Tom answered. He tucked a strand of fallen hair behind my ear, his hand lingering near my throat, then took my hand in his and led me through the house, until we reached Daniel's bedroom door.

"Tom," I whispered, feeling fragile. "I'd like to talk to him alone."

Tom stepped back and pulled his hand loose from mine. I exhaled, not wanting to hurt him. He had been through enough already. But I had to do things my own way, and right now, I needed the only flesh and blood that remained to be with me, and only me.

"Okay," Tom said, echoing his earlier approval. I pulled his face towards mine and placed a soft, gentle kiss on his lips. Tom sighed, slowly tugging out of my embrace, then turned away from me with a nod, understanding.

When I entered Daniel's room, a strange calm fell over me. I wasn't used to feeling like I belonged. But Daniel smiled at me like I had been gone for many years and had just returned to offer gifts from my foreign travels.

I stepped towards Daniel and sat on the edge of his bed, taking his hand in mine. He had aged in the short time that I had known him, his face more gaunt, and the lines of stress beneath his eyes more pronounced. But Daniel felt calmer, like he had finally established peace with the world. I wondered what that felt like.

"Would you like to paint me something else?" Daniel smiled, gazing up at me expectantly. His blue eyes had never been more still, a side effect of the medicine, no doubt.

Overcome with glee, I rushed over to Daniel's closet and opened the door. Several of my paintings lay stacked against the wall. The sight of them filled me with warmth. I pulled out the easel and a blank canvas, as well as a small wooden stool, then set everything up by the window.

"How about a portrait this time?" Daniel suggested, folding his hands over the covers. I returned to the closet to gather brushes and paint, mulling over the idea in my head. With Daniel's help, I had been painting objects and landscapes for weeks, but a portrait?

"Of who?" I wondered, cheerfully waltzing over to the window.

"Me," Daniel suggested, waving a hand over his resting body.

"Okay," I agreed, swiftly rearranging the easel and canvas, and then the wooden stool, so that I was facing Daniel. "I've only *sketched* people before," I commented, feeling ill-qualified. Just because I could draw a face, didn't mean I could paint one.

"Stop being so afraid of it, Addie," Daniel commanded. "Just paint."

And I did, not thinking about Jeffrey or Eleanor, or the fact that I had school in the morning. All traces of anxiety dissipated, soon replaced by blooming, brilliant colors. I gave myself up to that blank piece of canvas, forgetting the entire world around me, until Daniel's blue eyes were centered within it and staring back at me.

Daniel's was the first portrait I had completed of the last remaining member of my family, my flesh, my blood, my life. It wasn't a perfect portrait, and certainly not a great one, but I was always glad that I had taken the time to do it.

Chapter 42

The day before prom, I sat in the den at Daniel's house, working on homework with Tom. For a Friday afternoon, we had gotten more studying accomplished than most students did in an entire week. While I made good grades for the sake of securing an acceptance letter into a great university, Tom did so for no particular reason at all.

I studied because I *had* to. Tom studied because he *wanted* to.

"Are you okay?" Tom asked, disrupting my daydream.

"Yeah." I nodded without smiling, then stared into the dark, empty fireplace before us and began chewing at the end of my pen cap. Recently, I had grown frantic, anxious, and paranoid. I couldn't sleep anymore and knew that it showed. My sixty days were about to run out, and I had yet to find the necklace.

"You've been acting strange all week," Tom complained, flipping to the next page of the open textbook before him. "What's up?" Tom lay on his stomach, with a palm to his head, as his elbow dug into the carpet. He looked like a grown man, too ruggedly handsome in his thin white t-shirt and relaxed blue jeans to be no more than sixteen.

When Tom set those golden eyes on me, I quickly looked away, wishing I could tell him everything, wishing I didn't have to, wishing he already knew.

"Nothing," I droned, "just trying to memorize all these formulas." I gestured to the spiral notebook on the carpet in front of me, hearing the weak, anxious sound of my own voice.

"Uh-huh," Tom mumbled, doubting my every word.

"What?" I exhaled, jerking my head in his direction. I didn't appreciate being questioned, as Tom stared into my eyes, never relenting.

"Why won't you tell me what's wrong?" Tom persisted, badgering me.

"Nothing's wrong, Tom." I shook my head and sighed, "I'm fine."

"No, you're not," he insisted, utterly unconvinced. I groaned, running a hand through my hair in frustration. "Addie," Tom pleaded, placing his hand on my knee. "You know that you can tell me anything."

"Yeah, I know," I breathed, then shifted my eyes to the carpet beneath me.

"So just tell me then," Tom goaded, trying to back me into a corner.

"There's nothing to tell." I placed the pen back in my mouth and chewed.

"It's not like you to lie to me, Addie." Tom glowered in my direction, then ripped the pen out of my mouth when I ignored him.

"I'm not lying!" I yelled, feeling red hot blood rush to the surface of my skin and color my cheeks. "What is wrong with you?"

"Nothing's wrong with me!" Tom snapped back. "What? I'm not allowed to worry about my girlfriend? After everything that's happened, I think I have every reason to."

"I don't want you to worry about me, Tom!" I countered, my blood boiling. I couldn't tell Tom the truth and risk not keeping Daniel alive. Couldn't he see that?

"Well, I'm not going to stop," he hissed, practically growling at me.

"Why not?" I griped.

"Because I love you!" Tom shouted, startling me. I hadn't expected him to say that. He caught his breath, then looked me over carefully, contemplating. When I failed to respond, Tom stood up and flung the pen across the room. It skirted the carpet before landing in the fireplace. "Don't worry," he muttered. "You don't have to say it back."

My eyes followed Tom's figure as he stormed off, leaving me alone in the den. Tears brimmed along the corners of my eyes. I felt so confused, so lost, so stuck. Tom's footsteps sounded in the distance, as I dried my eyes, still plagued by anger and sadness.

"I'm going into town," Tom announced. "I need to mail some things for Grandpa."

I turned my head towards Tom, looking up at him from where I sat on the floor.

"Tom, I-"

"It's okay," he interrupted, silencing me with the quickest flick of his wrist. "You're not ready to say it," Tom paused, his honey-colored eyes glistening like glowing amber. "I understand," he continued. "But one day you will be."

And with that, Tom turned on his heel, out the door, and into the daylight. I listened for the sound of him driving away, then went to Daniel's room and opened the door, sneaking a peek through the crack. Daniel slept soundlessly, apart from the occasional sound of his breathing. It was as if he hadn't heard us at all. Gently pulling the door closed, I took advantage of the moment and headed upstairs.

Since the night DeMilo and Hugh took me to the river, I had been able to search Daniel's house no more than a handful of times, when Tom had either been in the shower or fallen asleep while we were watching TV. On those rare occasions, I had managed to explore every room in the house with ease, apart from Daniel's and Tom's.

I couldn't risk waking Daniel, even though he was such a heavy sleeper, and doubted that I would have much success with him in the room anyway. But with Tom gone to the post office and many miles away, I finally had the opportunity to rifle through his room unchecked.

At the top of the staircase, I walked down the hallway and stopped in front of Tom's bedroom door. For a moment, I hesitated, regretting the fact that I was about to invade Tom's privacy and betray him in a way that I never had before. But I had Daniel's life to consider, so I let myself into the room anyway and left my inhibitions at the door.

Moving quickly, I stepped towards Tom's dresser and opened each drawer without allowing myself the time to think about what I was doing. Before I knew it, I had sifted through his t-shirts, jeans, sweatpants, and socks. My entire body froze once I reached his underwear drawer, spotting several pairs of neatly folded boxers.

I took a deep breath and thought, *this is so wrong*.

But I had to do it.

Exhaling, I shut all of the dresser drawers and sauntered over to the closet, where I found nothing but jackets on hangers and racks of shoes and belts. After searching the space more thoroughly, I groaned in frustration and shut the closet doors. Would I ever find this necklace?

I walked towards Tom's desk with a feeling of dread and sat down in his chair, as if it were my own. In the top drawer, I found a small notebook and scattered pieces of paper, full of notes, lyrics, and prose. Even though I longed to read every single word, the necklace preceded all else, so I tossed everything aside and kept on hunting.

"Addie?" I looked up to find Tom in the doorway, with a stack of envelopes in his hand. He didn't move.

"I was just," I cut myself off, gazing down at the desk as I searched for an excuse. "Looking for some paper," I breathed. "I ran out."

Tom narrowed his eyes at me, considering the lie, then came closer and set the envelopes down on the desk. I felt my pulse quicken, as Tom placed his hand at the back of his chair and leaned over me, in order to open the only desk drawer that I had yet to look through. While Tom collected a few sheets of notebook paper, I sat back in the chair, disarmed by the closeness of his body to mine.

"Here," Tom said, briefly touching my hand, as I took the paper from him.

"Thanks." I held his gaze, overcome by a subtle, electric sensation that left me without breath. "What happened?" I inquired, wondering why he had come back.

"I forgot the stamps." Tom smoldered, silently gazing over me.

"Oh," I whispered, unnerved by the look in his eyes. If I weren't sitting down, I surely would have toppled over, with my knees growing weaker every second.

Tom leaned back, against the edge of the desk, keeping a close distance between us. I spotted a booklet of stamps in the open drawer, but when Tom continued to watch me, without any intention of taking them, I spoke up.

"Tom, just because I haven't told you how I feel, doesn't mean I don't-"

Before I could finish, Tom planted his mouth against mine, pulling my face towards his own as I braced myself for the unnerving, electric sensation that would surely be the death of me. I weaved my fingers through his hair and kissed him back, reveling in the touch of his soft, gentle lips.

"I should go mail these," Tom panted between breaths. I locked my hands at the nape of his neck, not minding when the stubble of his five o'clock shadow tickled my chin.

"Or you could do it later," I suggested, tugging at his shirt sleeve. Without warning, Tom abruptly pulled away and bit the edge of his bottom lip. I looked up at him expectantly, while he sat down on the desk, batting his hands against the wood.

"You're very distracting," Tom sneered, a crooked smile on his face. It was times such as these, that he looked too beautiful to be real.

"And you aren't?" I countered. Tom looked sultry, yet guarded, carefully folding his arms across his chest. When he turned his head, observing the open desk drawer that I had rifled through, I felt a wave of uneasiness return.

"What were you really doing in here, Addie?" Tom scanned the length of my face, then stared into my eyes the way a cop would before interrogating a criminal.

"I told you," I sighed, "I was just looking for more paper. I ran out."

"Addie." Tom smiled, patronizing me. "You have a notebook downstairs with plenty of empty pages." His golden eyes burned with suspicion and disbelief.

I lowered my eyes like a disobedient child, who had just been caught with her hand in the cookie jar. *Tom would make a great lawyer*, I thought to myself, because that's what Jeffrey would have said, had he been there.

"Addie, I don't mind you being in my room," Tom stated. "I trust you."

That surprised me. If the roles were reversed, and I had found Tom in my room, ransacking my desk drawers, would I have been able to say the same?

"But I still want to know why you're in here." Tom eyed me austerely.

I felt cold all of a sudden, placing my hands over my arms to warm myself. I couldn't relax when Tom refused to take his eyes off mine. Didn't he need to blink?

"I was just..." I faded out, seamlessly paralyzed by Tom's honey-colored eyes, until I garnered enough courage to say the word, "curious."

"You were just *curious*?" Tom questioned, throwing the word back in my face.

"Yeah." I nodded. "Just *curious*." I added emphasis at the end, just as he had.

"Well," Tom grunted, clearing his throat. "Now I guess I am too."

Chapter 43

On Saturday night, I found myself in the guest room at Daniel's house, getting ready for prom. Everything seemed out of place, and when the sun went down, I felt a deep wave of nausea fill my stomach. I only had three days left until DeMilo would come to collect.

Standing in front of the closet mirror, I took a deep breath and looked at myself.

The green satin gown draped over my skin like royal silk, inviting me to feel of its soft, glossy texture. I held my arms across my chest, turned in front of the mirror, and sighed.

My hair fell in long, golden waves past my shoulders, drawing further attention to my bare, naked back. I looked thinner, weaker, and younger than I ever had before. Regardless, I couldn't help thinking that I was the same girl. I wondered if Antoinette had ever felt the same, hopelessly devoid of choices. Perhaps it was the Tony DeMilo effect.

Lifting my chin in scrutiny, I studied the subtle touches of makeup on my face. A thin layer of foundation added more color to my complexion than I had proffered in days, while the slightest strokes of blush and eye shadow created a healthy, balanced tone.

Cosmetics worked well that way, masking the deepest sentiments by embellishing the ones that looked better on the surface. No one would question the synthetic nature of my smiles tonight, because the students at Maple Creek High were equally familiar with disguising the truth. We were a deceptive lot, every last one of us.

I left the guest bedroom and walked down the hall in a pair of strappy, silver heels, not minding the clicking noise that sounded with every step. When I entered the den, Tom stood before the empty fireplace, with one hand in his pocket and the other on the mantle. I glided towards him, reveling in the way the soft satin moved over my legs.

"Wow," Tom inhaled. "You look beautiful, Addie."

I smiled without showing any teeth, though could not help blushing when Tom took my hand in his and knotted our fingers together, his eyes shining like pure honey.

"And you look mighty handsome," I replied, fluttering my lashes at Tom.

Dressed in black tie, Tom looked like Hollywood royalty, with his strong jawline and chiseled cheekbones. I noted the black tuxedo, bow tie, cummerbund, and dress shoes. Tom couldn't have looked more perfect if I had drawn him myself.

"I'm sorry about yesterday," he began, gently shaking his head. Tom looked down, then shifted his eyes to me, revealing the doubtful, lamenting nature of his thoughts.

"I shouldn't have been in your room," I admitted, prepared to accept the blame.

"You can go in there whenever you like." Tom took my face in his hands and brushed his lips against my forehead. It was such a sweet, innocent gesture, yet

I felt nothing more than guilt, because I was the one with the intent to deceive.

"Grandpa wanted to see you before we left." Tom beamed. I nodded as he pulled me towards the hallway and into the bedroom, where Daniel was waiting.

"Addie," Daniel began, holding his hand out for me to take. Smiling, I sat down on the edge of his bed and clasped his rough, wrinkled hand. Tom lingered in the doorway, with his arm against the frame. He looked like an angel, watching over us from where he stood.

"You look beautiful," Daniel began, echoing Tom's earlier compliment. "Your eyes have never been more green." When Daniel's expression faltered, I knew that his thoughts had drifted to Antoinette. Looking at me must have been painful. How could he bear it?

"I'd like to show you something," Daniel announced, hardly giving me time to react. "Go into my closet and look for a black photo album on one of the shelves," he softly directed, "then bring it in here."

I rose from the bed and exchanged a look with Tom, then opened the closet door and walked inside. After switching the light on, I scanned the wooden shelves above me, soon spotting the photo album between an old transistor radio and a stack of quilts.

"Is this it?" I walked into the doorway of the closet and held the album up for Daniel to see. When he nodded, I turned the light off and closed the door behind me. Returning to the bed, I sat down and handed the album to Daniel.

"Could you get my reading glasses?" he asked, though his focus remained on the photo album. His fingers slowly trembled above the worn, dust-laden cover.

"Sure," I answered, taking Daniel's glasses from the nightstand and handing them to him. "Here you go." Daniel slowly grasped the pair of glasses and slipped them over his eyes, then glanced down at the photo album in silence.

"For a long time, I couldn't look at these pictures and have her staring back at me with those eyes." Daniel looked at me, lifting his brow in admission. "But she would have wanted you to have this, and so do I."

Daniel offered the photo album to me, but I couldn't accept it. When I opened my mouth to speak, and hesitated instead, Daniel intervened. "It's all right. I have other pictures of her. And you never got the chance to know her, as I did."

"Daniel, I don't know what to say." I took the album from him and peeled the cover back, gazing at pictures from Antoinette and Daniel's high school days.

"She would have wanted you to have them, Addie," Daniel repeated.

Tom came over and sat down beside me on the bed, as we flipped through the album together. Each photograph had been sealed in a plastic sleeve, chronicling everything from their courtship, wedding, marriage, and beyond. There were baby pictures of Josette and Wesley, growing up beneath the summer sun, and then there were just pictures of Josette.

"That was the last picture taken of Antoinette." Daniel pointed to a photo of her on the beach, with Wesley and Josette playing beside her in the sand, both still just toddlers.

"Daniel, I'm so sorry. You should have had more time together with all of them," I sympathized, slowly understanding how precious my time with Tom was, since Daniel and Antoinette had been given no more than a few years.

"There's a really good picture of her from our wedding in the back," Daniel said.

Curious, I flipped to the end of the album to find Antoinette young, beautiful, and in love, her face like a radiant starlet's. She stood before the wedding cake with an enormous grin on her face, presumably waiting for Daniel to enter the frame.

"Wait a minute," I said, eyeing Antoinette's wedding dress. "That's the same dress from the portrait." I pointed at Antoinette in the white gown.

"Yes," Daniel faintly acknowledged.

"I had no idea that it was her wedding dress." I shook my head, gawking at the image. "I'm so sorry, Daniel," I whispered, nearly on the verge of tears. I couldn't help longing for the family that we had lost, because they didn't feel gone, not Antoinette, or Josette, or Wesley. They just felt out of reach.

"Don't be," Daniel softly murmured. "She gave me you."

"You look a lot like her there," Tom added. I glanced up and looked into his eyes, as he placed his hand against the side of my face.

Tom had every right to be jealous, but he wasn't.

Tom had every right to feel surpassed, but he didn't.

Tom had every right to resent me, but he hadn't.

Despite the most unusual circumstances and a slew of misfortunes, Tom loved me.

All of the eccentricities that should have deterred

him from me, that should have kept us apart from the beginning, had only brought us closer together. Reality had become an eerie, twisted mess that felt so unlike the life I had known before. But within the arms of the man I loved, I had never felt more alive.

"We should probably get going," Tom pressed, tugging at my elbow.

"Yeah," I sighed, because deep down, I wanted to stay. "You're right."

I flipped the final page over in reluctance, placing my hand at the back of the cover to close the album. But then, the faintest glimmer caught my eye, and I stopped to take a second look. Widening my eyes in disbelief, I gasped, unable to breathe. Within the plastic sleeve, on the other side of Antoinette's wedding picture, was her emerald necklace.

Chapter 44

For the longest time, no one said a word. Tom and I sat beside each other on the bed, too stunned to speak, while Daniel looked on, smiling. And all the while, that emerald necklace lay among the three of us, slightly obscured beneath the plastic photo sleeve, like some forgotten treasure that had been discovered by chance. Only the twinkle in Daniel's eye made me believe otherwise.

I gazed at Tom, then placed my palm over his hand, noting the rise and fall of his chest. He looked just as terrified as I was. Antoinette's necklace held more power than either of us could have imagined, though we did not know it. And yet, all I could think about was Tony DeMilo and the way he had wickedly grinned down at me, when Hugh had pinned me to the bathroom floor with a damp handkerchief over my mouth.

"Don't you want to try it on?" Daniel questioned, as though my silence had offended him. "I thought you might want to wear Antoinette's necklace tonight," he explained, "especially since you're wearing that dress."

Daniel gestured towards my silky green gown and nodded, assuring me of his approval. For the first time, he looked less vulnerable. I didn't know why.

"Isn't that dangerous?" I breathed, forcing myself to swallow.

"No," Daniel said. "Why?" He found the idea to be ludicrous.

"What about DeMilo?" I held Daniel's gaze, unable to rid myself of the cold, uneasy feeling that crept along my spine. When Tom exhaled, I flinched, still on edge.

"Addie," Daniel sighed. "Aren't you even going to look at it?"

Cringing, I darted my eyes at the sparkling emerald stone that lay beyond the plastic. I couldn't believe that the necklace I had been perpetually searching for was the same one that I was looking at now. The irony was not lost on me, because I finally had what DeMilo wanted most in this world, and I knew how to give it to him.

"Go on, Addie," Daniel commanded, growing impatient.

I slipped my fingers beneath the plastic sleeve and tugged at the silver chain, until the necklace spilled out, onto the bed. Cradling the necklace within the palm of my hand, I rubbed my thumb over the emerald stone, and then traced the surrounding white diamonds with my index finger. Of all the ways I could have found Antoinette's necklace, I had never imagined it to be like this.

"You've kept it here, at the back of a photo album, this whole time?" I lifted my eyes to Daniel, weighing the heavy, precious gem in my hand. Tom remained unmoved.

"It's the last place anyone would think to look," Daniel said. "Try it on."

Swallowing, I mulled the idea over carefully in my head, and then looked at Tom. We shared a brief, meaningful glance, as I parted my lips to speak. But then Tom lowered his gaze, and I closed my mouth. Words weren't necessary.

Tom cocked his head to the side, curiously evaluating the emerald. He placed his hand at the back of mine and turned it over, so that the necklace fell into his other open palm. Tugging at my wrist, Tom rose from the bed and pulled me across the floor, until I was standing in front of the mirror above Daniel's dresser.

I kept still, my heart pounding as Tom placed the stone against my sternum. The emerald felt cold, rigid, and heavy, though I did not show it. Tom's fingers traced the outline of the silver chain, where it lay along my throat and clavicle, before fastening the clasp at the back of my neck. Quickly inhaling, I felt my pulse quicken when Tom placed his hands over my bare shoulders, then withdrew them with the slightest caress.

"Well," Daniel prodded. "What do you think?"

I looked in the mirror and twisted my mouth into an ambivalent expression.

"I can't wear this. It's too much," I admitted, holding the emerald in my hand.

"Why? Don't you like it?" Daniel frowned.

"I love it," I replied, eyeing his reflection in the mirror. "It's perfect in every way."

"Then what's wrong?" Daniel chuckled, finding my distress amusing.

"It's too valuable to wear in public," I reasoned, turning around to face Daniel. "That would be like carrying a hundred pounds of gold in my purse."

"That necklace is worth a lot more than a hundred pounds of gold," Daniel noted, clearly dissatisfied with my inaccurate approximation of Antoinette's jewelry.

"Exactly!" I countered, placing my hands on my hips in self-satisfaction.

Daniel exhaled in frustration, considering. He could see that I was right.

I raised my brow at him, pleased to have won the argument, while Tom threw his hands up in the air, not wanting to get involved. Just as I thought that I had rendered Daniel speechless, his lips curved into a clever, unwarranted smile

"Then don't show if off," he remarked, leaving me baffled.

Understanding Daniel, Tom grasped my shoulders and turned me towards the mirror, then toyed with the silver chain around my neck. Before I could question Tom, his hands traveled to my collar bone. He pulled the front of Antoinette's necklace forward and loosened the chain, until the emerald stone slipped into the bodice of my gown. It was carefully concealed beneath the green satin. Only the top part of the chain, sans pendant, remained visible.

Tom stepped back, shoving his hands into his pockets, as I searched his eyes, blazing and golden. I remained speechless, unable to move, though Tom kept his cool, appearing less affected. As I held Tom's gaze, I couldn't help thinking, *did he just do that?*

"If the two of you don't leave soon, ya'll are going to be late," Daniel barked.

Tom took my hand in his and led me towards the door. I smiled, reveling in the touch of his skin against mine. A foreign, giddy feeling coursed through me, because I was about to go to prom with Tom Sutton. I had never felt so lucky. Maybe Nicki was right.

"Drive safe," Daniel ordered, eyeing Tom ardently.

"I will," Tom replied. He let go of my hand and walked towards Daniel, leaning over the mattress to give him a hug good-bye. Once Tom pulled away, I sat down on the bed and warmly embraced Daniel, before kissing him on the cheek.

"You kids be careful," Daniel said, patting the back of my hand.

"We will," I giggled, amused by his parent-like concern. Rising from the bed, I reached for Tom's hand and smiled. His expression mirrored my own.

"And Addie?" Daniel called, stopping us near the doorway.

"Yes?" I turned around at the sound of his voice.

"Guard your heart."

Chapter 45

T om held the car door open for me, then took my hand and helped me out as any true gentleman would. As he shut the door, I gazed down at the white corsage around my wrist. Deep down, I knew that they didn't make men like this anymore, because Tom always did what he was supposed to do.

"Ready?" he asked, tightly grasping my hand with his.

"Yeah." I nodded, nearly out of breath. I wasn't used to feeling this excited.

"Okay, let's go," he declared, just as eager as I was.

Tom and I walked across the parking lot, until we reached a set of heavy glass doors that led us into the main lobby of the hotel. On our way to the ballroom, I briefly recalled the last time I had been here, the night I had first met Jeanine, and then later dreamed of Tom. Only, it hadn't been a dream, though Tom had yet to explain how.

When we entered the ballroom, Tom pulled me towards the crowded dancefloor, all too happy to have arrived at the beginning of a slow song. As couples retreated towards the punch table, Tom found a spot at the center of the dancefloor, beneath an elaborate crystal chandelier.

I quickly scanned my surroundings, noting the DJ onstage before us, mindlessly bobbing his head to the soft, swaying rhythm of the music. A large white banner hung over the stage, bearing the words, *Maple Creek High*. Beyond the dance floor, a slew of round tables provided seating for those who would rather watch instead.

Tom wrapped his hands around my waist and pulled my body towards him. Blushing, I lifted my hands to the back of Tom's neck, unable to deny the pulse of my beating heart, against Antoinette's emerald stone. Tom grinned, sensing the effect he had on me, though his intentions, as always, seemed to be nothing less than honorable.

"You never told me about that dream," I murmured, gazing up at him.

"What dream?" Tom smirked. His eyes looked darker in the dim light.

"The one that you said I never had," I accused, jerking my chin at him.

"Addie," Tom exhaled, briefly glancing away.

"I need to know what happened that night," I goaded. My hands moved to either side of Tom's face, forcing him to look me in the eye. "I need to know why I can't remember." Tom glowered down at me, his expression turning into a beautiful smolder.

"Not here," he coaxed, though his chin remained taut. "I'll tell you after the dance, on the way home. Okay?" Tom promised, despite the distant fear in his eyes.

I nodded, content for the time being, then took a shallow breath of oxygen.

"Come here," Tom sweetly said, sensing my anxiety.

His fingers trailed the bare skin of my back, sending tingles down my spine. He pulled me into an intimate embrace, and then rested his chin on my shoulder. Sighing, I buried my face in Tom's chest and inhaled, finding comfort in the smell of his cologne. In that moment, I knew that I had never trusted anyone so implicitly.

"I have a surprise for you," Tom whispered, his warm breath caressing my ear.

Overcome with elation, I lifted my face from his chest and smiled. Before Tom could speak again, I leaned in and molded my mouth to his, not caring who might see. I felt a smile on his lips, as Tom returned the favor, eagerly anticipating every kiss to come.

Careless, I lost myself in his touch, tracing patterns across his lean, muscular back, feeling of the separation between his shoulder blades. Between breaths, I held my parted lips before Tom's and gasped, "I love you."

Tom froze in place, his jaw dropping in one swift motion.

I bit the edge of my lip, enjoying his beautifully astonished face; it was a rarity.

Shaking his head in disbelief, Tom cupped my chin in his hand and gazed into my eyes, as though he were seeing me for the first time.

"I'm yours forever, Addie," he vowed, brushing his thumb along my jawline. "And I'll do whatever you want to keep it that way." Tom planted a soft kiss at the corner of my mouth, then pulled me into his arms again.

With my head on Tom's chest, I listened to his strong, steady heartbeat and closed my eyes, imagining what it would be like to fall asleep every night, listening to that sound.

When the song ended, Tom abruptly pulled away, and said, "I'll be right back."

I watched Tom approach the DJ onstage, as a Rihanna song began to play. The dancefloor quickly filled with more students, presumably returning from their time at the punch table, while Tom yelled into the DJ's ear, in order to be heard over the loud, thumping bass line. Tom patted the DJ on the back, nodding in delight, then smiled at me from where he stood on the stage.

Shrugging my shoulders in confusion, I motioned for Tom to climb down from the stage and join me on the dancefloor. He merely laughed, amused by my impatience. As I waited for Tom to return, a rough hand grabbed my wrist, spinning me around and into the arms of Ricky Travis.

"Let go of me!" I shouted, though my voice could hardly be heard over the music.

Ricky circled his arms around my waist, forcibly pressing his body against mine, as I struggled, unable to pry myself out of his restricting grasp.

"Get off!" I shoved my hands into Ricky's chest, attempting to push him away, but he was too strong for me. When I protested further, Ricky twisted my arm, then forced his hard, greedy mouth onto mine. He reeked of alcohol and sweat.

Tom appeared out of thin air and slammed into Ricky, breaking the unwanted contact between us. Ricky stumbled to the floor, slowly rising before the crowd of students that had gathered around us.

"You're drunk," Tom accused, shoving him backwards. "Go home, Ricky."

Ricky cocked his head to the side, like a house dog listening to the sound of a tea kettle whistling, then glowered in Tom's direction. Nodding, Ricky took a few steps back and raised his hands in the air, lengthening the distance between us. I felt my body relax, as he neared the edge of the dancefloor. The feeling didn't linger.

"I want her," Ricky mumbled, pointing his finger at me.

When Tom failed to respond, Ricky bolted towards him and threw the first punch. Tom caught Ricky's fist in his hand and then pinned him to the ground, mercilessly beating him to a pulp. Blood trickled from Ricky's nose, as he lolled his head back in submission.

"Tom! STOP!" I yelled over the music. Growing frantic, I grabbed the back of Tom's arms and tried to pull him off Ricky, but he wouldn't budge.

"Get out of here, Addie!" Tom snapped.

I let go of Tom immediately, gazing down at him with a pair of wide, confused eyes.

"GO!" Tom glared, frightening me. I didn't know what he was going to do.

Regaining focus, Ricky punched Tom in the jaw, and then in the mouth. Tom gritted his teeth and winced in pain, before slamming his fist into the side of Ricky's face again. Fresh blood colored Tom's chin, making me feel cold all over.

I remained frozen, unable to move, as Tom and Ricky fought like savages. Dark thoughts filtered through my mind, though I tried to block them out. I could not help thinking and fearing, that one day, they might kill each other.

Nicki Caldwell appeared before me, dressed in a yellow floor-length gown. She placed her hand on my shoulder, eyeing me sympathetically, then marched towards the boys without the slightest ounce of fear. Like a strong Southern woman, Nicki dug her hands into Ricky's armpits and dragged him away from Tom, successfully separating the two of them.

Exhaling in relief, I rushed to Tom's side and grabbed him by the arm. My blood boiled like never before, as I steered him out of the ballroom and down the hallway. Once we arrived at the girls' bathroom, I opened the door and pushed Tom inside, then closed the door behind us.

A handful of girls stood in front of the sinks and mirrors, astonished by the sight of Tom's reflection in the glass. I scowled at their presence, not caring that every last one of them had chosen the wrong time to reapply foundation and lip gloss.

"Get out," I sternly commanded, though the girls didn't move. "NOW!"

Terrified, the girls fled the bathroom immediately, nearly tripping over each other to keep from being the last one out the door. Once they were gone, I checked every stall, glad to discover that they were all empty. Tom and I were finally alone.

"What was that?" I snarled, shoving my open palm into Tom's chest.

Tom turned away from me and rested his hands on the bathroom counter. He didn't look at his reflection in the mirror.

"Are you trying to get arrested?" I hovered, crossing my arms over my chest.

"What did you want me to do, Addie? Let him have you?" Tom glared down at me, waving his arm towards the bathroom door, in the direction of the ballroom.

"No!" I snipped, not liking the sound of my own voice.

"Well then what was I supposed to do? Let him

stick his tongue down your throat first?" Tom growled as he leaned into me, still boiling over with anger.

"No, but you didn't have to break his nose!" I retorted.

Tom turned around and paced the tile floor beneath him, in an attempt to cool off. Once he had, I grabbed a couple of paper towels from the dispenser and placed them under a running faucet in the sink. Tom removed his jacket and draped it over the bathroom counter, exposing the blood on his white dress shirt.

I turned towards Tom and lifted the damp paper towels to his mouth. Blood stained his chin, neck, and collar. He looked like a vampire, plagued with bloodlust.

Tom recoiled at the slightest touch, aggravating my degree of frustration.

"Your lip is bleeding," I grumbled, angry that he had pulled away from me.

"I know," Tom barked back. "Just let me do it."

Tom turned the faucet on and rinsed the blood off his face, splashing water against his chin, around his mouth, and over his throat. Afterwards, he snatched the paper towels out of my hand and pressed them to his lips.

"Are you ready to go?" he muttered, grabbing his jacket. "Because I am."

"Yeah," I sighed. "Just give me a minute."

"Fine," Tom said, on his way to the door. "I'll go get the car."

The heavy bathroom door slammed shut behind him, making me flinch. I gazed into the mirror and studied the silver chain around my neck, as my thoughts drifted to Daniel. What would he think when

Tom came home with a bloody lip?

I didn't understand how the night could have changed so unexpectedly.

I had finally told Tom that I loved him, not because he had said it first, or because he had wanted me to, but because I truly meant it. And now, I thought he hated me.

Had I done the right thing? Should I have thanked him first and scolded him second? I shook my head from side to side, feeling warm tears pool in my eyes.

Anytime Ricky laid a hand on me, Tom could not control himself. I didn't want to accept the fact that Tom had a violent, raging temper, the same temper that Ricky loved to ignite, but I had to. Regardless, I knew that Tom wouldn't hurt me, because his temper never surfaced unless he was provoked by others.

Still, I didn't want Tom to end up a juvenile delinquent, just because Ricky knew how to set him off. If they kept brawling, Ricky would eventually press charges, and his sophisticated, billionaire father would bribe the toughest prosecuting attorney in Georgia, until Tom was helplessly imprisoned behind the cold metal bars of a jail cell.

Shivering, I turned the faucet on and splashed warm water on my face to banish those thoughts from my mind. After drying my hands, I looked down at the white corsage around my wrist and toyed with its petals. They had managed to remain intact, somehow.

I took a deep breath and glanced in the mirror one last time, ready to go home. As I turned on my heel and headed for the door, I recognized the music playing in the ballroom and stopped in my tracks.

At the sound of Chris Martin's voice, I slowly melted, finally realizing Tom's surprise. I hoped that the students on the dancefloor liked the song, "Yellow."

Tom had requested that song, our song.

I couldn't stand to be apart from him any longer.

As I stepped forward, anxious to be wrapped in Tom's embrace, all of the bathroom lights dimmed, before going out completely. I was in total darkness. Swallowing, I opened my mouth and inhaled.

"Tom?" I stepped away from the mirror, feigning confidence.

"Tom?" I repeated, my voice a ragged whisper. "Is that you?"

Turning back to the mirror, I tried to remain calm as my eyes adjusted to the blackness. A dark image materialized in the glass before me, as I shrieked in terror. But the sound was muted, when someone placed a cold hand over my mouth.

"Don't scream," the stranger murmured, whispering in my ear.

I cried aloud, recognizing the familiar, surly cadence to his voice.

"You really shouldn't have worn this dress."

I felt his warm breath on my neck, as he stood behind me, planting rough, angry kisses along my shoulder blades. When his fingers dug into the flesh of my bare back, I stomped his foot with the pointed heel of my shoe, escaping his grasp.

Griping in pain, he grabbed my arm and tossed me across the bathroom floor.

I landed on the cold, hard tile, wincing as I hit my head on the wall.

"I want you, Addie," he panted, moving closer. "And I always get what I want."

I touched my head, unable to ignore the painful,

throbbing sensation.

"I can't wait to get you out of this dress," he mumbled, slurring his words.

When he struck my face, I dozed off, feebly surrendering to the blackness.

Chapter 46

Stirring awake, I found myself sprawled out in the back seat of a moving car. Everything smelled like leather, a rich, robust scent that reminded me of Eleanor's expensive taste in clothing. Despite the throbbing discomfort in my forehead, I forced myself to sit up, and then leaned back into the soft leather seat by the window.

The dark, moonlit forest greeted me through the glass, as I spotted him in the driver's seat, nursing the silver flask in his hand. I toyed with the lock on my door, then jerked at the handle, but neither would budge. Panicking, I leapt across the back seat to the other car door, then beat my fist against the window. I was trapped.

Chuckling, he parked among the crowded gathering of oaks and pines, then removed the car keys from the ignition and tossed them into the console beside him. I lowered my eyes to the floorboard and placed my hands over my thighs, feeling the soft, silky texture of my prom dress. Sweat gathered in the slits of my palms, as I quietly breathed through my nostrils, attempting to calm my heart rate.

"What do you want from me?" I inhaled, unable to mask my shaky voice.

"Something that you won't be able to get back," he slurred, taking one final swig from the flask, before tossing it aside. "Something that you've been guarding."

I felt the silver chain of Antoinette's necklace against my throat, yet kept still, not wanting to enlighten him. Flicking my eyes southward, I breathed an internal sigh of relief, for the emerald remained out of sight, hidden within the green satin bodice of my gown.

"What?" I murmured, assuming ignorance. It was the only weapon I had.

"Don't play coy, Addie," he barked, turning around in the front seat. "I'm not what you think." He wiped his mouth with the back of his hand, then gazed over me in carnal delight, his eyes like maple syrup. "I'm much worse."

Lunging towards me, he grabbed my shoulders, forced my body into the leather seat, and placed his knees on either side of my hips. I lay flat, utterly helpless beneath the crushing weight of his body, realizing that everybody had been right about him all along.

"NO!" I cried out, squirming beneath his grasp. He was too strong.

"Shut up, Addie," he growled, pinning my arms above my head. "We're in the woods." He lowered his face over mine and exhaled, his breath spilling into my mouth. "It's not like anyone is going to hear you."

He crudely clamped his mouth to mine, starving me of oxygen, while I wailed in torture, gagging on his sour, pungent stench. Tears streamed down my face, like pitiful, whimpering pleas of agony, as I felt his hands hug the space above my waistline.

"Please," I begged, flattening my palms against his chest, in an attempt to push him away. But he was too strong, too muscular, too skilled, because he had done this before. His sloppy, unwelcome mouth traveled the length of my neck, marking me, scarring me. I would never forget where his lips had been.

"Stop," I cried, though the sound was barely audible. My breath came in weak, choking sobs, as he forced my lips apart with his mouth, mercilessly taking what did not belong to him. Every kiss felt more painful than the last, because I knew that he wasn't going to stop, until he had hurt me in a way that could never be forgotten.

"Ricky," I beckoned, pulling his face away with my hands.

At the sound of his name, Ricky stilled, hovering over my body with raging, lascivious lust. He searched my eyes in desperate longing, impatient and greedy. He wanted me to touch him too.

"Don't do this," I whispered, running my thumb across his lower lip.

Ricky placed his palm over my hand and panted, slowly catching his breath. A wave of serenity washed over him, as I observed the change in his appearance, the light in his eyes. How could he act like a demon, and then look like an angel?

I felt hollow, indelibly haunted by the soft glow of his countenance. Perhaps Ricky would let me go, if I swore never to tell a soul what had happened. I opened my mouth to speak, to make Ricky whatever promise he desired, so long as he released me. But then his eyes turned ominous, frighteningly black, and I knew that my time was up.

"Why?" I whimpered. Fresh tears pooled in my eyes, blurring my vision.

Ricky looked into my eyes and sighed, "Because I just have to."

"NO!" I clawed the side of his face with my fingernails, kneed him in the groin, and then slammed his head into the car door.

"Ah!" Ricky groaned in pain, recoiling into the back seat.

I climbed into the driver's seat and unlocked the door, fleeing into the shadows of the forest. When Ricky yelled after me, I ran faster and faster, winding my way through the woods. Eventually, I found a vast, sprawling live oak tree where I could hide.

"ADDIE!" Ricky called, his drunken voice turning my skin ice cold.

Shaking, I pressed my back into the trunk of the tree and closed my eyes. The sound of his voice drew near, alarming my senses as I scanned the forest. We were nestled so deeply in the woods that I would have to walk for miles to find the nearest stretch of pavement.

Where else could I run?

Where else could I hide?

"Addie," Ricky coaxed, leaves crunching beneath his feet with every step.

Silently panting, I turned my head to the side and spotted his lurking figure in the darkness. There was nothing left to do but run.

"Addie," he called out again, creeping closer.

I crouched down behind the tree and unfastened the leather shoe straps around my ankles. When Ricky took a step towards me, I reared up and knocked him in the head with both shoes in my hand. He staggered backwards, cursing my name aloud.

Victorious, I sprinted through the forest barefoot, before tripping over a thick tree root and falling to the ground. With my palms against the dirt floor, I struggled to stand, unable to do more than sit up straight. I felt tired, dizzy, and defeated. My time was running out.

When I looked up, Ricky towered over me with a wicked gleam in his eyes. I swallowed, succumbing to the terror, the inevitability, the powerlessness, as soft tears left my red, swollen eyes. Every ounce of hope dissipated, because young girls didn't survive nights like these. They didn't make it out of the forest alive.

"You're different than your friend," Ricky drawled, stepping on the edge of my dress. "She wasn't as pretty as you." He kneeled down before me and grabbed my wrists, staking his claim. "But she didn't give in so easily."

"What friend?" I gasped, bracing myself.

"That girl I used to always see you with," Ricky muttered. "I used to think ya'll were sisters, because you looked so much alike. Blonde hair, smooth skin," Ricky murmured, brushing his fingers across my cheek and jawline.

Emily had been my best friend.

"Only her eyes were blue," he paused, smirking down at me, "not like yours."

Emily went missing two years ago. The entire family had moved to Atlanta.

"Not green," Ricky added. He slid his tongue across his teeth and smiled. "And I prefer green eyes," he sighed, tracing my left eyebrow with his thumb. "Green eyes and blonde hair."

"NO!" I howled, kicking his shins.

Ricky covered my mouth with his hand and then pinned me to the ground, beneath the weight of his body. When I struggled to fight him off, Ricky slapped the side of my face, sending a powerful burst of pain through my cheekbone.

"Ricky, please stop!" I begged, crying aloud in misery. "PLEASE!"

Ricky ignored my protests and slid his hands beneath my dress, touching my calves, my knees, my thighs. I felt his lips at my throat, like poison on my skin. I wanted to perish.

"Stop," I silently whimpered, "please."

But it was no use now, no point in screaming, no point in begging. No one was coming to save me. It was too late. All I could think about was Tom and how desperately I wished he were here right now. I had never wanted anyone to touch me but him.

Ricky unfastened his belt buckle, while I grew numb, lifeless. A sickening discomfort filled the pit of my stomach, as bile collected in my throat. Ricky lowered his face to mine and whispered in my ear, preparing me.

"It will only hurt for a minute," he claimed, then gazed over my body one last time.

"Okay," I sobbed, blinded by the tears in my eyes.

Ricky ran his fingers along my sternum, following the silver chain around my neck. I lay still beneath him and bit my tongue, in order to deal with the pain that would surely follow. But when nothing happened, I lifted my head in surprise as Ricky gasped.

"I can't believe it," Ricky said. He held the emerald stone in the palm of his hand, mesmerized by the stunning, glorious jewel. "He said you had it. I didn't believe him."

Two gunshots fired, one behind the other, as Ricky collapsed on top of me. Terrified, I lifted his face with my hands, unable to ignore the painful ringing in my ears. Ricky's mouth dropped open into a painful grimace, while I slid out from underneath him and rolled his body onto the ground beside me.

Ricky lay face down, on his belly, as I saw two round bullet holes at the top of his back, one in each shoulder blade. Blood surrounded each wound, slowly soaking through his white shirt. I sank into the dirt, too traumatized to move.

Ricky grabbed my hand and squeezed it, as he clenched his teeth and groaned. Shivering, I slowly turned my head from left to right and scanned the dark shadows of the forest, but no one was there.

"Addie," Ricky whimpered, tightening his grip around my hand. I kept my eyes on the trees, wondering who had been watching us and where they were now.

My body would not stop shaking.

My ears would not stop ringing.

Ricky would not stop bleeding.

I didn't know how to feel about any of it. I didn't know how to breathe.

Two beaming headlights blinded me, as a black Escalade pulled up beside us.

"What happened?" DeMilo jumped out of the passenger's seat and collapsed in front of Ricky's body, separating our hands. He turned Ricky over gently and then forced him to sit upright, though Ricky resisted.

"ANSWER ME!" DeMilo shouted in my face.

"I don't know," I faintly replied, feeling small. "I don't know."

"WHAT DO YOU MEAN YOU DON'T KNOW?"

Tears continued to stream down my face, while DeMilo hugged Ricky to his chest, rocking him back and forth. The bullet holes in Ricky's back leaked crimson, as he began coughing up blood. I watched Ricky's head loll back, hanging over DeMilo's forearm.

"HUGH!" DeMilo shouted, his booming voice like a weapon.

Hugh rushed to DeMilo's side and knelt down in front of him.

"Ricky's been shot," DeMilo explained. "He's bleeding too much."

Hugh's eyes widened at the sight of Ricky, cradled in DeMilo's arms.

"Take him to the hospital," DeMilo commanded. "NOW!"

Hugh lifted Ricky in his arms, hardly noticing my stunned, feeble presence.

"No," Ricky grumbled. "Granddaddy!" He cried out, reaching for DeMilo.

"You're going to be all right, son," DeMilo said. "I promise."

Hugh walked over to the vehicle, opened the back door, and laid Ricky down on the back seat, before shutting the door. With two swift steps, Hugh climbed into the driver's seat and slammed the door behind him, ready to drive away.

"WAIT!" DeMilo banged on the window, motioning for Hugh to stop. When he did, DeMilo turned around and jerked me onto my feet. "Ricky is my eldest grandson," he hissed, pulling me towards the back of the vehicle. "Would you like to meet the other one?"

DeMilo lifted the hatchback and revealed a handsome, black-haired boy with glistening, golden eyes.

Chapter 47

As soon as Tom climbed out of the trunk, Hugh sped off into the night, leaving the three of us alone. DeMilo patted Tom on the back, pulling him into a warm embrace. Tom stared at me over DeMilo's shoulder, as I took three steps backward, retreating from them both. I had never felt so wholly betrayed.

"Addie," Tom called, pushing DeMilo aside.

When Tom approached me, I slapped him across the side of his face. Tom gritted his teeth in frustration, clenching his jaw. I noticed the dried blood on his bottom lip, from the earlier scuffle with Ricky, and wondered exactly how they were related.

"Give him the necklace, Addie," Tom commanded, gauging me quietly.

I looked into his soft golden eyes and shook my head. How could I have been so stupid? The whole time I had been with Tom, I had never questioned his sincerity. I had truly believed that he cared. I had truly believed that he loved me.

"No," I refused, holding my chin taut.

"Addie." Tom placed his hands on my shoulders, his touch soft and gentle. "Just give it to him," he begged, narrowing his eyes at me.

When I turned my face away from him, Tom cupped my chin in his hand, forcing me to gaze into his gloriously warm, honey-colored eyes. In that moment, I knew that I still loved him, and that I would never be able to feel for another, what I already felt for Tom. Tears filled my eyes, constantly flowing, constantly returning, as they had been all night. I would never be able to look at him the same way again.

"If you do, all of this will go away," Tom whispered, holding my gaze.

"Will you?" I gently murmured, devastated by the mere thought.

"Hurry up, Tom. I don't have all night." DeMilo paced the ground nearby, smoking a thin, white cigarette to ease his impatience. "If she won't give it to you, then just take it."

Tom removed his hands from my face and searched my eyes one last time, then clasped the emerald stone in his palm and ripped the silver chain from my neck. I widened my eyes in surprise, silently gasping, as Tom handed the necklace to DeMilo.

Tom placed his hands on his hips, and then turned back to me, complacent as ever. I glowered in his direction, seething with molten, lava-like fury, until I couldn't stand to look at his smug, attractive face any longer.

Sighing in relief, DeMilo slipped the emerald necklace into his pocket, and then took one long, final drag on his cigarette. Just as he flicked the cigarette out of his hand, a gunshot sounded nearby, simultaneously slicing the cigarette in half, before it landed on the ground in pieces.

All of us froze in place, stunned by the proximity of the bullet and how easily it could have struck one of us. Lifting my eyes to the tree tops above, I scanned the shadowy thickets of the forest, but once again, no one was there.

"It's Daniel," DeMilo exhaled, deftly removing a switchblade from the front pocket of his trousers. The blade ejected from its handle so rapidly, that I blinked and nearly missed it.

"What?" Tom furrowed his brow in confusion, caught off guard.

"He's in the woods," DeMilo clarified. "He's the one who shot Ricky."

"No," Tom argued, shaking his head. "He hardly ever leaves his room. It couldn't be him."

DeMilo brushed past Tom, unconvinced. The switchblade remained firmly within his grasp, as DeMilo kept his dark, fleeting eyes on the trees above, watching and waiting.

"Besides, he's at home," Tom added. "I told you that already."

"Find him," DeMilo ordered, cutting Tom off. "NOW!"

"He's not here, I swear!" Tom yelled, gesturing his hands in the air.

"Find him," DeMilo repeated, then took a step forward. Before I could flinch, he grabbed me, locked his arm around my clavicle, and pressed the blade to my throat. "Or I'll kill her," he threatened, practically spitting the words from his mouth.

Yelping in panic, I shook within DeMilo's constricting hold and gripped his forearm with my hands. He held me at the point of a fine, decisive blade. The metal felt cool against my skin, too close, too sharp. I knew that if he wanted to kill me, he would.

"You said that if I gave you the necklace, you'd let her live," Tom chided, his eyes widening in alarm. He lifted a critical finger and pointed it at DeMilo. "You promised that you wouldn't touch her."

"Yes," DeMilo agreed. "I did. But that was before Daniel shot Ricky, your cousin."

Tom blinked, contemplating, while DeMilo's restrictive force began to feel more like a chain, with his chest pressing deeper and deeper into my back.

"I'm your grandfather, Tom. Not him. Remember?" DeMilo coaxed. "Just because he raised you, that doesn't mean anything. Daniel is her blood, not yours, not *ours*."

Two gunshots sounded as I screamed aloud, aware of the sharp blade at my throat. The bullets had just skimmed the ground before us, barely missing our feet. Tom looked to the wilderness that surrounded us, slowly scanning from one angle to the next. His golden eyes stilled for a moment, then continued searching, as if he had seen nothing at all.

"You see him, don't you?" DeMilo barked, his breath hot on my neck.

"No," Tom denied. He looked DeMilo in the eye and said, "I don't."

"Don't lie to me boy!" DeMilo shouted, his raspy voice terrifying me further.

I closed my eyes in an attempt to calm my breathing, yet my heart thumped rapidly, just the same. My body had never felt so aggravated, so exhausted, so fragile.

"You can't protect them both," DeMilo hollered, lengthening the duration of the sharp, high-pitched ringing in my ears. "You're going to have to make a decision, Tom."

"No," Tom mouthed, violently jerking his head back and forth.

"You're going to have to choose between them," DeMilo continued.

"No!" Tom shouted, as he weaved his fingers through his hair.

"It's Daniel or Addie," DeMilo asserted, cruelly brusque. "Reveal the old man to me, and the girl goes free. Don't, and I'll slit her throat."

Wailing in terror, I squirmed within DeMilo's strong, unyielding grip and felt the loud, throbbing pulse of the artery in my neck, where the blade remained.

"You told me she would go free before," Tom uttered, choosing his words carefully. He looked like a little boy. "How do I know you're not lying?"

DeMilo snickered in my ear, then removed the blade from my throat, as I took a deep, hesitant breath, sighing in relief. Just as I began to have hope, DeMilo grabbed my left wrist, turned it over, and, with a quick, clean swipe, cut my open palm with the blade.

I yelped in pain, then looked down at the bloody gash he had made.

"Is that enough of a promise for you?" DeMilo arrogantly asked.

Tom blankly stared at DeMilo, unable to speak, unable to move.

"Just show me where Daniel is," DeMilo implored, his voice syrupy sweet.

Tom turned his head away and sighed. He had never looked more indecisive.

"I know you just saw him," DeMilo badgered, sounding like a child. "Use your head, son," he continued, unwavering. "Daniel is the one that I want, not Addie. I don't have to kill her, but I will if you don't listen."

Tom pressed his lips into a firm line, and then flicked his eyes to the forest floor.

"DECIDE!" DeMilo snarled, quickly returning the blade to my throat.

"Let her go." Daniel appeared through the trees with a pistol in his hand.

My mouth dropped open at the sight of Daniel, mirroring Tom's reaction.

"Drop the gun, or I'll kill her," DeMilo snarled. And there it was again, that same imminent threat that hung overhead, waiting to end everything, the taking of my life.

"You're bluffing," Daniel remarked. He stepped closer, until he was standing beside Tom, though the pistol was still aimed at DeMilo, cocked and ready to fire.

Despite Daniel's protective measures, I felt all the more distressed, because my body was the only shield that DeMilo had at the moment. If Daniel pulled the trigger, he couldn't miss.

"Just let her go," Daniel sternly asserted. "You have the necklace," he commented matter-of-factly. "We've given you what you want."

DeMilo kept his arm around my body, constricting me like a snake, as he lowered the blade from my throat, and then slipped it into his pocket.

The minute DeMilo released me, I rushed towards Daniel, wanting him desperately, needing to be wrapped in his embrace. But Tom grabbed my arm and jerked me away from Daniel before I could reach him, because that was when DeMilo pulled out a pistol of his own.

Chapter 48

Every gunshot filled my ears with a piercing, painful ring, even as Tom dragged me deeper into the forest, away from the noise and danger. I nearly tripped over my own two feet, hardly able to keep up with Tom, until he slowed down at the sight of a tremendously over-grown live oak tree. Jerking me to the ground, Tom forced me behind the trunk of the tree, and then crouched down beside me, though only long enough to catch his breath.

"Stay here," Tom commanded, ready to abandon me.

"No," I cried, clasping his hand with mine. "Don't go."

"I have to," Tom admitted, then let go of me, and rose to his feet.

"No!" I protested, grabbing hold of his shirt sleeve. "Don't go! Please!" I wailed, because I knew what would happen if he did.

Desperate, I leapt into Tom's arms and kissed him, as if it were for the last time. Sensing my struggle, Tom sighed against my mouth, his lips moving fast and fervently, in order to match every kiss that I offered. My fingers dug into Tom's shoulders, as his hands found their way to the small of my back, supporting my weak, exhausted frame.

When Tom pulled away, I folded my hands at the nape of his neck and returned his lips to mine. I felt his breath on my mouth, his hands on my back, tracing patterns over my bare flesh. I hardly noticed the tears spilling from my eyes.

"TOM! ADDIE!"

Tom and I broke apart, paralyzed by the sound of Daniel's pleading voice in the distance. I withdrew from Tom's intimate embrace and turned on my heel, until he clutched my wrist and jerked me back.

"What do you think you're doing?" I snarled, struggling to free myself from his grasp, but Tom wouldn't budge. "LET GO OF ME!"

"Stay here," Tom begged, echoing his earlier sentiment.

"ADDIE!" Daniel cried from afar.

"He wants me," I declared, my voice trembling. "Please, let me go to him."

When Tom released me, I ran into the night, rushing through the crowded thickets, chasing the sound of Daniel's voice, hoping that I wasn't too late. Tom kept pace with me, just as terrified as I was. Neither of us was prepared for what happened next.

We found Daniel on the ground, lying flat on his back, with two bloody bullet holes pierced through his shirt. The first was in his shoulder, the second in his chest.

"DANIEL!" I screamed in agony, dropping to my knees before him. "Daniel," I cried, burying my face in his chest. His ragged breathing was painful to listen to. I wanted to give him my lungs, my heart, whatever he needed to survive.

Tom stood at Daniel's feet, watching the trail of blood that led into the distance. I looked through the trees, as far as the eye could see, and spotted two red tail lights dissipating into the darkness. *Ricky's car*, I thought to myself.

DeMilo had gotten away.

Tom knelt down on the other side of Daniel and swallowed, while I placed my hand behind Daniel's head and held him upright. He was struggling to breathe and choking on his own blood, yet looked into my eyes and smiled.

"It's better this way," Daniel sputtered, his eyes glazing over.

"No," I sobbed, holding his hand in mine.

"I don't want to live like this." Daniel showed me his trembling hands.

"Daniel." I shook my head, crying out in agony. "Don't go, please!" I begged, insisting, "Tom and I are here. And we love you."

Warm red blood coated Daniel's torso, soaking through his clothes. Tom sat in stunned silence, as I grabbed his hand and placed it over Daniel's chest, above his still-beating heart. Before long, our hands were covered with Daniel's blood.

"I've lived without Antoinette long enough," Daniel spoke, his voice becoming less and less clear. "I don't want to anymore."

Crying, I caressed Daniel's cheek with my hand, then kissed him on the forehead. "I love you," I whimpered.

"I'm sorry for all the time we lost," Daniel said. "I wish I had been there to watch you grow up. There were so many things that I had left to say." He placed his hand against the side of my face and coughed, "I love you."

"Tom," he called, barely having the strength to turn his face.

"Yes Grandpa, I'm here." Tom squeezed Daniel's

hand and then wrapped an arm around his shoulder, helping me support his limp body.

"I'm sorry I never told you where you really came from. Don't listen to Tony. You're not like him, Tom. You're the son I always wanted, the one I lost, and I love you," Daniel cried, as blood spilled from his mouth.

"I love you too, Grandpa." Tom wept, hugging him close. "I love you."

"You will both be taken care of. I have already made all the arrangements. I love you, both of you. Promise me that you'll take care of each other," Daniel pressed.

"I promise," I said, as Daniel took Tom's hand and placed it over mine.

"I promise," Tom echoed, looking at me, though only for a moment.

"It's not..." Daniel wheezed, his sentence breaking off. "It's what's inside of it."

"Daniel, I don't know what you're talking about," I helplessly whimpered.

"It's at the center." Daniel forced the words out, struggling to breathe.

"What is?" I asked, watching his blue, still eyes.

"Life," he exhaled, and then let go of my hand.

"Daniel," I cried, blinking in disbelief, at the sight of his lifeless body. "DANIEL!"

But Daniel did not move. His blue eyes had turned silent, frozen in place, like some motionless image set in stone, like a painting.

"DANIEL!" I screamed, burrowing my face in his chest. I lay beside Daniel and held him for the longest time.

I didn't want to let go.

I didn't want to leave him there.
But he was gone.

Chapter 49

Later that night, Tom and I found ourselves at the police station. Jeffrey and Eleanor arrived with the speed of a fighter jet, practically materializing from wherever they had been. I knew that things were going to be different between us from now on.

For the sake of criminal justice, Tom and I were split up, then taken to separate rooms, where we were each forced to recount the events of the past several hours. I had to relive the memory of Ricky's hands up my dress, DeMilo's knife at my throat, and Daniel's bloody, lifeless corpse on the dirty forest floor beneath me. I just wanted to wake up from the nightmare that my life had become. But I couldn't, because I wasn't dreaming.

Once Tom and I were finished at the police station, Jeffrey and Eleanor took us home and quickly became the kind of parents that I had always longed for. Jeffrey warmed some left-over soup for the two of us to eat, even though we weren't hungry. Meanwhile, Eleanor chattered on and on about how terribly sorry she was, eventually offering to clean our blood-stained clothes. It was the first time she had ever used the washing machine.

Jeffrey and Eleanor surprised me further, when they let Tom spend the night and stay with me upstairs, in my room. They were being too nice, too apologetic. And while I appreciated their newfound concern for my well-being, I resented the fact that it had taken such a gruesome tragedy for them to care. Perhaps they were finally sorry for their unwavering absence and all of its consequences.

Regardless, I lay awake all night, unable to stop crying. I cried until it physically hurt, until I thought my bones might break, until I thought it might kill me. All the while, Tom lay beside me, quiet, still, motionless, with his eyes wide open and staring at the ceiling.

Tom wouldn't move.

Tom wouldn't speak.

I didn't know how long I could go on like this, not talking, not touching, not mourning Daniel's loss together. I craved the comfort of another, especially when I realized that Tom was going to shut me out again. Only this time, I wasn't sure if he would ever let me back in.

* * *

Just after sunrise, Ricky's body was found by the side of an old dirt road, in a ditch, just a few miles south of the woods where he had taken me. The police also found a black Escalade and a shiny, new BMW. Both cars were parked no more than 500 yards away from the body.

DeMilo and Hugh were discovered inside the BMW, and then willingly taken into custody, where they would await trial for Daniel's murder. I found it strange that the two men who had given their lives to defy the law, would crumble so easily at the sight of it.

No, I didn't believe it. DeMilo and Hugh had wanted to be found, arrested, and charged, though I couldn't begin to fathom why.

The emerald necklace, however, had gone missing.

Chapter 50

We attended Ricky's funeral one day and Daniel's the next, yet Tom remained voiceless, distant, guarded. He hadn't cried since Daniel had drawn his last breath. I, on the other hand, hadn't stopped.

Ricky's body had been too marred for an open casket; Daniel's had not. And though I hardly possessed the courage to view the body, I did so anyway.

But Tom didn't want to look, didn't want to grieve, didn't want to be touched. He could be standing right beside me, and yet, it would feel as though he were miles away, on some other planet, in some other universe. I didn't know who he was anymore.

In the meantime, poor Jeanine had fallen to pieces over the death of her brother. Despite Ricky's shortcomings, she had loved him, and he had been her family. Somehow, Jeanine and I found a way to bond through the tragedy, and rely more on each other, now that we were sharing common ground.

We had each lost a piece of ourselves that we wouldn't be able to get back.

Foolishly, I had thought that Tom would want to develop a relationship with Jeanine, and let her in, maybe even tell her things that he wouldn't tell me. After all, she was his cousin. But once again, to my absolute dismay, I had thought wrong.

* * *

After Daniel's funeral, a heavy rain descended over Savannah and lasted into the night. I lay awake crying, as had become my evening ritual, because all I could recall was the haunting memory of Daniel's lifeless body being zipped inside of a black bag, like he was some object to be packed away and discarded.

Shifting, I grabbed my pillow and plopped it down on the end of the bed, then sprawled out so that my feet lay where my head had been. As a child, I had moved to the opposite end of the bed when I couldn't sleep at night, hoping that a change of scenery might fix the problem. Unfortunately, it hadn't worked then, and it still didn't work now.

Unable to lie still, I rolled onto my side and faced the window, where rainwater continuously washed over the glass. When lightning flashed in the distance, something caught the corner of my eye, so I stumbled out of bed and ambled towards the window. As thunder shook the house, I widened my eyes at the sight of Tom, for he was perched on the tree outside my bedroom, thoroughly soaked from head to toe.

Stunned, I lifted the window and yelled, "Are you crazy?"

"We need to talk," Tom announced, as raindrops skirted down his face.

Stepping back, I walked into the bathroom and grabbed a fresh towel, while Tom climbed through the window, and then shut it behind him. I carefully approached Tom, profoundly confused by his recent, erratic behavior. He was no longer rational.

I lifted the towel to the front of Tom's shoulders and began drying him off. He was dripping wet, dressed in a thin t-shirt and blue jeans, with no rain jacket. I wondered how long he had been out there, quietly waiting by the window, in the middle of a storm.

"I got it," Tom snapped, jerking the towel from my grasp.

I froze in place, hurt by his cold, biting remark.

Tom walked into the bathroom with the towel in his hands, while I sat down on the edge of my bed and wondered if the man I loved would ever make an appearance.

"I can't sleep," Tom started, alarming me.

I looked up to find him in the bathroom doorway, rubbing the towel over his hair. Swallowing, I took a shallow breath as Tom turned around and tossed the towel onto the bathroom counter behind him.

"I can't sleep in that house," Tom continued. He leaned forward, hugging the door frame. "All I can hear is his voice. And knowing he's not there, it's just..." he trailed off, holding my gaze with his own.

"Then stay here," I pleaded. "Mom and Dad already said that you could."

Tom exhaled, then walked over to the window and watched the rain.

"Why are you so mad at me?" I asked, as tears clouded my eyes.

"I'm not mad at you," Tom replied. He pressed one palm against the window pane and slid the other into his pocket, quietly gazing out at the storm.

"Then why won't you look at me, or talk to me, or even touch me?" I sobbed.

"We are talking, Addie," Tom droned, impassively staring through the glass.

"Why are you doing this?" I waited for an answer, then rose from the bed when he didn't give one.

"Tom, I know that you're hurting, and I know that it's never going to be the same without him, but I loved Daniel too."

Tom swallowed, lowering his gaze, as I placed my hand on his shoulder. He stiffened at my touch, then said, "It's my fault that he's dead."

"What?" I gasped the word, practically an inaudible breath.

Tom turned around and peeled my hand from his shirt, breaking all physical contact between us. I crossed my arms over my chest, in reaction to the hollow coldness that swept through me. He might as well have spit in my face.

"DeMilo wanted me to choose between the two of you," he said, "I did."

Tom searched my eyes, then quickly looked away, as if he were ashamed of me.

"Daniel revealed himself, Tom. You didn't do that for him," I mentioned.

"True, but when he got shot, where was I?" Tom paused, fixing his eyes on my face. "I was with you," he muttered. "I chose you over him."

"What are you saying? That you wish you hadn't?" I snapped, growing defensive.

"No, it's just that..." Tom drifted off, gauging me carefully. His eyes traveled from my eyes to my mouth, as he said, "If I hadn't been kissing you, he might still be alive."

"Oh," I choked, feeling accused. "So now it's my fault?"

"I didn't say that!" Tom barked.

"Well, you might as well have," I snarled, before turning my back to him. "DeMilo killed Daniel, Tom. Not you. Not me." I turned on my heel and moved towards him, closing the distance between us, as I lifted my face to meet his eyes. "Why won't you believe it? Why can't you just accept the fact that DeMilo is a murderer?"

"Because he's my grandfather!" Tom yelled. His roaring voice sent chills down my spine as I stilled before him, vaguely wondering if Jeffrey and Eleanor had heard him from their bedroom downstairs.

"And what if I turn out just like him?" Tom murmured. He sank into the chair by my window and held his head in his hands. He looked like he might finally cry.

"Tom, you won't." I knelt down in front of him. "Just because he's your grand-"

"Look at Ricky," he interrupted, cutting me off. "Look at what he tried to do to you," Tom paused, letting his words linger in the air, before saying, "again."

"Again?" I repeated, glad that he hadn't pushed me away.

Tom tightened his jaw, then gazed down at me with a pair of quiet, discerning eyes.

"Ricky's done this before?" I felt my mouth go dry, because everything was finally starting to make sense. "It was in December, wasn't it? At the dance?"

Tom's face shifted into an unpleasant grimace. He didn't want to remember.

"You never told me what happened that night," I persisted, desperate to know the truth. "The night that I saw you in my dream, only you swore that it wasn't-" I broke off in midsentence, noting the uncomfortable glint of despair in Tom's eyes. "What happened?"

"I think you know," Tom quietly spoke. "I think you've known for a while now."

"Saturday wasn't the first night that Ricky laid his hands on me. Was it?"

"No," Tom remarked, his face expressionless.

"Then why can't I remember?" I rose to my feet, disturbed by the thought.

"You said that Ricky poisoned the punch," Tom explained, the words like a vague memory that I couldn't grasp. "I'm pretty sure that has something to do with it."

"Tell me, Tom," I begged, crossing my arms over my chest. "Please. Tell me what happened that night." I kept my eyes on him, unwilling to drop the subject.

Tom leaned forward in the chair, folding his hands together as he looked up at me. When his mouth pressed into a hard line, I knew that he was about to tell me everything.

"After the dance, you took Jeanine home," Tom began. "Then you stopped by the grocery store, and I just so happened to be there at the same time."

I looked away from Tom and out the window, trying to think, trying to remember.

"Ricky followed you there. He was waiting for you in the parking lot, and on the way to my car, I heard you screaming." Tom fell silent, contemplating, then added, "I grabbed you before he had the chance to do anything and brought you back to Grandpa's for a little while. When you were ready to leave, I took you home."

I took one step back, then another, plagued by the feeling that I was trapped in a strange dream. I wanted to leave. I wanted to stay. I didn't know what I wanted.

"How could you not tell me any of this?" I scowled at Tom. "All this time..."

"I don't know." He shrugged. "When you didn't

recognize me that first day at school, I didn't know what to think. I never imagined that you wouldn't remember."

Exhaling, I ran a hand through my hair, unable to comprehend all of it at once. "This is too complicated," I grumbled, before setting my eyes on Tom.

"Do you want me to leave?" He stood up, prepared to climb through the window.

"No!" I moved towards Tom, longing to be wrapped in his embrace. But he quickly turned away, wounding me further. Tears filled my eyes, because I couldn't understand him. If he didn't want to touch me, then why was he here?

"Maybe you don't need me," I confessed, sobbing. "But I need you."

"Addie, just because I've been distant, that doesn't mean that I don't need you, or want you, or care about you," Tom coaxed, his voice soft and silky.

I glowered at him through my tears, my sadness, my pain.

"What?" Tom glanced over my face in concern, but I didn't care.

"I guess I don't believe you," I mumbled, drying my eyes with the back of my hand. "Maybe you should go." I placed my hands on my hips and nodded my head towards the window, sniffling all the while. Would I ever stop crying?

"Addie, please," Tom begged, for what exactly, I don't know.

"You've already hurt me enough," I admitted on my way to the bathroom. Stopping in the doorway, I took a deep breath and said, "I don't think I can take anymore."

I walked into the bathroom and shut the door behind me, slowly sinking to the cool tile floor. A fresh set of tears arrived, as I surrendered to the pain. I let it overwhelm me, until I became so exhausted that I could hardly stay awake. I wasn't certain if I even had the strength to stand.

When the door creaked open, I lifted my head from my lap and found Tom lurking in the doorway. My eyes stilled at the sight of him, distressed and lethargic. Tom knelt down before me, took my face in his hands, and sighed.

"I'm sorry," he whispered, brushing his thumb along my cheekbone.

"Go away," I griped, sniffling and groggy. "You don't want me, so just leave."

When I lifted my hand to push Tom away, he grabbed my wrist, and then tilted my chin forward, compelling me to look into his eyes. I felt his breath on my face, a soft, fleeting caress, as he said, "The only place I want to be right now is with you."

I opened my mouth to speak, but Tom planted his lips on mine, silencing me. His hands moved to my throat, and then my shoulders, as he held me against the wall, hardly allowing me the chance to breathe. I tugged at his shirt sleeve and pulled him closer, despite the fact that I could barely move my arms.

"Addie," Tom breathed against my mouth. "I need you to promise me something."

"Okay," I panted, surprised by his abruptness.

"Promise me that from now on, we're going to be completely honest with each other," he implored, still gasping for air. "Promise me that we're going to tell each other the absolute truth about everything, no matter how bad it is. No lies, no half-truths, nothing but complete and total honesty. Promise me Addie," he sternly begged, tantalizing me.

"I promise," I sighed, and fell limp in his arms, my body aching with fatigue.

"Let's get you to bed," he softly murmured, noticing my state of weariness.

Tom picked me up and carried me into the bedroom, then gently laid my body on the mattress and pulled the covers up to my chin. I rolled onto my side and relaxed, resting my head against the soft, cool pillow, as I fought to keep my eyes open.

"Stay," I crooned, sounding like a child. "Don't go. Please."

I closed my eyes and exhaled, succumbing to exhaustion. Before dozing off, I recalled the faintest image of Tom, making himself comfortable in the chair by my window.

Epilogue

Tom and I sat down beside each other, in a pair of matching leather chairs. I looked around the room, a nice, stately office that had been cleaned and adorned to perfection, with an enormous row of bookshelves that lined either wall. An obscure painting hung against the back wall, by the window. I wondered if it was one of Daniel's.

"Good morning," a deep voice greeted us.

A tall, stocky man entered the room and took a seat at the finely polished desk before us. His shiny black mane had been combed to the side, and despite his receding hair line, I figured that he was in his early to mid-forties. A handful of deep pockmarks scarred his pale, placid, and otherwise unblemished face, yet his steely blue eyes were striking enough to divert all attention away from anything other than his pleasant, charming gaze.

His name was Walter James, and he had been Daniel's attorney.

"Before we start, I would just like to say how terribly sorry I am for your loss. I've known Daniel for many years, and I was pretty stunned when I heard the news. My condolences to you both." Walter nodded, then shrugged remorsefully.

"Thank you." I forced a smiled, while Tom stared blankly ahead.

A wave of silence fell over the room, until the

attorney spoke again.

"Well," Walter grunted, clearing his throat. "I understand that you've both already looked over the will. Did you have any questions?"

I turned to Tom and waited for him to respond.

"Not really," I replied, privy to Tom's disinterest.

"I guess you're wondering why I called the two of you in here today," Walter mentioned, his smile polite and caring. "I know that nothing can bring Daniel back, and money is hardly the thing to be thinking of right now. But just think, in a few short years, you'll be millionaires."

Tom grumbled aloud, then continued to sulk beside me.

I averted my eyes in modesty, because it was true. Daniel had split all of his financial assets between us, right down the middle. Together, we would inherit the house, the land, as well as all of Daniel's personal belongings. However, until we reached the age of majority, Walter would be at our financial beck and call. It was a reality that did not sit so well with Tom and his private, reticent ways.

Presently, Daniel had left us with enough money to cover living expenses, upkeep on the house, and college tuition, so that our needs would be met for the next several years. But at the age of twenty-two, each of us would be granted access to a trust fund worth $3.5 million, meaning our collective inheritance would total $7 million.

"I don't say that to be pretentious," Walter continued. "I say it, because Daniel wanted both of you to be taken care of." Walter opened a drawer and placed two small, square boxes on the surface of his desk. "He also wanted you to have these."

Curious, I leaned forward and picked up the box nearest to me. It felt soft against my fingertips, covered in black velvet, just like a jewelry box. When I gave the other one to Tom, he stilled for a moment, then hesitantly clasped the box in his hand.

"Don't open them here," Walter commanded, startling me. "Daniel would like no one but the two of you to know what is inside."

* * *

"I didn't like that guy," Tom grumbled, joining me at the kitchen table.

Sighing aloud, I rested my head within the palm of my hand, and then looked down at the two boxes. It felt so strange to be in Daniel's house without him.

"You know, he probably opened them already," Tom said, following my gaze.

"What?" I twisted my face into an irritated expression.

"Yeah," Tom insisted. "I bet he knows exactly what's in there. He probably just thinks we're a couple of stupid teenagers, Addie."

"Why are you so critical?" I snapped back. "Don't you know Daniel better than that? I don't think he would put someone in charge that he didn't trust."

Tom scowled at me, then leaned back in his chair and exhaled.

I pulled one of the black boxes towards me and placed my thumb over the lid. But when I tried to open the box, it wouldn't budge. Frustrated, I threw my hands up in the air.

"Why won't it open?" I groaned, my blood beginning to boil.

"Let me see." Tom held his hand out, as I gave the

box to him.

Amused, I sat back and watched Tom struggle. He couldn't open it either.

"The other one's like that too," I noted, after toying with the second box. "I don't know how Walter could have opened these, Tom. They're practically glued shut."

"Maybe he did it," Tom mused.

"Tom!" I scolded, as my degree of irritation continued to escalate. "Did you ever think that Daniel glued them together?" I fluttered my eyelashes for dramatic effect.

Tom stood up, walked into the kitchen, and began rifling through drawers.

"Walter was right," I admitted. "Whatever's inside of these boxes, Daniel doesn't want anyone else to see but us."

I let my thoughts linger in the air, until Tom returned with a box cutter.

"This is probably going to ruin the box," he said, lifting the object in the air.

"Just do it," I proclaimed. "I want to know what's inside."

Tom darted his eyes across my face, then sat down at the table and pressed the blade into the closed mouth of the first box. After several minutes of griping and cursing, Tom managed to pry the box open, as a shiny golden object fell out. My brow furrowed with intrigue, for the top half of a broken key lay on the table before us.

Tom and I exchanged a meaningful glance, breathless and alert. I didn't have to ask. We both knew where to find the other half.

Impatient, I grabbed the partial key in my hand

and nodded to Tom. When he finished prying the second box open, the other half of the key slipped out, equally gold in color. Tom gingerly collected the new piece with his fingers, then dropped it into my hand, as the two halves quickly became an instantaneous whole, emphatically magnetized.

"It looks like the key to a door," Tom remarked.

Somehow, we both knew where to go.

Grabbing Tom's hand, I left the kitchen and pulled him behind me, as we headed up the staircase. At the top, I turned left and approached the old wooden door, then twisted the handle and stepped inside. Tom trailed behind me, while I gazed across the room and spotted Antoinette's portrait, hanging silently on the wall, as if she had always been there, watching.

I wandered towards the back of the room and stopped before that dark, mysterious door, which I had favorably glimpsed just months before. When I took a step closer, Tom let go of my hand and crossed his arms over his chest.

"Go on," he encouraged, before turning on his heel.

"You're not coming with me?" I held his gaze with a sorrowful expression.

Tom pressed his lips together, stalling, contemplating.

"Why?" I asked, disappointed.

"You just go ahead," Tom softly spoke, waving me towards the door.

"But-"

"All of this is yours anyway," he confessed, staring into my eyes.

With the absence of Daniel, I had lost the last

remaining member of my family. I had lost my blood, my connection to the past. Yet somehow, I knew that from what Daniel had left behind, I could hope for the future. Tom and I could build a new life together.

Gazing at him now, I noticed that the light had gone from his eyes. No more gold, no more honey, no more flecks of glowing yellow or glistening amber. But I would find a way to get it back. I had to find a way to get that light back.

I would restore the color to his eyes.

"No," I shook my head, then rested my hand against his face. "It's ours."

Grinning, Tom took my hand in his and steered me towards the back of the room. I looked at the golden key in the palm of my hand, wondering what other secrets Daniel had kept hidden, secrets that no one else would know, but the two of us.

With a deep breath, I placed the key in the lock and opened the door.

Tell Me Your Favorite Part!

If you enjoyed Emerald Green, I invite you to head over to Amazon and let me know your favorite part. Reviews are so important to an author's career, because they help new readers like you discover the book. Even if you didn't enjoy Emerald Green, I'd still love it if you could take three minutes to let me know what you think of the book.

Leaving a review is super easy:

1) Go to Emerald Green Book Page on Amazon

2) Scroll Down and click "Write a Customer Review"

3) Sign in to Amazon if prompted

4) Select a star rating

5) Write a few short words (or long words, I won't judge)

6) Click the 'submit' button

I thank you in advance!

Acknowledgements

First and foremost, I would like to thank my mother and father, for refusing to let me give up on my dreams and for showering me with a perpetual supply of unconditional love and support.

The rest of my family—grandparents, aunts, uncles, all of my "little" cousins, and my lifelong friends—have been the best support system a girl could ask for. Thank you for believing in me.

About the Author

Lindsay Marie Miller was born and raised in Tallahassee, Florida, where she graduated from high school as Valedictorian. At sixteen, she started writing her first novel, *Emerald Green*, after being inspired by Stephenie Meyer's International Bestselling *Twilight Saga*. During her time in college, Lindsay wrote 5 more novels and over 100 songs. After graduating Summa Cum Laude from Florida State University, she put her B.A. in English Literature to good use and published her debut novel, *Emerald Green*. An author of over 10 Romance Titles, Lindsay currently resides in her hometown of Tallahassee where she is always working on her next novel.

To learn more, please visit:

www.lindsaymariemillerauthor.com

Sign up for Lindsay's newsletter:

lindsaymariemillerauthor.com/claim-your-free-book/

Join Lindsay on Facebook at:

facebook.com/LindsayMarieMillerAuthor

Follow Lindsay on Twitter at:

twitter.com/Lindsay_MMiller

LOOK FOR THE NEXT BOOK

HONEY GOLD
LINDSAY MARIE MILLER

AVAILABLE
NOVEMBER 2017

www.ingramcontent.com/pod-product-compliance
Lightning Source LLC
Chambersburg PA
CBHW030016180626
46810CB00001B/70